FEATHERED SERPENT DARK HEART OF SKY

MYTHS OF MEXICO

FEATHERED SERPENT DARK HEART OF SKY

MYTHS OF MEXICO

David Bowles

CINCO PUNTOS PRESS
www.cincopuntos.com

FIRST EDITION
10 9 8 7 6 5 4 3 2 1

Library of Congress Cataloging-in-Publication Data

Names: Bowles, David, author.
Title: Feathered serpent, dark heart of sky : myths of Mexico / by David Bowles.
Description: First [edition]. | El Paso : Cinco Puntos Press, 2018.
Identifiers: LCCN 2017021739 (print) | LCCN 2017035543 (ebook) |
ISBN 978-1-941026-73-1 (e-book) | ISBN 978-1-941026-71-7 (cloth : alk. paper)
ISBN 978-1-941026-72-4 (pbk. : alk. paper)
Subjects: LCSH: Indian mythology—Mexico.
Classification: LCC F1219.3.R38 (ebook) | LCC F1219.3.R38 B69 2017 (print) |
DDC 972/.01—dc23
LC record available at https://lccn.loc.gov/2017021739

Book and cover design by Sergio A. Gómez

cover and interior
illustrations © 2017 LxsDos
(LxsDos is Christian and Ramon Cardenas)
maintainstudio@gmail.com

All good things come from El Paso!

Para mi abuelo
MANUEL GARZA
que en paz descance.

Table of Contents

Introduction

Five hundred years ago, Mexico was quite different. The Triple Alliance of Anahuac—what we now call the Aztec Empire—dominated an area that stretched from the Gulf of Mexico to the Pacific coast. Arrayed all around them were dozens of other nations: the Maya, the Purepecha, Zapotecs, Yaqui, Huichol, Huastec, and Tarahumara, among many others. All of these peoples had different languages, gods, and traditions. Over the centuries, though, migration, trade, and conflict had spread certain common cultural traits widely.

Twenty million people lived in this land when the Spanish arrived in 1519. But the conquistadores were not interested in the cultural richness of Mexico. In their single-minded hunger for glory and gold, in their zealous drive to see the "Indians" kneel to the Christian god, the Spanish swept across the landscape with their steel swords, their guns, their armored horses. They also brought with them diseases that devastated the indigenous population.

It was genocide. Seventy-five years later, only one million people remained. Most of these survivors converted to Catholicism. Many blended with the Spanish colonists who came to occupy lands emptied by conquest. That fusion of races and ethnicities is called mestizaje. In time, a caste system was created to carefully separate this new hybrid population into special groups. Spaniards—both those born in Spain, peninsulares, and those born in Mexico, criollos—had the greatest rights and privileges. Below them others were ranked by how much Spanish blood ran through their veins: castizos (75%, with 25% indigenous), moriscos (75%, with 25% black), mestizos (50%, with 50% indigenous), mulattoes (50%, with 50% black). Pure indigenous and black individuals were at the very bottom of this social hierarchy.

As a result of this caste system, the sort of life a person had was essentially determined by the number of Spanish ancestors they laid claim to. Light skin and eyes, European features—such attributes brought advancement and opportunity. As a result, those who were products of mestizaje often turned away from their own native heritage and sought to be more like the Spanish conquerors, even oppressing people with less Spanish blood than they had.

Even after the caste system broke down and Mexico won its independence from Spain, traces of this old prejudice stubbornly survived. A fledgling Mexican identity was arising, however. The late 19th century saw a renewed interest in the pre-Colombian glories of the nation. But much had been lost. The few traditions that survived were diluted and fractured. And so they have remained, even down to my own generation.

By the time my grandfather Manuel Garza was born, his family's indigenous past had been wiped away. They were Spanish-speaking Mexicans, then Mexican-American Texans, heirs to traditions from across the sea. Ranches and cattle were the lifeblood of their community in northern Mexico and deep South Texas.

Their norteño music and weekly mass were also European, if flavored with native spice. One of the worst insults was *indio*. Everyone swore their ancestors were pure Spanish.

Even though the stories my grandparents, aunts, and uncles told me when I was child were thick with local lore—strange boogeymen and wailing women—no trace remained of the old gods, the ancient priests, the vaunted heroes of Mexico's pre-Colombian past.

In school, I was taught—like my father—the myths of the Norse, the Egyptians, the Romans, and especially the Greeks. I devoured the *Odyssey*, hungry for those Bronze-Age sensibilities, that interweaving of human and divine. On my own, I read other great epics of Western mythology: the *Iliad*, the *Aeneid*. I widened my net, plunged into India and its *Ramayana*, sought out the *Sunjata* of West Africa.

But it wasn't until I took a world literature class in college that I read a single Aztec or Maya myth. Amazing. I had attended schools just miles from the Mexican border, but not one of my teachers had spoken of Quetzalcoatl or Itzamna, of Cihuacoatl or Ixchel. My family also knew nothing of these Mesocamerican gods.

Something important had been kept from me and other Mexican-

American students. At first I was shocked and a bit angry. Yet who could I blame for five centuries of syncretism and erasure? Rather than lash out in response to the loss I felt, I began to scour the local libraries for every book I could find about pre-Colombian Mexican myths. In the end, I realized, it was my responsibility—knowing of this lack on my part—to reconnect with that forgotten past.

That duty to the history of one's people has never been better expressed than in one of the few remaining poems of the Maya, from the colonial-era manuscript *Songs of Dzitbalché*:

It's vital we never lose count
Of how many long generations
Have passed since the faraway age
When here in this land lived
Great and powerful men
Who lifted the walls of those cities—
The ancient, awesome ruins,
Pyramids rising like hills.

We try to determine their meaning
Here in our humbler towns,
A meaning that matters today,
One we draw from the signs
Those men of the Golden Age—
Men of this land, our forefathers—
Urged us to seek in the sky.

Consecrated to this task,
We turn our faces upward
As darkness slowly falls
From zenith to horizon
And fills the sky with stars
In which we scry our fate.

I found quite a lot of meaning in those scattered myths. They helped me through some very dark moments in my life. In time I became a school teacher, then a university professor. Though no standards required it, I did my best to share the heritage I had rediscovered with my students. My passion for our lost past drove me even further: I began to study Mayan and Nahuatl, wanting to decipher the original indigenous texts myself without the filter of a translator's voice.

The difficulty was that so much had been destroyed. The Conquest not only decimated the native population of Mexico. It also eviscerated their literature, their history. Conquering soldiers and zealous priests had burned many of the indigenous manuscripts, and converted native minds shrugged off the lore of millennia. Though some Spaniards and mestizos sought to preserve what they could of the venerable old words, setting down songs and sayings using the foreign alphabet, the damage had been done.

Today, we cannot just pick up the indigenous equivalent of the *Odyssey* and read it—beyond the *Popol Vuh*, a *Quiché* Maya text from Guatemala, no such work has survived in Mesoamerica. What we have are stories and fragments of stories, preserved piecemeal across multiple codices and colonial histories or passed down word-of-mouth for centuries in remote communities.

As a result, the work of a chronicler or teacher is made very difficult: we have no cohesive narrative of Mexico's mythic identity, no mythological history to rival other classical epics. As I pondered the dilemma, I saw a need for an exciting fusion of the different stories, one that could make Mesoamerican mythology come alive for a Western audience the way William Buck's abridged take on the *Ramayana* did for Hindu epics, one that employs engaging, accessible, yet timeless language, much like Robert Fagles' translations of the *Iliad*, *Odyssey*, and *Aeneid*.

So I set out to write the book you hold in your hands.

Of course, I am hardly the first to retell these tales. The collections I found as a college freshman in different border libraries existed because of wonderful scholars and authors who gathered together written and orally transmitted myths and legends. What makes the present volume different is that—instead of telling the tales separately, discretely—I craft a single chronological narrative.

Drawing from a variety of sources (especially Nahuatl and Maya texts such as the *Popol Vuh, Cantares Mexicanos,* the *Codex Chimalpopoca, Primeros Memoriales,* and the *Florentine Codex*), this fresh take blurs the line between the legendary and the historical. My intent has been to stitch together myths and legends, organizing the tales so that they trace the mythic past of Mesoamerica from the creation of the world to the arrival of the Spanish.

As a Mexican-American author and translator, I see myself as one of many transmitters of tradition down the generations. My renditions treat these stories with respect and intimacy, as though they depict actual events. Because of the state of the existing lore, however, I have used several different techniques to create English-language versions. A few of the pieces are simply translated with some editorial adjustments to fit the larger narrative. Others are looser adaptations of myths and legends with some partial translation. Many are straight-up retellings, often of orally transmitted stories.

Quite a few of the myths are themselves syntheses of multiple sources, interwoven into a coherent narrative that I have quilted into the chronological sequence of the book itself. For the most part, I have synthesized several texts together from a single cultural tradition. A few times, however, I have blended Maya and Aztec cosmovisions wherever their overlap suggested an older Mesoamerican mythology from which both may have drawn. In such instances, I am not trying to erase the distinctiveness of the two very different cultures, but to reflect the hybrid mestizaje that has long been a characteristic of the Mexican identity.

I have provided notes on my sources and a comprehensive bibliography. My hope is that readers will become intrigued or excited by the mythological history I have woven and feel compelled to dive into the original texts as I once did, seeking to find some part of myself reflected in those ancient, enduring words.

DAVID BOWLES
August 22, 2016

The First Three Ages of the World

Convocation

Look upon our beloved Mexico. The ancient singers gave her such lovely names—

Navel of the Moon.

Foundation of Heaven.

Sea-Ringed World.

From jungle-thick peninsula and isthmus to misty highlands and hardy deserts, Mexico has cradled dozens of nations through the millennia, all worshipping the divine around them, shaping names and tales that echo one another while remaining distinct.

If you listen close, you can hear the voices of our ancestors, whispering down the long years in a hundred different tongues, urging us never to forget where we came from, how Mexico came to be, the price they paid to make us who we are.

Can you hear that ancient chorus, chanting to the rhythm of the wooden drum, accompanied by the throaty shrill of the conch? That is the flower song, the holy hymn. Listen closely, sisters and brothers: catch snatches of the melody. Let us sing the old thoughts with new words.

Can you see the looms of our grandmothers, shuttling out colors, the weft and woof of so many tribes? They unfurl through the ages, frayed or unraveled by time and conquest like well-worn, rainbowed rebozos. Take up the threads, each of you, and weave with me the multi-hued fabric of our history, from the obsidian darkness of the void to the flash of foreign steel upon these shores.

We start at the beginning.

Origins

The Dual God

There was never nothing.

Before you or I or anything else existed, the universe was filled with a mysterious vital force we call *ku* or *teotl*. Still and calm, this divine energy stirred slow, hushed murmurs spreading in languid ripples across the immeasurable expanse.

Then, at the very heart of the cosmos, the force compressed, coalescing into a powerful being of two complementary halves—what we might call male and female. This dual god, Ometeotl in the Nahua tongue, the ancients lovingly called *our grandparents*. Ometeotl began to dream and to speak to itself about those dreams, describing a vast world and multi-tiered sky, peopled with creatures so diverse and wonderful that the very thought of them brought joy to our grandparents' hearts.

And there, in that primal place of authority at the center of everything, Ometeotl understood that it could be a mirror in which these dreams would be reflected, from which they would emerge into existence.

Though still one, its two halves became more distinct. For this reason, we give them both many names: Builder and Molder, Lord and Lady of the Two, Goddess and God Who Sustain Us, Matchmaker and Midwife, Grandmother and Grandfather. They pulled the vital force in two directions, molding it to form the vast cosmic sea below and the empty heavens above. From the very depths of the eternal waters, our grandparents drew a massive leviathan, Cipactli. With its knobby skin and razor-sharp teeth, the beast prowled the sea, a frightening mixture of reptile, amphibian, and fish. Always hungry, Cipactli would not remain still, but kept diving in search of food. Our grandparents, who had hoped to build a world atop the monster's back, understood that creation was a more complex task than they had imagined.

They would need help to finish their work.

Time Lord and Old God

Perhaps formed from the cycling of endless currents in the cosmic sea, another figure appeared, delighting Ometeotl. Turquoise-blue and very young, the newcomer wielded flinty stones in each hand, which he struck together, sending sparks and warmth throughout the universe. With his birth, time was set into motion at last, its interlocking gears slowly but ceaselessly marking the days and the years. As a result, our grandparents named him Xiuhtecuhtli—Lord of Time—and made him God of Fire.

Like Ometeotl, the Lord of Time had a dual nature: he could transform at will into his nahualli or spirit form, a dragon-like fire serpent whose coiling body matched the circular cycling of the ages. Eventually, as the complex wheels of time were deciphered, he would establish the two calendars that govern life in Mesoamerica: solar and sacred years, interlocking, ever-turning.

As the first year of our universe began to wind down, a change came over the Lord of Time: he began to grow weaker, to stoop over, to shamble slowly through the cosmos. His hair thinned, turned gray. His skin wrinkled and sagged. He became, in a word, old. Finally, this old god lay down, overcome by the shadow of something that had not yet entered the universe: death. But as the last flame of life flickered weakly in his soul, our divine grandparents, having learned the value of time, sacrificed a bit of the mysterious force from which they had formed themselves. Speeding that energy into the dying god, they restored his youthful vitality for another cycle. So it is that we renew every year by giving up something we hold dear, sending what little power we possess to the heart of the Lord of Time.

Brothers and Stewards of the Earth

Our grandparents realized that they could unfold themselves, bringing powerful, divine children into existence to assist them in creating and maintaining the world they had envisioned. First they brought two sons into existence, opposite but complementary forces: Feathered Serpent burst from the cosmic sea and took flight through the endless sky, his long body rippling with bright red, green, and blue plumes. Heart of Sky swirled to life in the heavens before dropping to the waters and spinning like a violent cyclone, dark smoke curling from the black mirror on his forehead. The two looked upon their dual parent and awaited instructions.

"Mighty sons," Ometeotl said, "you both hold one half of the key to creation. Feathered Serpent, you embody order and loving care, structure that comes from compassion. Heart of Sky, you wield force, passion, conflict—the willingness to tear down and begin again. Together you will build a world on which our children can thrive and work to keep the wheels of time forever turning."

At first, the brothers spent years testing the limits of their powers. Each discovered he possessed a nahualli. Feathered Serpent could transform into a massive hound that wielded lightning and fire. In this guise, he was called Xolotl, twin or double. Heart of Sky was able to shapeshift into a huge jaguar (Tepeyollotl, Mountainheart) whose very steps would make the earth tremble one day.

At last the brothers came together and considered their parents' vision of a world upon the waters of the vast cosmic sea. They thought long and hard about how to realize this dream, and then they debated with each other for many cycles of time. Finally, Feathered Serpent convinced Heart of Sky that they should try to reason with the great, hungry leviathan Cipactli. He called to it with his lulling, resounding voice, and the beast emerged from the depths.

"Powerful Cipactli," Feathered Serpent said, "you have been chosen by our mother-father the Dual God to bear the earth upon your back. Your strength makes you the only being capable of this feat. All the inhabitants of the sea-ringed world will glorify your name, calling you Ruler of Earth."

"I AM HUNGRY," growled Cipactli. "WHAT CARE I FOR PRAISE?"

Heart of Sky drew closer to the leviathan. "Those who live on your broad back will curb that hunger with many sacrifices, beast. As many as you demand."

Snarling, Cipactli twisted in the waves and clamped fearsome jaws upon one of Heart of Sky's feet, tearing it away and swallowing it. "I AM HUNGRY *NOW!*"

Heart of Sky, angry and in pain, began to spin violently, attacking the leviathan. Feathered Serpent rushed to his brother's aid, coiling himself around Cipactli so it could not move. Together they broke that massive beast in two, leaving it unable to ever dive again.

"Now the true work begins," Feathered Serpent said to his brother. "A livable world must be crafted upon this craggy back. Then can we create new life, creatures for which we will be caretakers, stewards."

Heart of Sky looked down at his leg. A bit of bare bone protruded where once he had possessed a foot. Pulling the smoking mirror from his forehead, he attached it to his mangled limb.

"Caretakers, for certain. But also judges, ready to punish when wrong is done."

Feathered Serpent regarded his brother silently. He understood Heart of Sky's outrage, but he hoped in time he could temper the anger that flared in his brother's soul. Now, however, he took up Cipactli's tail, which had been severed in the fight, and planted it at the center of the newly formed earth.

"Become a tree!" he cried out. "Sink yourself deep in the bowels of the world. Let those roots spread to the four corners of earth, sprouting into four saplings. Grow tall, spreading branches wide to hold the heavens away from the land, so that the future inhabitants of the sea-ringed world may live and breathe and contemplate the universe in awe."

Thus the five world trees came into existence, ready to serve as passageways between the vast expanse of heaven, the surface of the earth, and the dark hungry recesses that were once the leviathan's innards.

The brothers looked upon their work, satisfied at this beginning.

Mother, Protector and the New Gods

The female aspect of Ometeotl, our beloved grandmother, came to understand the need for motherhood, for someone to bear, nurture, and protect the generation of gods required to ready the earth for its future inhabitants. So she unfolded herself, bringing into existence the Divine Mother and the Protector. As they stood before her, hand in hand, she addressed them in this way:

"You, Divine Mother, embody love, care, and selflessness. Down the ages you will be called by many names: Quilaztli, Tonantzin, Queen of Heaven. Gods and mortals alike will turn their eyes to you for comfort in the darkest moments, and you will pour compassion on their heads.

"And you, Protector, reflect the other elements of motherhood: strength to face great pain, unyielding struggle, fierceness in keeping children safe. Ixchel, they will name you. Cihuacoatl, female serpent. Midwives and those giving birth will cry out to you in anguish, fear, and despair, and you will aid them in the battle to bring life into the world."

Then the Divine Mother gave birth to the second generation of gods. There was the goggle-eyed and fanged god of rain, Tlaloc, whose power could feed or drown the world; the god of spring, Xipe Totec, who shed his skin each year like a dried-up husk in order to renew life; the goddess of flowers and fertility, Xochiquetzal, who clothed the earth in color; Chalchiuhtlicue, goddess of rivers and lakes, who poured sweet water down her jade-green skirt for drinking and baptism. And these were just the beginning. More and more divinities were born, from gods of corn and maguey to deities of stone and stars and death itself. The Divine Mother and the Protector gathered them up and called their home Tamoanchan, place of misty sky. There, above the newly formed earth, the divine beings learned their destinies.

In time, the young gods began their work. With loving hands, they transformed the insatiable and broken Cipactli into the nourishing and verdant Mecihtli, Earth Goddess and source of fertility. Upon her ample flesh they formed mountains and streams, grew trees and plains, shaped beasts and birds to gladden the eye and heart. They readied the world for the arrival of human beings, the creatures whose praise and sacrifice would keep the wheels of time forever turning.

The Heavens and the Underworld

As the younger gods prepared the earth for the arrival of humanity, Feathered Serpent and Heart of Sky began to arrange the universe to sustain the fledgling world. Upon the boughs of the World Trees they set themselves to building, layering heaven in swaths of holy energy. The levels numbered thirteen, reflecting the perfection of the sacred calendar. The first level was set aside for the moon, which the brothers agreed would illuminate the night. Above that was the heaven of stars, thousands of glittering gems that would bring joy to wandering souls. But the brightest of lights would sail the sky in a third heaven beyond these astral jewels: a brilliant sun whose creation would be the brothers' crowning accomplishment.

Feathered Serpent, wanting to be close to his handiwork, claimed the fourth heaven for himself. He set comets and shooting stars over his head in the fifth level to separate him from the somber sixth space of deepest green where his chaotic brother chose to whirl blackly.

The seventh layer was blazingly blue, the daytime sky we see when the sun arcs from horizon to horizon. Above it, Heart of Sky set the heaven of storms, a violent region of wind and lightning and thunder like the clash of enormous obsidian blades.

The remaining levels were set aside for the gods. After the dazzling heavens of white, yellow, and red, the brothers set Tamoanchan in the twelfth heaven at the celestial summit, a paradise which earthly words could never do justice. Thus were our Divine Mother and the Protector forever enthroned on high in an awesome metropolis built by divine hands, towering ziggurats, and broad avenues that cast a pale shadow in the minds of men: Teotihuacan, city of the gods.

Beyond all lay the thirteenth heaven: Omeyocan, Place of Duality, abode of our beloved grandparents. Deep in its inscrutable heart stood Tonacacuahuitl, the Mother Tree, where the souls of human beings began to bud, nourished like babes at the breast. There also, aflame with energy from every holy sacrifice, the Lord of Time watched the wheels of the cosmos turn and turn and turn.

These labors complete, Feathered Serpent and Heart of Sky descended to the sea-ringed world, which sat at the heart of the vast cosmic sea, the canopy of heaven spreading above it. They divided the world into four parts—North, South, East, and West—with the World Tree at the intersection of a vast cross, an axis for the universe.

"Now," said Heart of Sky, "life has a home, with caretakers to sustain it. Likewise, my brother, must we make a realm for death." Just as the Lord of Time grows old, dies, and is renewed, so the earth must grow cold and fallow before rebirth. And humans must feel mortality's sting. Their souls must be cycled through the cosmic wheels. Come, let us fashion an underworld, layered like the heavens, to purge their souls upon death and return them to their source."

But Feathered Serpent objected. "Not all souls should face the same fate, my brother. What of those who willingly give their lives to keep the wheels turning? Or children dead before their lives have truly begun? Exceptions must be made."

They argued for a time, and finally Heart of Sky strode away into the North, where he descended into Cipactli's interior, split into enormous caverns by the roots of the World Trees. There he unfolded himself into two more beings: Newborn Lightning and Sudden Lightning, also called Blue and Red Tezcatlipoca.

"We three are as one," he said to them. "Together we will delve deep into the bowels of this creature, heedless of its pain, and fashion a scourging path for the human soul. Nine levels will contain the Realm of the Dead. First, a roiling river, swift and deep and broad. Alone no man or woman will ford its rushing waters, a reminder of their inherent weakness. Instead, a companion will they need, an animal faithful and true. Yes, families will bury a dog with their dead, and upon its back will be the crossing.

"Below we will erect mighty mountains that move and clash, grinding stone to sand. Here the dead will learn they cannot dawdle: speed is of the essence in death as well as life. Next they descend into a level of razor-sharp obsidian that begins the work of shearing the flesh away. Another region of biting winds that flail with frigid cruelty continues the task, until they become so light that the swirling winds of the fifth level whip their forms about like ragged banners.

"Deeper still we will set a narrow path along which the dead must travel while pierced by thousands of arrows and darts till they emerge at the seventh level, where jaguars will at last eat their hearts, freeing the core of their soul. Beyond this we will carve a vast basin to fill with the blackest, coldest water in the cosmos. Traversing that lake, the human soul will have every memory, every shred of physical existence, stripped away.

"Finally, at the heart of the Realm of the Dead, we will raise a mighty palace, carved from the very bones of the earth. Here those souls will stand before a puissant king and queen, rulers of this black domain. If truly shorn of the flesh, they will be admitted into oblivion and, should such be the will of Ometeotl, possible rebirth."

So Heart of Sky declared, and with his sons he went to work. When the Underworld had been wrought to suit his purposes, he set a dark lord over each layer to oversee its function. Then he brought down from the twelfth heaven Mictecacihuatl and Mictlantecuhtli, the goddess and god of death, and placed them on their thrones there at the very nadir of the universe.

"Behold your realm. Rule it wisely and well. Fill it with such terrors as you deem fit. Make of it a place of fear. Only when humans fear death will they value life. And fear will help strip away their flesh on their journey here, till naught but bones and soul remains. Let none but the dead enter. None. Not even my brother."

Upon the sea-ringed world, Feathered Serpent busied himself with death as well. Seeing the entrance to the Underworld off in the North, he fashioned paradises in the other three directions. In the East he set Tonatiuhchan, the House of the Sun, misty land of flowers and birds of bright plumage. This would be the destination of men who gave their lives, whether in sacrifice or upon the battlefield, to keep the wheels of the cosmos in motion. Each morning, transformed into butterflies and hummingbirds and other precious winged things, these souls would accompany the sun as it ascended to its zenith, returning to enjoy the cool beauty of their eternal home. Every four years they would fly again to the sea-ringed world, to sip from its blooms and sing divine songs to gladden the hearts of the living.

In the West, Feathered Serpent established Cihuatlampa, the Realm of Noble Women, an eternal resting place for mothers who died during childbirth. Transformed into fearsome warriors for having lost their lives in the most important battle of human existence, these women would accompany the sun each afternoon as it slid down the western sky. Feathered Serpent wanted to allow the fierce mothers earthly visits like he would male warriors, but he understood that their longing for the children they lost would make them dangerous. Their trips to the sea-ringed world would only take place once every fifty-two years.

In the South, the creator god wrought a verdant Tlalocan, Kingdom of Water, a land replete with fountainheads and streams, lakes, and mountain springs. Every good and useful fruit grew with abundance, and every corner echoed with the croak of frogs and chirp of birds. To this paradise Feathered Serpent brought the young god Tlaloc.

"From this fount of fresh water you will provide the world with rain. But the precious liquid, so vital for life, does not spring eternal. Like all else, it must be renewed. Every death caused by water will channel divine energy to your realm. Those who drown, who are struck by lightning, who suffer from disease, or who struggle with deformities— they ensure the fall of life-giving rain. In times of great drought, humans may elect to give their lives to draw water down from the heavens. Their sacrifice will be yours as well.

"The souls of all these dead will populate your realm. Here they will suffer no more, but delight in the bounty I have prepared for them."

Finally, Feathered Serpent thought upon the greatest tragedy he knew would face humanity: the death of infants, the foreshortening of their young lives. For an answer, he spread his shimmering green wings and ascended to Omeyocan itself. In the presence of our grandparents, looking with hope and love upon the human souls just beginning to blossom on the Mother Tree, the creator god made his case.

"The souls of children who have not yet begun to truly live," he argued, "ought to return here, to their place of origin, to await another birth, another chance at joy."

Ometeotl agreed.

Feathered Serpent's heart rejoiced. Despite the angry will of Heart of Sky, death could now inspire hope as well as fear.

The First Three Ages of the World

The First Age

The moment had come. After caring lovingly for creation, the younger gods had departed for their celestial home. Feathered Serpent and Heart of Sky stood upon the sea-ringed world and readied themselves to create thinking, speaking beings much different from the mute creatures that the young gods had set roaming earth, water and sky. Taking the very bones of the world, the brothers fashioned a man and a woman—towering, imperious giants of rugged flesh and snow-white hair. Infusing the pair with teotl, the brothers named them Oxomoco and Cipactonal. Enlisting the help of the Lord of Time, the brothers also formed a ball of fire to hang in the third heaven. But this meager sun was weak. Life wilted in its half-light. The giant humans shivered with cold.

Feathered Serpent understood. "A god must sacrifice himself to bring light to this world, must meld with that flame and become a full sun, pouring tonalli, radiant teotl, down to sustain life."

Seeing that his brother meant to offer himself and become the most revered of all the deities, Heart of Sky swirled up into the heavens and plunged himself into the conflagration, becoming the very first sun to spread its warmth over mountain, sea and field.

To Feathered Serpent fell the labor of teaching the primal couple. He gave them language, taught them the names of every beast and tree, showed them how to work stone and cultivate each useful plant.

With the Lord of Time, he helped them devise a calendar to measure the solar year with all its attendant rites and agricultural seasons—eighteen months of twenty days, plus an unnamed period of five—365 days.

Each of the days of the month had a different sign, twenty in all: crocodile, wind, house, lizard, snake, death, deer, rabbit, water, dog, monkey, grass, reed, jaguar, eagle, vulture, earthquake, flint, rain, flower.

The gods gave the first people another calendar to keep track of the passing of time and to divine probable futures: twenty weeks of thirteen days—260 days.

The two calendars interlocked like gears. As the twenty-day months turned, so did the thirteen-day weeks. Our ancestors named days by combining the number of the week with the sign of the month. The very first day in the universe, then, was 1-Crocodile, as crocodile is the first day sign. The following days were 2-Wind, 3-House, 4-Lizard, and so on.

The ancients also named each year by its first day. Therefore do we know that creation began in the year 1-Crocodile, on the day 1-Crocodile.

The two calendars came into alignment once every fifty-two years, completing a cycle. A new year and fresh cycle would then begin on 1-Crocodile.

As each evening fell and Heart of Sky slipped past the horizon into the Realm of the Dead to be attended to by his minions there, Feathered Serpent taught Oxomoco and Cipactonal not to fear the dark, but to delight in the stars and give each one a name.

In time the couple had a child, a son they called Piltzintecuhtli, Young Prince. He grew to be a handsome, strapping young man, but there was no maiden yet alive to be his wife. Seeing his need, the Divine Mother took strands of long, black hair from the head of Xochiquetzal, goddess of beauty and fertility, and with them wove a lovely bride.

The years wore on, one calendar cycle after another. The giants multiplied and spread across the sea-ringed world. They lifted mighty temples and monuments in order to better worship the gods. There they performed their penances and bloodlettings and sacrifices so that the cosmic order would be sustained.

Heart of Sky looked down on the earth and was not pleased. The sacrifices seemed paltry to him, even the New Fire Ceremony meant to restore his strength every fifty-two years. Listening to the worship and prayers the giants lifted toward heaven, Heart of Sky was convinced that they favored his brother, Feathered Serpent. Temples to Feathered Serpent seemed finer, his priests more richly arrayed, the offerings sweeter.

The god of the smoking mirror coldly resolved to exterminate all the giants. Calling up vast reserves of divine energy, Heart of Sky sent his huge jaguar nahualli down to the sea-ringed world. Mountainheart sought out giants whose calendar day sign, determined by their birth, was jaguar. He taught them dark sorcery, how to transform into their nahualli and bend the minds of others, then he twisted them to his own purpose. When he had trained them to despise other giants utterly, he led them in a vicious war against their brothers and sisters.

In the year 1-Reed, on the day 4-Jaguar, Mountainheart and his army of jaguars devoured nearly every giant on the face of the earth. It was the 676th year since Heart of Sky had become the sun, the end of the thirteenth calendar cycle. A handful of men and women survived in the mountains. They cried out to Feathered Serpent, who descended to find his beloved creation despoiled and bereft. Seeing Mountainheart leap up at the sun to rejoin with his divine form, the creator god knew his brother was to blame.

Driven by indignant rage, Feathered Serpent attacked the sun at its zenith. Their struggle was great. It nearly rent the heavens in its violence. Twinning into Feathered Serpent and Xolotl, the creator simultaneously gripped Heart of Sky, his own plumage aflame, and uprooted one of the World Trees. Wielding it like a gargantuan club, he struck his brother from the third heaven, sending him plunging into the cosmic sea with such force that the god of the smoking mirror was nearly obliterated.

Thus did the first age of the world come to a tragic end.

The Second Age
Soon the gods descended once more to repair the damage done to the sea-ringed world.

The Divine Mother worked with Feathered Serpent to carve new humans from wood. Once he had bled life into them—his own chalchiuhatl, precious liquid—the men and women arose and lived their lives much as the giants had before.

This time Feathered Serpent became the sun, smiling down on his creation as they begot and bore children, erected wooden homes and temples, lived their small lives in honor, worshipping their magnanimous gods.

As the cycles wore on, however, a dark swirl began to form unnoticed in the cosmic sea, slow at first, but spinning ever faster down the years, a furious typhoon of spite and vengeance.

Then—at the end of the seventh cycle of this second age, on the day 4-Wind of the year 1-Flint, the 364th since Feathered Serpent had become the sun—Heart of Sky, Hurricane, the Smoking Mirror emerged from the trackless ocean and stormed across the earth.

His winds blasted and scoured the mountains, shredded fields and forests, emptied lakes and wore boulders down to pebbles. The wooden abodes of humans were ripped entirely from the face of the earth, and people themselves—much lighter than giants—were lifted by the gales and flung into the void.

Feathered Serpent, horrified and impotent, reached out to the few remaining men and women and gave them a desperate gift: tails to anchor them to whatever trees remained and feet that gripped the branches like a second set of hands. Thus were born the tlacaozomahtin, ape-men, who still live in dark corners of the world.

Mere moments after saving this small remnant, Feathered Serpent was beset by the howling, apocalyptic winds of his brother's long-simmering wrath. Though he lifted flaming wings to beat aside the blast, the sun was torn from the sky and hurled beyond oblivion.

Thus did the second age of the world end in vengeance.

The Third Age

Hurricane—for he had truly ceased to be Heart of Sky—spent his ire
and then stood alone upon the rocky, desolate earth. He called down
the gods to begin again the work of creation, restoring flora and fauna,
filling rivers and lakes, smoothing the rugged contours of the world.

With his red and blue sons, the god of the smoking mirror took clay
from the guts of the earth and fashioned beings to serve and worship him.
Wanting to more closely watch and rule them, he persuaded Tlaloc, lord
of rain and lightning, to leave his paradise and his new bride Xochiquetzal
to become the sun.

For several calendar cycles, Hurricane was content with the sacrifices
and adulation of his creations. But the envy that had taken root in the
dark god continued to grow. He looked upon Tlaloc's wife Xochiquetzal
and saw that she was the most beautiful being in the universe. It was
intolerable that she pair herself with a lesser god.

So Hurricane entered Tlalocan and stole the goddess of fertility,
forcing her to marry him and live within his dark heaven. Tlaloc,
devastated, burned even brighter in the sky, glowering with betrayal and
anger. With no lord or lady to instruct them, the tlaloques—servants of
Tlaloc, the goggle-eyed god—ceased pouring water from the sky. Rain
stopped falling. A great drought swept the world.

The people of the Third Age cried out to Tlaloc, begging for rain and
a surcease from his anguished heat. But their prayers annoyed the sun.
This attempt at humanity had been fashioned by his enemy's hands, so
why should he care? He spitefully refused to provide moisture, insisting
that every thinking creature suffer as much as he did without his beloved.
The men and women of earth continued to beg him as the rivers and lakes
gradually dried up.

Hurricane allowed the suffering for a time, enjoying the constant stream of
supplications and sacrifice. But he finally tired of Tlaloc's tantrum. He descended
to confront the god of rain.

Tlaloc would not heed the commands of his betrayer. They clashed above the parched earth, the sun bombarding Hurricane with massive waves of fire that were churned and spun away by typhoon whorls—toward the sea-ringed world. The whole earth burned, great storms sweeping across the land on screaming, furnace-like winds. Most people died, but a few found shelter in mountain caves. Furious that any of his foe's creations should survive, Tlaloc had his servants draw magma from deep within the earth, making it explode out of vast volcanoes and flow hungrily over the surface of the world.

At that moment, 312 years after being expelled from creation by his brother, Feathered Serpent returned, glowing with renewed power, determined to save what he could. Struggling against Hurricane and Tlaloc both, he subdued them and forced them to their respective spheres before they could wreak the utter devastation of the world.

The small bands of survivors now begged Feathered Serpent to have mercy on them. The creator god transformed these last people, giving them wings and pulling quills from his own flesh to cover them. Now gifted with flight, his brother's creations rose above the lava sear, borne aloft by drafts of heated wind.

Feathered Serpent knew that remaking this burning world would task the very limits of the gods' abilities. He hoped that he could avoid the mistakes and envies of the past as he sought to craft humans who could be his partners in preserving the order of the cosmos. But the winged survivors of this destruction he allowed to make their homes in the high crags and cliffs of the new world as long as they kept to themselves.

For their age, the third, had ended in conflagration after only six calendar cycles, on the day 4-Rain of the year 1-Flint.

The Fourth Age and the Hero Twins

Convocation

Follow me now into the dim beginnings of the Fourth Age. The cataclysm is over, the conflagration has snuffed itself to ash, and the sea-ringed world is dark but for the light of the stars and a faint smear of perpetual dawn on the eastern horizon.

It is an epoch of gods, great and small, who strive to restore the shattered earth.

Some bend their knee to the cosmic order, to the competing wills of Feathered Serpent and Hurricane, carrying out their appointed tasks without a word of complaint.
Others choose to forge a different path.

A few become heroes.

Two in particular survive down the years in some form or another throughout southern Mexico: bright paint in crumbling friezes, curling lines on rotting pages, stone statues in which their young profiles are captured forever, rebellious and brave.

Two brothers. Twins.

They are depicted again and again with distinctive headbands, one dark, the other sewn from a jaguar's pelt. We often find them with their father, a god of maize.

The millennia have effaced their names from most Mayan tongues. Archeologists, crafting a code to categorize forgotten deities, call the father God E. His sons are God CH and God S.

But in the highlands of Guatemala, despite all odds, the K'iche' Maya preserved these ancestral stories, even after the glyphs of mighty empires had fallen into disuse. With letters learned from Spanish priests, they transcribed those ancient words in their native tongue.

The *Popol Vuh*, they called this sacred scripture. *The Book of the People*.

Come closer, friends. Let me open that tome, let me find the right page, and I will tell you of the wondrous deeds of the Hero Twins:

Xbalanque and Hunahpu, as the K'iche' name them, playful and courageous young men who mocked death itself.

Then let us weave strands of Aztec lore into this epic to explore the short but unforgettable age that ended—as peoples across the globe affirm—with the greatest flood our world has ever seen.

The Hero Twins

The Tragedy of Their Fathers

During the long night before the dawn of the fourth sun, two brothers were born, minor gods of the milpas, those tangled fields of corn and bean and squash. They were named One Hunahpu and Seven Hunahpu, for the day signs of their respective births. They lived with their mother, Ixmukane, a maize goddess.

In time One Hunahpu married Lady Egret, and she bore him two sons: One Monkey and One Artisan. The small family continued to live with One Hunahpu's mother and brother in the gloom of a world with no sun.

Other gods hailed One and Seven Hunahpu as knowledgeable and wise, the foremost seers on the earth. They taught young One Monkey and One Artisan many skills, and in time the boys became like their father and uncle: singers, musicians, poets, sculptors, and workers of jade and metal.

Though the brothers possessed a singular, innate goodness, they tended to shirk their responsibilities in order to roll dice and play ball. Every day the boys played with their father and uncle, two against two in the ball court. As each game began, a falcon would descend to watch them, sent by Hurricane and his sons. The falcon could fly in an instant from the sea-ringed world to Hurricane's abode in the sixth heaven, or just as well descend to the Land of the Dead to do his master's bidding there.

Lady Egret left the earth, returning to the Divine Mother, but the four ballplayers remained behind. Their ball court was located at Great Hollow, on the road to the Underworld, the dark land that men would one day call Xibalba, Realm of Fright. The King and Queen of Death could not help but hear them.

Disturbed by the riotous sounds, the god and goddess called together their council, all the dark lords in that place of fear, tasked with bringing death to humans in a variety of savage ways.

"Who are these middling fools that shake the earth with their running and that disturb the stillness of the grave with their shouts?" demanded the King of Death. "They show no proper fear and run roughshod over the natural order. We should bring them here to play ball. Since they have no respect for us, we shall beat them at their favorite game and then destroy them."

The dark lords all agreed with their sovereign, adding that upon winning they could seize the brothers' gear, the pads, yokes and plumed helmets that made up their kits.

The task of summoning One and Seven Hunahpu was given to the Royal Guard, four fearsome owls from the very throne room of the Land of the Dead. They flew from the Underworld in an instant, alighting in the stands above the ball court. The four players halted their game and approached the messengers.

"We have been sent by the Lords of the Underworld," announced Strafer, chief among them. "Harken unto the words of the King and Queen of Death: 'You must come. Do us the pleasure of playing ball in our dark courts. Your skill amazes us. Bring your gear, your yokes and pads and rubber ball.'"

"Is that what the gods of that fearful place truly said?" asked One Hunahpu.

"Yes. Now, come along. We shall accompany you."

"Fine, but wait while we let our mother know. She'll have to watch over my sons while we're gone."

One and Seven Hunahpu took the boys back home and explained the situation to Ixmukane, their mother.

"We've no choice but to go. These are messengers of the King of Death himself. But we'll be back, we promise. Here, we'll leave our ball behind as a token." They hung the rubber sphere in the rafters. "Don't worry, we'll be kicking it around again very soon."

One Hunahpu turned to his sons. "You two keep practicing your music, your art, your skill at games. Keep this house—and your grandmother's heart—warm in our absence."

Their mother began to weep at their words.

"We're off on a journey," they told her, "not to our deaths. Don't be sad."

Then the brothers left. Guided by the Royal Guard, they headed north toward the entrance to the Underworld. They descended through strange canyons, past streams of scorpions, over rivers of blood and pus. None of these obstacles slowed them down.

But then they came to a vast crossroads that offered four paths to the Land of the Dead: the Red, the Black, the White, and the Green. The messenger owls indicated the Black Road. "That is the one you should take. It is the King's Road."

And here was the beginning of their defeat, for the brothers heeded the Royal Guard, not suspecting that this was the path of the dead. They were led along its gruesome length to the council chambers of the dark lords, where their doom was further sealed. The horrid aristocrats of that fell place were seated in a row, but the first two—the king and queen themselves—were clever statues carved and arrayed by the artisans of the netherworld.

"Greetings, Your Majesty," they said to the first statue.

"The dawn shine upon you, Your Majesty," they said to the second.

The chambers erupted with laughter, for the brothers had failed again. Chortling, the dark lords mocked them.

"Foremost seers, indeed! Those are mere manikins, fools!" In their hearts the nobility of the Realm of Fright felt certain they had already won.

The real king and queen entered, smiles on their skeletal faces.

"Perfect. You have arrived. Tomorrow you will show your skill with yokes and guards. For the present, however, take a seat upon the bench we have prepared."

When the brothers sat down, they realized the bench was a burning hot slab. They squirmed around for a time, trying to save face, but finally they had to leap to their feet or risk real damage. The dark lords once more burst out in howls of laughter. They laughed so hard their innards ached. Even writhing in pain, they could not stop their chuckles and hoots.

Now the Underworld is full of torments of every kind, among them five terrible houses of torture. But as fate would have it, the brothers would only experience one. They were escorted to their supposed sleeping quarters by the rulers of that fearful place, who smiled and said:

"Enter, friends. Get some rest. In a moment you will be brought a torch and two cigars."

One and Seven Hunahpu went inside, greeted by inky blackness. Unbeknownst to them, the brothers were lodged in Dark House, a place devoid of light.

Meanwhile, the dark lords conferred. "They are certain to lose. Let us sacrifice them tomorrow. It will be quick. We shall use our bone-white blade to kill them both, and then we shall keep their gear."

The king and queen sent a messenger with a torch of *ocote* wood and two lit cigars. "Here you go. You are expected to return these in the morning—whole, just as they are now."

The brothers took the torch and the cigars, and once again they were defeated. They let the torch burn down to ashes. They smoked the cigars down to stubs. In the morning they were led back to the council chambers, fear mounting in their hearts.

"Where are my cigars? Where is the torch that I lent you last night?" demanded the King of Death.

In that moment of terror, a vision winged its way to the brothers from the heavens above. They saw their doom.

Then, in the depths of their despair, they also saw their victory.

So they admitted defeat. "They're all gone, Your Majesty."

"Very well. Today your days are ended. You will die here. You will be ripped from the world. Your faces will remain hidden. You will be sacrificed!"

And there and then the brothers were slaughtered. Their bodies were buried together in a single grave near the ball court, except for the head of One Hunahpu, which was removed at the king's command.

"Take his head," the god of death instructed, "and set it in the forked branches of that bare tree beside the road to serve as a reminder of our might."

But as soon as the head was fixed in place, the tree miraculously bore fruit, round and heavy like a skull. It was the calabash, and it hung now from every branch so that it was no longer clear where the head of One Hunahpu had been deposited.

The dark lords gathered round in amazement. It was clear that the sudden appearance of fruit was an ill omen. So the king and queen issued an edict:

"Let no one pick fruit from this tree. Let no one even sit beneath its boughs."

And all the inhabitants of that dreadful realm obeyed. Except a maiden.

The Victory of their Mother

The dark lord Blood Gatherer had a daughter, a maiden named Lady Blood. He told her of the tree and the prohibition of their king, trusting that she would obey. But Lady Blood was curious. She wondered about the taste of the fruit and pondered its possible origin.

Finally, she could not resist looking on the miracle herself, so she went alone to where the tree stood, near the ball court and the graves of sacrificial victims.

"Ah!" she exclaimed. "What sort of fruit is this? It simply has to be sweet. If only I could pick one and not be killed or banished. Just one."

Then the head of One Hunahpu spoke from the fork in the tree.

"Come, you're not really interested in these round things hanging from the branches. They're just skulls. You can't possibly want one."

"But I do," answered Lady Blood.

"Alright, then. Stretch out your right hand."

"Fine." Lady Blood reached toward the source of the voice, and the head squirted a bit of spit into her palm. Startled, the maiden drew back her hand and stared at it closely, but the saliva was gone.

"The spittle I've given you is a sort of symbol," explained the voice of One and Seven Hunahpu, for they had merged and spoke with a single mind. "You see, my head here has been stripped bare: all that's left is just the bone. But that's the way it is even with the head of a great lord. He only looks decent because of the flesh on his skull. Once he's dead and rotted away, though, people shrink in fear from that naked bone.

"His sons, now…they're like his saliva, which still contains his essence even after leaving his mouth. Whether they be the sons of a lord or a wise man or an orator, they preserve the basic nature of their father. His face isn't wholly lost, but passes to the children he leaves behind. That's what I'm doing through you. Now abandon this land of fright. Go to the surface of the sea-ringed world before they kill you. Find my mother, Ixmukane. Trust in my words."

The skull gave her many more instructions before she was on her way. By the time she reached her home, the saliva had sparked life in her womb, and she conceived twins, sons of One and Seven Hunahpu both. But instead of leaving the Land of the Dead, she remained in her father's house.

When six months had passed, Lord Blood Gatherer noticed that his daughter was pregnant. He went to the council chambers and addressed his king and queen:

"That daughter of mine is with child. A bastard."

"Very well," said the queen. "Question her. If she refuses to reveal the truth, you must punish her. Have her taken to some distant place and sacrificed."

So Lord Blood Gatherer confronted Lady Blood. "Whose child is in your belly, girl?"

"There is no child, lord father. I have not known the face of a man."

"I see. So you have given yourself to the pleasures of the flesh without my leave." He summoned the Royal Guard, and when those four fearsome owls arrived, he gestured at his daughter. "Take her away for sacrifice. Bring back just her heart, in a gourd, and surrender it to our king and queen this very day."

The Royal Guard departed, bearing aloft in black talons Lady Blood, a gourd and the council's bone-white blade, with which they were to sacrifice the maiden. Once they had traveled far from the center of the Underworld, the owls alighted and reluctantly readied themselves to complete the task.

Lady Blood begged them to reconsider. "It is not right that you should kill me, messengers. There is no disgrace carried in my womb, but a miracle, begotten when I went to visit One Hunahpu's head there beside the ball court. There is a greater power at work here, respected friends. You must not sacrifice me."

The owls looked upon her unblinking for quite some time. They had known her all her life, had watched her grow into a delightful young woman. Deceit was not her nature. And even if she were lying, they realized with a start, they did not wish her to die.

"But what can we take in place of your heart, Lady Blood? Your father demanded we bring it to the king and queen today."

"My heart will never belong to them. And you, friends, must no longer call this place your home. Never again let them force you to kill someone unjustly. There, upon the sea-ringed world, you can harry true villains. From now on, let the King and Queen of Death taste only blood, sap, resin. No more hearts burned in their presence. Not mine, not anyone's."

She placed her palm on a cochineal croton tree. "Drain the sap from this plant. Collect it in your gourd."

They used the blade to slice the trunk until sap dribbled out. The red resin congealed in the makeshift bowl, forming a lump like a heart surrounded by what appeared to be clotted blood.

"On the surface of the world you will be blessed," said the maiden to the owls with a happy smile. "You will have all you desire."

"So be it, Lady. We will accompany and serve you. But go on ahead while we present this false heart to the dark lords."

When the Royal Guard arrived in the council chambers, the fell aristocracy of the netherworld had already gathered.

"Has it been done?" asked the King of Death.

"Indeed, Your Majesty. Here is her heart in this gourd."

"Very well. Let us see." The king lifted out the coagulated sap, which looked for all the world like a heart glazed with ruddy gore.

"Excellent. Stir up the fire—let us set it among the coals."

Once the resinous clump was thrown upon the fire, the dark lords delighted in the aroma of its burning. They stood near, leaned into the smoke, delighted at the sweet smell.

As they watched it bubble and hiss, the owls slipped away, overtaking the maiden and leading her up through caverns, out of the bleak Land of the Dead and onto the surface of the earth.

And that is how the dark lords were first defeated, every one of them tricked by a maiden.

Their Birth and Childhood

Following the instructions she had been given by One and Seven Hunahpu, Lady Blood finally arrived where Ixmukane lived with One Monkey and One Artisan. She carried sons in her womb—soon they would be born, twins named Hunahpu and Xbalanque.

Standing before the grandmother, the maiden announced:

"Here I am, Lady Mother—your daughter-in-law, your own sweet child."

"What?" demanded Ixmukane. "Who are you? Where are you from? How can you be my daughter-in-law when my boys have both died in the Land of the Dead? Look upon these two: One Monkey and One Artisan, their true blood and heirs. Now go. Get out!"

Wincing at the shouts, Lady Blood did not move. "Regardless, I am still your daughter-in-law. I belong to your sons. One and Seven Hunahpu are not dead, Lady Mother. They live on in what I carry. They have turned dark tragedy to brightest hope, as you will see for yourself in the faces of my sons."

The other woman scoffed. "Daughter-in-law indeed. No, you lying wench, I have no need of you or the fruit of your disgrace. My sons are dead, I tell you. You are clearly an impostor!"

Lady Blood remained where she was, head high. After a few moments, Ixmukane frowned. "Right. You claim to be my daughter-in-law. If that is true, then go bring food for these boys. A netful of ripe ears of corn from our milpa."

"As you say," the maiden replied. She walked along the road that One and Seven Hunahpu had cleared until it opened onto the family milpa. One lone clump of cornstalks stood in its midst, with a single ear dangling from it.

"Oh, I am but a sinner, a debtor!" Lady Blood cried. "Where will I get the netful of food she has demanded?"

Then she remembered who she was, a noblewoman from the Land of the Dead, powerful and commanding. Lifting her hands, she called out to the guardians of food:

"Arise now, come, O Lady of Tribute, O Lady of Maize-Gold, O Lady of Cocoa Beans, O Lady of the Shameless Day! Come, you guardians of the food of One Monkey and One Artisan!"

Then, seizing the cornsilk at the top of the ear, she yanked upward. Though she did not pick the corn, it multiplied magically, filling her net till it overflowed. Calling to the animals of the field, she enlisted their help in transporting the load back to the house. Once they had arrived, the creatures brought her a carrying frame, and she made herself break out in a sweat so her mother-in-law would believe she had brought the net alone.

Ixmukane emerged from the house and was astonished at the mound of food. "Where did you get that corn? Did you steal it? Let me go see if you have stripped the milpa bare!"

She rushed to the field to find the clump of cornstalks intact and the impression of the net sunken deep in the earth. Something miraculous had occurred. And where there was one miracle, there could be others. She hurried back home and spoke to Lady Blood.

"This is surely a sign that you are, in truth, my daughter-in-law. I will keep watch over all that you do. Those grandchildren of mine you carry must already be as magical."

The day at last arrived, but Lady Blood was on the mountain, so Ixmukane did not witness the birth. Labor came upon the maiden suddenly, and the twins were born: Hunahpu and Xbalanque.

When their mother finally brought them down to the house, they could not sleep and made quite a fuss.

"Take them back to the mountain and leave them there," Ixmukane told her other two grandsons. "They just will not stop screaming."

So One Monkey and One Artisan dumped them on an anthill, hoping they would die, but the babies slept soundly and were not harmed. The jealous half-brothers then threw them in the brambles, from which their mother soon rescued them. Neither had a scratch.

In the end the older boys simply would not accept their half-brothers or Lady Blood into their home. The maiden had to raise her sons in the mountains, aided by animals and other beings. Over the years they learned to harness the divine energy that was their birthright, to communicate with the animals, to hunt with a blowgun, to coax melodies from the flute, and, above all, to play ball with such skill as to make their fathers very proud.

When they were able to fend for themselves, Lady Blood left them, knowing their destiny could not be fulfilled at her side. Once their mother was gone, Hunahpu and Xbalanque spent their days shooting their blowguns and felling prey. Though they had never received love or food from their fathers' family, the boys began to visit their grandmother's home again, avoiding mealtime in order to minimize conflicts. Silently, understanding their low rank in the family, they suffered the rudeness of their grandmother and older brothers, making a gift of fowl each day with the full understanding that they would never have a bite from the fruit of their own labor, which was devoured by their older siblings without a word of thanks.

One Monkey and One Artisan had suffered greatly from the loss of their father and uncle, but they had grown in stature through the years, becoming in many ways the equals of One and Seven Hunahpu. However, though as talented and wise as their father, the brothers felt such envy of the twins, their half-brothers, that their hearts were filled with hate, keeping them from showing true wisdom. Their natural foresight told them that their young brothers were destined for greatness, but they did nothing to encourage those abilities.

Finally, Hunahpu and Xbalanque decided to put an end to their siblings' cruelty. "We'll just turn their beastly nature against them. It'll be a fitting payment. If they'd had their way, we would've died as babies or been lost as little kids. They treat us like slaves. To their minds, we're nobodies. Time to make an example of them."

That evening they arrived at their grandmother's house empty-handed.

"Why have you not brought any birds?" she demanded.

"Well, grandmother, we shot some birds, but they're stuck in the top branches of a tree. We're pretty clumsy and can't climb up there, so we were hoping our older brothers would come help us."

"Very well," said One Monkey and One Artisan. "We will go with you in the morning."

The next day the twins led their brothers to a large madre de cacao tree replete with countless singing birds. They loosed a barrage of darts, but not a single bird fell to the ground.

"See? They're getting stuck. Climb up and fetch them here."

"Fine." One Monkey and One Artisan clambered up into the very top branches of the tree, looking for the birds. As they did so, the twins caused the trunk to swell and stretch toward the sky until it was monstrously big. When their brothers realized what was happening, they tried to get down but couldn't.

"Little brothers!" they called down. "Take pity on us! What can we say? This tree is frightening to behold."

"Look, it's your loincloths that are keeping you from moving freely. Loosen them and then retie them so the long end sticks out behind you. You'll be able to get down easier."

One Monkey and One Artisan did as they were told. The moment they pulled out the long ends of their loincloths, these instantly became tails. The spell had been triggered. Within seconds, the older brothers were transformed into spider monkeys. They leapt from the gigantic madre de cacao into the branches of smaller nearby trees and then went swinging their way into the dense mountain forests, chattering and howling wildly.

And so One Monkey and One Artisan were defeated by the divine magic of Hunahpu and Xbalanque. The matter of their grandmother still remained, of course. When they got home, they immediately called to her.

"Grandmother! Something's happened to our brothers! Their faces have changed: now they look like animals!"

"If you have done something to them, boys, you will break my heart. Please tell me you have not worked your magic on them!"

"Don't be sad, Grandmother. You'll see our older brothers' faces again. They'll be back. But this is going to be a test for you. You can't laugh at them, okay? Now, let's see what fate has in store."

They sat down outside the house and began to play the flute and drum, singing a song they called "Hunahpu Spider Monkey" in which their brothers' names were repeated. Soon One Monkey and One Artisan approached, excited, and began to dance to the music. When she saw their ugly little simian faces, Ixmukane could not contain her laughter. Her guffaws startled the monkeys, and they scampered off into the forest.

"Grandmother! Didn't we say not to laugh? Look, we're only going to try this four times. Three more. You simply have to keep yourself from laughing next time."

They started up the tune once more, and their transformed siblings rushed to the patio to dance with wild abandon. Ixmukane struggled not to even giggle, but the monkeys had truly funny faces. Their little potbellies jiggled and their genitals were showing. Their grandmother could not help herself: she burst into gales of laughter that made them run off toward the mountains.

"What else are we supposed to do, Grandmother? Here goes attempt number three."

Again the song. Again the dancing. Now, however, their grandmother kept her composure. So the monkeys clambered up the wall, making foolish expressions. They puckered up their red lips and snorted at the twins. It was too much. Ixmukane cackled and howled, and her grandsons left in a hurry.

"This is the last time," Hunahpu and Xbalanque warned, and they struck up the melody again. But the monkeys did not return. They stayed in the forest instead.

The twins shook their heads in disappointment. "We tried, Grandmother. They're gone. But don't be sad. You still have two grandsons, right here with you. You can give your love to us. Our older brothers will always be remembered, you know. For they were given names and titles. Down the ages, musicians and artists and scribes will call on them for inspiration. Yes, they were prideful and mean, and their cruelty brought ruin on their heads. But people will always remember that One Monkey and One Artisan accomplished great things, in a distant time, when they lived with their grandmother in a small house near the mountains."

Their Journey to the Realm of Fright

And so Hunahpu and Xbalanque took their rightful places as their fathers' heirs. For a time they tended the family milpa, enchanting axes and hoes and animals to do the brunt of the work while they went hunting with their blowguns.

After a while, however, they found their fathers' rubber ball in the rafters. Strapping on their siblings' gear with great joy, they headed down to the ball court. For a long time they played there alone, sweeping the field of their fathers.

The dark lords of the Realm of Fright could not help but hear. "Someone has started a game again there above our heads. Are they not ashamed to be stomping about like that?" the King of Death asked. "Did not One and Seven Hunahpu die precisely for this reason? Just like these knaves, they wanted to prove their importance. Go, then, messenger: summon these fools as well."

Hurricane's falcon, who had watched many of their fathers' games, winged his way to the surface to call the twins before the nether council. As he approached, he cried out, "Wak-ko! Wak-ko!"

"What's that sound?" Hunahpu exclaimed, dropping his yoke. "Quick, grab your blowgun!"

They shot the bird out of the air, a pellet impacting against his eye. When they went to grab him, they asked why he was there.

"I've a message for you, but first heal my eye."

They took a sliver of rubber from their ball and used it to cure his wound. As soon as his vision was restored, he spoke the words in his belly:

"You are commanded by the King and Queen of Death to present yourself in the Realm of Fright in seven days. Bring your kit, for you will be playing ball against the dark lords of the netherworld. They promise it will be great fun."

The twins went to their grandmother, who was devastated by the news.

"We've got to go, of course," they told her. "But first let us be your advisors. Each of us will plant an ear of unripe corn here in the center of the house. If one dries up, you'll know that grandson has died. But if they sprout up, you can be sure we're alive."

After the planting, the twins took up their gear and their blowguns and departed. They wended their way down toward the Realm of Fright, over the rim of the world, along the canyons, through flocks of strange birds. They came to the river of pus and the river of blood, intended as traps by the dark lords. But the brothers caused their blowguns to swell as they had the madre de cacao tree and simply floated across without a care.

Then the brothers came to the crossroads, but their mother, the Lady Blood, had taught them about the roads: Black, White, Red, and Green. Hunahpu plucked a hair from his knee and with a whispered spell transformed it into an insect he called mosquito, the perfect spy.

"Go, little guy. Bite each of them in turn till you've tasted them all. Then forever the blood of travelers will be yours."

"Good," said the mosquito, and it flew down the Black Road. When it reached the council chambers, it alighted first on the wooden statues that had been dressed up to resemble the king and queen. It bit the first, but got no response. The second said nothing either.

Next he bit the third one, the real King of Death.

"Ow!" he cried.

"What, Your Majesty?" asked the dark lords. "What is it?"

"Something stung me!"

The queen looked at him. "It is merely a...ow!"

"What, my queen?" asked the king. "What is it?"

"Something stung me!"

"Ow!" cried the fifth one seated there.

"What, Peeling Scab?" asked the queen. "What is it?"

"Something stung me, Majesty!"

Then the sixth one was bitten.

"Ow!"

"What, Blood Gatherer?" asked Peeling Scab. "What is it?"

"Something stung me!"

And thus went mosquito to every dark lord, biting him or her to learn the face and name of each: Pus Demon, Jaundice Demon, Bone Scepter, Skull Scepter, Wing, Packstrap, Bloody Teeth, Bloody Claws.

Xbalanque and Hunahpu, meanwhile, had been approaching down the Green Road, the only one living beings should travel. As the mosquito heard the dark lords' names, so did Hunahpu, who shared them with his twin.

Finally the brothers reached the council chamber.

"Greet the King and Queen of Death, seated here before you," the dark lords commanded.

"Uh, no. Those aren't the king and queen. They're just statues," said the twins. They turned to the rest and greeted them by name.

"Morning, King of Death.   Morning, Queen of Death.

Morning, Peeling Scab.   Morning, Blood Gatherer.

Morning, Pus Demon.   Morning, Jaundice Demon.

Morning, Bone Scepter.   Morning, Skull Scepter.

Morning, Wing.   Morning, Packstrap.

Morning, Bloody Teeth.   Morning, Bloody Claws."

And the dark lords were taken quite by surprise.

"Greetings to you, as well. Have a seat on that bench," directed the king.

The twins were not defeated by this ruse. "Uh, that's no bench, Your Majesty," Xbalanque replied. "It's just a heated stone."

"Well done. Your journey has been long. You require rest before our game. You may enter yonder house now."

The brothers headed toward Darkness House, the first of the torments in the Realm of Fright. The dark lords felt certain that these two would be defeated there, so they sent a messenger with a torch and two cigars.

"Take these and light them," he instructed. "Our king bids you bring them back to him in the morning, intact."

"Will do!" the twins replied. But they did not light the torch. Instead they substituted consuming flame with the tail feather of a macaw that shimmered with magic. The night sentries saw it and believed the torch lit. In the same fashion the brothers called fireflies and set them dancing at the tips of their cigars. So Darkness House was aglow all night long.

"We have beaten them!" exulted the sentries.

Yet in the morning, when the brothers went before the council, the torch had no mark of fire and the cigars were whole. Then the lords consulted together:

"What sort of beings are they? Whence did they come? Who sired them? Who gave them birth? Our hearts are deeply troubled, for they will do no good unto us. Their appearance, their very essence, is wholly unique."

The king and queen confronted Hunahpu and Xbalanque. "Tell us, truly—whence do you come?"

"Well, we must've come from somewhere, but we just don't know." They would say nothing more.

"Very well. Let us go play ball, boys."

"Great."

They arrived at the ball court of the Underworld. "So, then, we will use this rubber ball of ours," said the dark lords.

"No, let's use ours."

"Not at all. We will use ours."

The twins shrugged. "Fine."

"The ball is just embossed with an image," clarified the dark lords.

"No, it's pretty clearly a real skull," the brothers countered.

"It is not."

"Sure. If you say so," said Hunahpu.

The dark lords hurled the ball at Hunahpu's yoke. He batted it away with a twist of his hips. The ball struck the ground and burst open, sending the bone-white dagger of sacrifice spinning around the ball court, threatening death.

"What's this?" shouted the brothers. "So that's why you sent a messenger to summon us: you want to kill us! What do you take us for? We're leaving!"

And indeed, that had been the dark lords' plan: for the twins to be killed right then, defeated by the blade. Hunahpu and Xbalanque had once again frustrated their design.

"Do not leave, boys. Let us continue the game, using your ball instead."

"In that case, alright," the brothers agreed, dropping their fathers' rubber ball onto the court.

"Let us discuss prizes," said the dark lords. "What will we receive if we win?"

"Whatever you want."

"We request merely four bowls of flowers."

The boys nodded. "Okay, but what sorts of flowers?"

"A bowlful of red petals, one of white petals, one of yellow petals, and one of the large petals."

"Done."

The game began. The strength of both teams was equal, but the boys made many plays, for their hearts were full of goodness. In the end, though, the twins allowed themselves to be beaten. The dark lords reveled in their defeat.

"We have done very well. We vanquished them on the first attempt. Now, even if they survive the next torment, where will they go to pluck our flowers?"

Since the only possibility was the garden of the King and Queen of Death, the council instructed the feathered guardians of those royal flowers:

"Keep a diligent watch over these blossoms. Do not permit them to be stolen, for they are the tool for the boys' defeat. Think what would happen were they able to obtain these as our prize! Do not sleep tonight."

Returning to Hunahpu and Xbalanque, the council reminded them of the agreement. "You will give us our prize of petals early in the morning."

"Sounds good. First thing in the morning, we'll play again."

Then the brothers reviewed their plans together until they were sent into Blade House, the second trial of the Realm of Fright. Inside, blades spun through the air constantly, and the hope was that the twins would quickly be sliced to ribbons. But they did not die. Instead, they called out to the blades, instructing them in this way:

"Be still and the flesh of animals is yours forever."

The blades stopped spinning. One by one they lowered their points to the ground.

As the brothers rested in the Blade House that night, they called to the ants:

"Cutting ants, conquering ants, come! Go fetch us flower petals as prizes for the dark lords."

The ants marched down to the garden of the King and Queen of Death and began swarming over the flowers, but the winged guardians did not notice a thing. Out of sheer boredom, the birds perched in the branches and squawked or ambled through the garden repeating their song:

"Whip-poor-will! Whip-poor-will!" And that is indeed what we call them to this day.

The guardian whippoorwills did not notice the ants, thronging blackly on the stems and leaves, carrying off what the birds were meant to guard. The ants clambered up trees to harvest more flowers, with the guardians none the wiser, even though their wings and tails were chewed on as well.

By dawn, the ants had harvested enough flowers to fill the four bowls. When the messengers arrived at Blade House, they were discouraged to find the brothers alive.

"The lords summon you both," they announced. "They demand you deliver their prize into their hands."

"Right away," the brothers said. When they arrived before the lords, they placed the bowls on the council table. The dark lords looked upon the petals with woeful expressions. They had been defeated. The faces of the council members went pale with fear.

Realizing the flowers were from the royal garden, they summoned the whippoorwills before them. The birds, tails and wings ragged from the ants' chewing, had no answer for their incompetence, so their mouths were split open so that they would always gape when cawing their song.

A second game was played, but this one ended in a tie. After it was over, each side began making plans.

"At dawn again tomorrow," said the dark lords.

"We'll be there," responded the twins.

They were escorted to a third torment, Cold House. Upon entering, they encountered cold beyond measure. The interior was thick with snow and hail. But the boys immediately dispersed the cold with divine magic, melting the ice and halting the hail. Though the dark lords intended them to die, they survived the night and were fine in the morning when the sentries summoned them.

"What is this? Did they not die?" asked the dark lords.

Once again they marveled at the deeds of the twins Hunahpu and Xbalanque.

That evening they entered Jaguar House, which was crowded with ravenous jaguars. But the brothers were prepared.

"Wait. Don't eat us. We'll give you what's yours."

Then they scattered bones before the beasts, the remains of humans from the first three ages, which they had collected during their journey through the Land of the Dead. The jaguars crunched the bones contentedly while the brothers rested.

In the morning the sentries were delighted to see these skeletal remains scattered among the beasts. "They are finished! They gave themselves up. The jaguars ate their hearts, and now they gnaw upon their bones!"

But, of course, the twins were fine. They emerged from Jaguar House to the amazement of the dark lords who had gathered.

"What kind of beings are these? Whence did they come?"

The next evening they stepped into flame—Fire House, the fifth torment of that Realm of Fright. Its interior was pure conflagration, but neither Hunahpu nor Xbalanque was burned. The dark lords intended for them to be roasted to a crisp, but they were proof against such flame and emerged unscathed in the morning.

The dark lords were losing heart. The next evening they escorted the twins to the final place of torment, Bat House, replete with death bats, enormous beasts with razor-like snouts they used for slaughter. The dark lords were certain that this would finish them off, but the brothers made their blowguns bigger and slept snugly inside.

During the night they awoke to the sound of flapping wings and horrible screeching. The twins prayed for wisdom for hours until the house fell quiet and the bats stopped moving.

Xbalanque called to his brother. "Hunahpu, are they asleep? Is it morning already?"

"Let me check."

Hunahpu crawled to the end of his blowgun and poked his head out to see, but at that instant a death bat swooped down and snatched his head from his shoulders.

After a few moments, Xbalanque called again. "And? Is it morning?"

There was no response.

"What's going on? What's wrong?"

Nothing moved, however. All he heard was the rustling of leathery wings.

"Ah, damn it. We've lost already," Xbalanque groaned.

Soon the sentries entered. Xbalanque dragged his brother's body from Bat House, but the King and Queen of Death ordered Hunahpu's head placed atop the ball court. The dark lords rejoiced now that they believed the youth dead.

But Xbalanque was inspired to action. He called to his side all of the animals, great and small, telling them to bring him the various foods that they ate. The coati brought a chilacayote or Siam pumpkin, rolling it with her snout as she came. Xbalanque saw that the round squash would make a perfect replacement for his brother's head.

So he carved features into the rind, calling on wiser deities from the heavens to descend and help him. Together, they hurried to make the pumpkin a perfect duplicate of Hunahpu's head, endowed with the ability to speak. When it was placed on Hunahpu's shoulders, the youth returned to life.

"Not bad," he said.

"Okay, time for the ruse," Xbalanque told him. "Don't even try to play ball. Just look enigmatic and threatening. I'll take care of things."

Turning to a rabbit, Xbalanque instructed:

"Head to the far end of the ball court and hide in the tomato patch. When the ball lands near you, hop away until the deed is done."

The dark lords were shocked when the brothers challenged them.

"What trick is this?" they demanded. "We have already triumphed! There sits your head, boy, proof of your defeat. Surrender!"

Hunahpu merely called out:

"Wrong! That's just a ball in the shape of my head, foolish lords. Strike it toward us. We're not afraid of any harm…are you?"

So the dark lords took up the head and threw it down. It rebounded before Xbalanque. He used his yoke to send it sailing over the court. It bounced into the tomato patch, and the rabbit immediately hopped away. All of the dark lords rushed after the animal, shouting and rushing about. They believed it was the ball.

While their enemies were thus distracted, Xbalanque retrieved and reattached his brother's head. He then set the pumpkin down on the court.

"Hey, come on!" the brothers cried. "We found the ball!"

The dark lords returned, confused about what they had been pursuing. The game resumed, each team equally matched, until Xbalanque struck the pumpkin so hard it burst, strewing seeds before the startled nobles of that Realm of Fright.

"Impossible! It was a head, not a pumpkin. How did that get here? Who brought it?"

They soon realized that they had been solidly defeated by Hunahpu and Xbalanque. Despite the best efforts of the dark lords, the brothers would not die.

Their Death and Resurrection

Hunahpu and Xbalanque knew, however, that the King and Queen of Death would not let them leave the Realm of Fright alive. They summoned the two great seers, Xulu and Paqam, whom the dark lords would consult concerning the proper disposal of the dead boys' bones.

"It's heaven's plan that we die here. But we need a favor. When they ask what to do with our bones, have them grind them up like flour and sprinkle that dust into the river that wends its way through the mountains. Then our destiny will be fulfilled."

The dark lords had meanwhile dug a pit oven, hot with coals and burning rock. They tried to trick the brothers into leaping over it in sport, but Hunahpu and Xbalanque called their bluff.

"You can't fool us. We've known the form of our deaths for a long time. Just watch."

Facing each other, the twins lifted their arms and dove into the pit. As they died, the maize withered in their grandmother's home, in their family milpa, across the entire face of the sea-ringed world. Without the brothers or their fathers to ensure their survival, the golden and silk-tasseled ears of corn could not grow.

When the two corpses had burned down to barest bones, the dark lords consulted with Xulu and Paqam, who recommended the grinding down and sprinkling the brothers had requested. Their ashes were not borne away by the current, however: they sank right away beneath the water.

Five days later they appeared again, as tritons in the river. The inhabitants of the Land of the Dead stared in shock at their fishlike faces. The next day they appeared as poor orphans, dressed in rags. The dark lords hurried to see them when they heard the news. They found the strangers doing dangerous dances and swallowing swords. The two seemed to set fire to a house, but then they recreated it from ashes.

As the dark lords looked on in amazement, first Hunahpu, then Xbalanque would leap from a high place, killing himself, only to be resurrected by the other. No one realized that this show laid the groundwork for the eventual defeat of the Land of the Dead.

The king and queen summoned the orphans before them. The two reluctantly allowed themselves to be herded to the dread palace. Pretending humility, they threw themselves upon the ground, covering their faces with rags as if desperately ashamed.

"Whence do you come?" the king asked.

"We do not know, Your Majesty. Nor do we know the faces of our mother or father. They died when we were small."

"Very well. Let us have a spectacle. What payment do you request?"

"We ask nothing. We are truly afraid."

"Do not fear. Be not timid. Dance! Demonstrate how you sacrifice and then revive yourselves. Burn this palace down and rebuild it. Let us behold your repertoire. As you are poor orphans, we shall pay whatever price you name."

The brothers began their routine, the dangerous dances and swallowing of swords. The word spread, and soon the place was overflowing with spectators.

"Sacrifice my dog," the queen commanded.

"As you wish," they replied, killing the dog and bringing him back to life, tail wagging for joy.

"Now burn the palace down," instructed the king.

They used illusion to make the vast fortress appear to burn down with all the dark lords within, but no one was consumed, and the palace was restored straightaway.

"Now kill one of these lords," the queen told them. "Sacrifice him, but do not let him actually perish."

They complied, holding down a lord, killing him, extracting his heart, and setting it before the king and queen, who marveled to see the noble immediately revived and rejoicing.

"Very well done. Now sacrifice yourselves, boys. We yearn to see this feat with all our hearts."

And so they did. Xbalanque killed his brother, severing his arms and legs, removing his head and placing it far away, digging out his heart and setting it upon a leaf. The dark lords became giddy at the dismemberment. Xbalanque continued his dance.

"Arise!" he shouted, and his brother was restored immediately to life. The dark lords roared their approval. The King and Queen of Death celebrated as if they themselves had wrought the miracle. So caught up were they in the spectacle that they felt part of the dance.

The king surged from his throne. "Now do the same to us!"

The queen stood, trembling. "Yes, sacrifice us in the same way!"

Xbalanque and Hunahpu nodded. "As you wish. No doubt you will be revived. After all, are you not the gods of death? And we are here to bring such joy to you, to your vassals, to your servants."

Dancing forward, they seized the king of that fearful place and slaughtered him, ripping away his limbs, tearing out his heart. They reached for the queen, but she saw that her husband was not revived, and she began to grovel and weep.

"No! Have pity on me!" she cried out, disoriented.

But the brothers stopped their ears to her laments as they eviscerated her as well.

The dark lords and their servants fled along the Black Road to the canyon en masse, filling it up, packed tight in that gloomy abyss. Then the ants came, millions of them, herded by the brothers' power, streaming down the canyon walls. They drove those twisted nobles from their hiding place. When the rulers of the Land of the Dead arrived once more before the twins, they bowed in abject and silent surrender.

"Listen! It's time to tell you our names and the names of our fathers. Behold us, little Hunahpu and Xbalanque, sons of One and Seven Hunahpu, the ones you killed. We're here to avenge the torment and afflictions of our fathers: that's why we put up with your torture. Now we've got you where we want you, and we're going to kill you, every last one!"

But the dark lords pleaded and begged for their lives. They showed the twins their fathers' grave and the tree in which a skull still sat.

"Fine. We'll spare you," the brothers agreed. "But you'll never be what you were. The great and noble sacrifices of humanity aren't yours to savor. You will never again touch the souls of men and women born in the light, good and honest folk there above. No, your offerings will be broken things, clumps of sap, insects and worms. And only the scum of the earth will offer themselves to you: the wicked, the corrupt, the wretched, the deviant. Only when their sins are clear can you attack—no more snatching the innocent!"

On the sea-ringed world, their grandmother—anguished and bereft for days at the signs of her grandsons' death—rejoiced at the sprouting of new corn in the heart of her home. And in the fearsome depths of the netherworld, the brothers resurrected their fathers, who curled up through the earth like tendrils and burst through the crust, emerging as a maize god, forever renewing that precious source of human sustenance. The place of their emergence was called Paxil—Rivenrock—revered down the ages as a most holy site.

And the hero twins? They were swept up into heaven, there at the heart of all light, to guard the sun and moon as they poured their brilliance out upon the heads of a newborn human race.

The long dawn had ended, and the fourth age had begun.

The Fourth Sun and the Flood

While the Hero Twins' adventures wound down to their finale, the work of restoring the earth neared completion. Feathered Serpent and the Divine Mother stood together and gave each other counsel.

"The dawn approaches, and our labor has not reached an end. No humans exist to populate the sea-ringed world, to glory in the light of the coming sun."

So they joined their minds in the midst of the gloaming, pondering how best to form a new race of women and men. During that long twilight, they discovered an answer to their need.

Feathered Serpent called out for aid, and four animals rushed to his side: Sly Coyote, lover of games. Stealthy Fox, sharp of hearing. Eloquent Parrot, clever and colorful. Crow, black and wild and oblivious.

"Stone and clay and wood were poor materials, our first creations flawed and weak. New humans we shall craft from richer stuff. Loyal birds, fly south in search of maize, staple of life, gift of the Divine Mother. Coyote and Fox, find me a spring, sulfur-rich and warm, bubbling from below."

So Parrot and Crow spread their wings and took to the sun-bright skies. After many days of searching far and wide, they spied a tor, crested with wild corn, cloven by some mighty force. This was Rivenrock, the place where the maize god had emerged from the Underworld. Hungry, Crow landed and devoured the blue kernels and the red. Parrot winged her way back to the Feathered Serpent to report their rich discovery.

Coyote and Fox had slunk through jungles, glens and mountain meadows, hunting for the perfect fount. After a time they found a brackish pool fed from nether streams not far from the craggy hill and its crown of hearty maize. Naming the water Bitterflow, Coyote stopped to drink and bathe while Fox hurried to inform the Divine Mother.

The animals guided the gods to Rivenrock and Bitterflow, where they delighted in the abundance of rich foods, not only yellow and white corn, but also cacao and papaxtli, zapote and jocote—every vital, edible plant.

The Divine Mother took the white and yellow corn and ground it down nine times in her metate. Feathered Serpent fetched water from Bitterflow, sprinkled it with lime, rinsed the hands of the goddess, and used the liquid to form a paste which he kneaded and worked, molded and modeled, making arms and legs for the first man and woman, giving them frame and shape and expression as dawn lightened the sky. The man they named Tata, his wife Nene, and they bade them repopulate the sea-ringed world.

A new sun was needed, but the gods wanted to avoid the disputes of the past. After a time they looked to Chalchiuhtlicue, she of the jade-green skirt of living water, new wife of Tlaloc and mother to Tecciztecatl, handsome young god of shell and stone. Powerful enough to sustain the world yet sufficiently loving and gentle to care for her charges, Chalchiuhtlicue seemed an ideal candidate.

Hurricane agreed immediately, seeing her selection as a way to further avenge himself on Tlaloc, who would be separated from his love. Feathered Serpent approved for nobler reasons. In the end even her husband and son, filled with pride at her fate, joined their votes to the unanimous acclamation.

So the goddess was transfigured and began her daily track across the heavens. Tata and Nene had many children, and those had many more. The earth began to fill up with human beings whose praise and sacrifice sustained the sun and pleased the gods.

Twelve calendar cycles passed in this way, idyllic and serene.

Then the heavens began to fill with water.

It is not clear precisely why or how, but some say that Chalchiuhtlicue wept for fifty-two years, her tears accumulating in the sky until it bowed with the weight of her sadness. The source of that weeping will be forever a mystery, though circumstances suggest that Hurricane was somehow responsible. He was, at least, the only god aware of the danger.

"Tata and Nene," he said, descending from his black heaven to greet the ancient parents of the human race. "Cease your foolish labor. A deluge is coming. Fell a cypress tree and hollow it out. Fill it full of ripened corn. When the skies begin to fall, get inside. After you have consumed the last of the corn, the waters will have receded. Then will I instruct you further. Do not leave your ship or eat anything else until you have heard my commands."

The couple prepared their log. Then it began to rain in spectacular torrents that seemed to efface the very air. The man and woman quickly entered the cypress and sealed themselves within.

Then the firmament shuddered, cracked, and ripped wide open. The heavens fell, flooding the sea-ringed world till it seemed a part of the cosmic sea, obliterated from existence entirely. Most of humanity drowned, but Feathered Serpent, rushing into the breach, attempting to staunch the tide, transformed a small number of survivors into merfolk, doughty sirens and tritons who dove deep to avoid the pounding storm. Their descendants, it is said, live there still, harrowing sailors and fishermen alike.

So the fourth sun was snuffed by a deluge in the year 1-House, on the day 4-Water. It was the 676th year since Chalchiuhtlicue had begun to shine, the end of the thirteenth calendar cycle.

Feathered Serpent called upon his brother. "The heavens must be lifted back into place, supported again by the World Trees."

Hurricane agreed. His sons Blue and Red Tezcatlipoca joined them, and together the four knelt at the edges of the sea-ringed world and took the multi-tiered sky upon their backs, heaving up against the void to restore order to the cosmos. To prevent another celestial collapse, the brothers created four Bacabs or sky bearers, powerful beings who would protect the World Trees and shoulder the heavens if the need arose.

With heaven settled back in place, the brothers looked up into the massive fracture the water had caused in the sky. Together they walked into it, sealing the wound as best they could with stars and magic, but a black scar remained, limned with ghostly light. Men, who grasped it was a road of sorts to places beyond their ken, would later call it the Milky Way.

It was dark for twenty-five years. The waters receded little by little until the mountains began to appear again. The ageless Tata and Nene finished the last of their corn, and their log came to rest on a mountain peak. They emerged onto the starlit summit and saw fish scales glittering in the water. Avidly hungry, they caught a few fish and set to drilling fire from the cypress log in order to cook a meal.

The lord and lady of the stars, Citlalatonac and Citlalicue, first noticed the curling wisps of smoke. "Gods, who has started a fire before the appointed time? Who sends cypress ash wafting into heaven?"

Hurricane spun from his black realm to confront the human couple.

"What are you doing? Did I not tell you to wait for my instructions? What possessed you to start a fire *now* of all times?"

Furious, he lopped off their heads. But death was not punishment enough. With a snarl, he reattached their heads above their buttocks and blazed dark energy at them until they transformed into dogs, their capacity for speech forever gone.

Such was the end of the last two humans of the Fourth Age.

The Fifth Age and the Reign of Demigods

Convocation

Watch with me as the floodwaters slowly subside, as the great deluge is absorbed into the cosmic sea. We stand on a growing expanse of dry land, contemplating a sunless sky once more.

It is 4-Movement, the first day of the Fifth Age. The present era. Our time.

The gods, having learned from their mistakes, make a better race of people. Humanity. Yet before we can rise to prominence across the sea-ringed world, we must be nurtured, taught, guided.

The gods sacrifice much to ensure our survival, to give us light and sustenance. And then they set wise creatures and demigods over us, agents of order who keep us on the path of sacred fate.

Feathered Serpent is determined that we will succeed and thrive, that we will make ourselves worthy of his love and trust.

Heart of Sky—Hurricane—mocks our attempts, jeers at our failures, ignores our progress. Ever hungry for chaos, he seeks allies and vassals who will destroy the world once more.

We look into this distant past through the tales of the ancients, passed down through the centuries in the cultures of the Mixtec, Cora, Mazatec, Otomi and Huichol. The words of the Aztec elders were themselves written down after the Conquest on the broad leatherbound pages of what we know today as the *Florentine Codex* and the *Codex Chimalpopoca*.

Let us turn to those precious books, friends, casting our eyes from time to time as well at the *Popol Vuh* and that lovely collection of Maya verse from the heart of the Yucatan, the *Songs of Dzitbalché*.

Once more we raise the chorus of our voices, point and counterpoint, combining melodic lines of old into a new harmony.

The Creation of Human Beings

The Fourth Age had come to an end. The gods, saddened at the destruction of the earth, gathered in Teotihuacan.

"The sea-ringed world emerges. The heavens have been restored. But who will sing us songs? Who will worship us? Who will keep the cosmic wheels turning?"

Feathered Serpent turned to the Divine Mother. "We must once more strive to make human beings. Let this new attempt combine all the strengths of the previous."

"To do so," she told him, "we will need the bones of those who have died."

Hurricane smiled. "Brother, if you want them, you will have to descend to the Land of the Dead and petition the king and queen of that fell demesne."

"So be it," Feathered Serpent declared, departing.

He came to the river at the edge of the Underworld, which the dead can only cross on the back of a hound. Twinning himself so that his nahualli stood before him, he addressed that hairless spirit dog:

"Xolotl, double of my heart, bear me across broad Apanohuayan so that on its farther shore I may seek the bones of the dead."

"Gladly, my plumed master. Seize the folds of flesh upon my back, and I will swim you to your destination."

And so all dogs buried with their owners for this purpose are called xoloitzcuintle to honor the nahualli of Feathered Serpent.

With Xolotl's aid, the creator god easily navigated the next eight obstacles and stood before the King and Queen of Death in their eldritch, windowless palace at the heart of the Underworld.

"What brings you to our realm now, after so many years, O Feathered Serpent?" asked the king, his eyes like pinpricks of fire in the black orbs of his skull, framed by his owl-plume headdress. The god's tilma and breechcloth were spattered with blood, and round his neck he wore a chain of human eyeballs.

"I am come to take the precious bones that you have guarded with such diligence."

"And what will you do with them, Lord Creator?" asked the queen.

"The gods in Tamoanchan need humans to ease their sadness. With these remains, I will fashion a new race of men and women to praise and honor us. They will be mortal, so their bones will return to your hands, as will the bones of their children and their children's children, for as long as this Fifth Age shall last."

"Very well," replied the king. "First, however, as a sign of honor, take this my conch and travel four times round my realm, sounding an exultant call as you go."

Feathered Serpent agreed, but as he prepared to sound the shell trumpet, he realized the conch had no hole for blowing. Summoning worms, he had them burrow in at the apex of the spire and smooth its hollow interior. Then he had bees and hornets fly inside, adding their distinctive buzz to the air he sent rushing through the whorls of the conch. The resulting call could be heard in every corner of the Underworld, even in the very throne room of Lord and Lady Death.

After his fourth circuit of the Land of the Dead, Feathered Serpent made his way back to its center and stood once more before the sovereigns of that realm.

"Very well, take the bones," growled the King of Death.

Once Feathered Serpent had departed the palace to collect the bones, however, the skeletal god called together his council, the lords of that frightful realm.

"Go after that plumed snake, my vassals, and tell him that I have changed my mind. He must leave at once without the bones."

The ghastly messengers caught up to the creator god and repeated their sovereign's command.

Feathered Serpent reluctantly agreed. "I will leave then. Tell your king and queen."

The lords of the netherworld watched him fly off, heading out of the Land of the Dead by the eastern route the sun once took to emerge at dawn each day. They themselves traveled back to the eerie castle to inform their masters.

But they were deceived. Earlier, when Feathered Serpent had heard in his heart the command of the King of Death, he had told Xolotl:

"I must take these bones, forever. I need you to change shapes with me. Having assumed my form, you will agree to the king's wishes. Once you and the messengers have gone, I will steal the remains and flee."

So it was that he emerged from a place of hiding in the form of his nahualli, gathered the bones of men and women, wrapped them in a bundle, then rushed like the wind to avoid detection.

The god of death became aware of the ruse, however, and he called again to his council: "Lords, Feathered Serpent is at this very moment stealing the precious bones! Use all haste to cut him off before he emerges in the sea-ringed world: dig a pit into which he will fall and be trapped!"

Using hidden routes known only to the rulers of the Realm of Fright, the dread lords raced ahead of the Feathered Serpent and fashioned a vast and cunningly disguised pit. The creator god, startled by a covey of quail that swirled about him on the king's command, tumbled into the trap, smashing the bones into smaller bits.

Shooing away the birds, which had begun pecking and nibbling at the fragments, Feathered Serpent gathered up the remains and assumed once more his true form. "Ah, Xolotl, how was I so easily deceived? Not one of them is whole."

The twin of his heart answered from within. "All is as it must be. The bones have been shattered, but they will have to suffice."

Feathered Serpent seized the bundled bones in his jaws and

ascended to Tamoanchan. He placed the bones in the Protector's hands, crying out:

"Divine Mother, the bones are broken! What can we do?"

The Divine Mother smiled. "All must be broken before it is made whole. We will now grind the remains into powder, my sister and I. Then all of us must do the proper penance to moisten the bone flour so it can be kneaded and shaped."

When the Divine Mother and the Protector had used metate and mano to pulverize the bones, Feathered Serpent pierced his flesh and bled into the flour. Then each of the gods in turn did the same. The resulting dough was shaped into men and women who were brought to life by the spirits wending their way down from Omeyocan, sent by our grandparents to inhabit the sturdy new forms.

Feathered Serpent bowed his head as the humans opened their eyes. "Thus is our hope born. We did penance to ensure their existence. Now they will do penance to preserve ours."

Hurricane looked down on the fragile forms. "And what do you propose they eat, my brother? There is no sun, no vegetation. The work of restoring the earth has barely begun. Behold. Even now they wander about, searching for nourishment."

Casting his gaze wide, Feathered Serpent spied a red ant bearing a kernel of corn upon its back. "Tell me where you found this, my friend."

The ant did not at first wish to respond, but Feathered Serpent persisted. "Follow me then. It is over there."

The ant led him to what remained of Rivenrock, that mountain of edible plants. Feathered Serpent transformed himself into a black ant and accompanied the red ant through the cleft in the tor and found a vast store of maize, set aside for such times by the clever deities of the milpas. He gathered up all he could carry and returned to Tamoanchan. The gods chewed the kernels and placed the food on the humans' lips to nourish and sustain them.

So that humans would have ready access to the maize, Rivenrock needed to be split wide open. Tlaloc had his vassals, the tlaloques, puissant lords of rain—who could smash open the great jars of rain in Tlalocan—do this. None of them could widen the crack, though, not the Blue or the White or the Yellow or the Red Tlaloque.

Feathered Serpent then called upon a new god, covered in pustules, decrepit and old. "Nanahuatzin," he commanded this stranger. "Burst Rivenrock open!"

The ugly god nodded with a sigh and lifted a bolt of lightning, hurling it toward the sea-ringed world. The tor fairly exploded, exposing its rich stores to the starlight.

The men and women, seeing such an abundance of food, rushed to horde what maize they could. The rest, however—beans, chia, amarath—was stolen away by the tlaloques, shamed and jealous at the power of the strange new arrival.

"Who is he?" the other gods demanded.

"He is my son," Feathered Serpent simply said, offering no further explanation.

Now there were four human couples at the dawning of the age: Jaguar Forest with his wife Sky Sea House. Jaguar Night with his wife Shrimp House. First Crown with his wife Hummingbird House. Black Jaguar with his wife Macaw House. They came to be individuals, able to speak, to converse, to look and to listen.

These excellent people, these chosen ones, were far-sighted and wise. Because their sight was perfect, so was their knowledge of everything under the heavens. Everywhere they looked, they immediately saw and comprehended all that was in the heart of earth and sky. There was no need to travel the breadth of the sea-ringed world. From where they stood, they saw and understood it all.

Knowledge crowded their minds. Their vision passed beyond the trees and rocks, the lakes and seas, the mountains and valleys. Those couples, our ancestors, were greatly esteemed.

Then the four eldest gods—the Divine Mother and the Protector, along with Feathered Serpent and Hurricane—put questions to the men and women:

"Explain your existence. Do you grasp it with your senses? You can look and listen, your speech and stride are sturdy. Now behold, therefore, the root of the sky. Are the mountains not clear to your eyes? Can you see the valleys?"

At that moment, the humans' vision was complete. They gave thanks to their creators:

"In truth twice, *thrice* over, we give you thanks for creating us, giving us mouths, giving us souls. We speak and listen, ponder and move. Much do we know, for we learned far and near. We saw the great and the small at the four corners, on the four sides, in the heart of the earth and sky. Thank you for giving us shape and form. We exist because of you."

Conferring alone, the divine brothers and sisters, original children of Ometeotl, were concerned at these words.

"They claim to have learned everything in the heavens and on earth," Hurricane reminded them. "Such knowledge is inacceptable and dangerous. They are creations, shaped and framed by greater hands. By letting them become like gods, we have committed a grave mistake."

The Protector agreed. "What can we do to them so that their vision is foreshortened, so that only a little of the sea-ringed world is visible to them?"

Feathered Serpent urged caution. "We must not go too far, however. If they do not multiply and increase in number, when will they begin to plant? When will the dawn begin?"

"Then we must merely undo them a little now," the Divine Mother said. "That is best."

Hurricane rumbled in satisfaction "Yes. We cannot allow their deeds to be equated with ours. If their knowledge continues to spread, it will reach into every corner of the cosmos, and they will see everything."

The task fell to Hurricane. He simply blurred their eyes. Like breath upon a mirror, a haze clouded their vision so that objects and creatures were only clear when they were close. Likewise their understanding was limited to the surface of earth and sky—no longer could they peer into the heart of things. Thus the wisdom of the first four couples was lost there at the beginning, at the very root of human existence.

The Fifth Sun and the Harbingers of Darkness

Once people had been created for the fifth time, all the gods came together in the darkness that had engulfed Teotihuacan, and the Lord of Time built a great fire in the sacred hearth. For the cosmos required a sun, and the only way to bring it into existence was for one of their number to sacrifice himself.

At first, none of them seemed willing to volunteer. Finally, Feathered Serpent approached his scarred and ugly son. "You are the one who must sustain the heavens and the earth, Nanahuatzin."

"But how? Look around you, Father, at all these mighty gods. I am but a scabby invalid at their side. Understand me: I speak not out of fear. Let me instead become the moon, that lesser light. I am not worthy to be the sun."

Tlaloc spoke as well to his son, handsome god of shell and stone. "Tecciztecatl, both your mother and I have served as the sun. Think of the glory you would bring to Tlalocan, to your parents, to yourself."

Tecciztecatl immediately agreed. "There is none more apt than I. Of course I will accept the charge."

So the two young gods began their preparations, fasting and doing penance for four days. Nanahuatzin took maguey spines and pierced his flesh to draw holy blood in offering. Tecciztecatl used feather shafts and shards of jade.

On the final day, they bathed and dressed in ritual paper robes. They were then blanched with chalk and festooned with feathers, as would ever be the custom for sacrificial victims.

The others had fed the bonfire till it raged hot enough to anneal divine flesh with sacred flames. They called out to Tlaloc's son:

"Come, Tecciztecatl—your time has come!"

Puffing up, he strode toward the hearth, but the flames leapt so high and the heat was so intense that he quailed in fear, pulling away. Grim before the disapproving stares of his elders, he rushed again toward the fire, but once more stopped short and retreated. After four tries, the other gods pushed him aside.

"You, Nanahuatzin! Will you enter the hearth first and become the new sun?"

And the sore-covered, humble god closed his eyes and leapt into the fire, which began to screech and sputter as it devoured his body.

Tlaloc glared at his son in rage. Tecciztecatl, overcome with shame, threw himself onto the slackening flames and glowing coals.

As the fire burned down, leaving only cooling ashes, the gods knelt and waited for the newborn sun to emerge. They had been waiting for some time when finally the sky began to glow red all about them, dawn splintering the dark in seemingly every direction. Confused, many of the deities thought the sun might ascend the sky not in the East, but elsewhere. They began to spin about, each trying to determine the exact location of Nanahuatzin's arrival.

Only Feathered Serpent and Hurricane were looking to the East when two lights began to shine upon the horizon, illuminating the cosmos with equal brilliance. Feathered Serpent looked upon the glowing orbs and was not pleased. He addressed the others:

"It is not just that both the sun and the moon should burn with the same splendor. Nanahuatzin was the more valiant of the two. He should be revered as the sun. We must diminish Tecciztecatl to some degree."

They agreed with him completely, so Feathered Serpent took up a rabbit and hurled it at the son of Chalchiuhtlicue and Tlaloc, dimming his brilliance and leaving the dark marks we see on the moon to this day.

But the sun would or could not blaze a path across the sky. The gods sat and watched it wobble redly on the horizon, its rays spraying wild and deadly in all directions.

Feathered Serpent entreated his son to continue his circuit, but the brilliant god remained where he was.

Indignant, the first Lord of the Dawn, the deity who accompanied the sun as both Morning and Evening Star, cried out:

"Move! Do you not see the destruction you cause by sitting there on the horizon?"

So saying, the Lord of the Dawn strung his bow and unleashed a hail of arrows against the sun, every one of them missing its mark. Nanahuatzin, reacting instinctively to defend himself, sent a sizzling flare like a massive plume from a scarlet macaw. It struck the irate god of Venus and sent him hurling to the heart of the Underworld, his face covered forever by nine layers of death.

At that moment, Feathered Serpent understood the true price of giving humanity enduring light: the gods would have to offer themselves up in sacrifice in order to set the sun in motion. He called them together in council and explained what must be done. They all agreed except for Hurricane, who insisted on certain conditions.

"This sacrifice demands an even greater one from human beings, dear brother. If our lives are required to give vitality and movement to your son, then he will continue to require an infusion of teotl. Every cycle, the turning of great cosmic wheels brings the two calendars, sacred and solar, back into alignment. That will become a perilous time, the universe unstable for five nameless days, time enough to snuff the sun. To stave off apocalypse, humans will cease their laboring, perform ablutions, fast and pray and draw blood from their flesh. Everything old in their homes must be destroyed: crockery, clothing, footwear and mats. All fires will be extinguished. Silence will fall across the sea-ringed world.

"On the final day of the cycle, as the sun sets perhaps forever, a man must be sacrificed and new fire drilled to life in his hollowed chest. Thus will the former years be bound and a new calendar round begun. The flames will be fed into a bonfire that will light bright torches to be carried to every temple so holy hearths may be quickened and feed each family's private coals—ten thousand glowing points of hope, infusing the sun with energy till the first dawn of a new year splinters the eastern dark."

Feathered Serpent, respectful of the balance between entropy and creation, approved these terms. Then he killed each and every god gathered there in Tamoanchan, releasing their essential sacredness. Drawing this energy into himself and assuming his aspect of Ehecatl, Lord of the Wind, Feathered Serpent released a gale of divine power at the sun, restarting its climb to zenith.

As the only god still able to accomplish the task, Feathered Serpent then twinned himself and took on the responsibilities of the fallen Lord of the Dawn. His nahualli Xolotl became the Evening Star, accompanying the sun into the Underworld at twilight, leading it to the great hearth where the god of fire would feed Nanahuatzin at night. Feathered Serpent performed the labors of the Morning Star, guiding his son out of the Land of the Dead at dawn each new day.

The gods were reborn in Tamoanchan and resumed their several roles. But he of the smoking mirror, Hurricane, resolved to use the binding of the years as a way to bring about the destruction of the Fifth Age. He enlisted the aid of Itzapapalotl, Taloned Butterfly, patroness of women who died giving birth and children who died in infancy. Together they established the tzitzimimeh, an order of goddesses who would ensure that humanity remembered the necessity of sacrifice, willing to threaten the very sun itself.

These harbingers of darkness worked with the moon to mount attacks on the sun. During these eclipses, Tecciztecatl attempted to cover and consume Nanahuatzin with the help of the tzitzimimeh, who would leap from the heaven of stars in terrifying skeletal forms. Human beings would have to sacrifice light-skinned victims to keep the moon from devouring the sun and the harbingers from falling like vicious arrows on the sea-ringed world to annihilate the inhabitants of the Fifth Age.

The tzitzimimeh would also bring misery to the earth during the five nameless days at the end of each solar year. They were aided in this dark task by the King and Queen of Death, who were permitted within that span of time to unleash banes upon the world. No one could stop them. Goodness seemed to disappear, leaving groans and cries.

Eighteen months of twenty days—one whole year named and closed. Now it began: sorrowful nights of sinister black on forsaken earth. During five days the gods would measure the sins of every human: woman and man, great and small, rich and poor, foolish and wise. From the bishop to the chief of the town to his deputies, officers, sheriff and councilors to the priests of the rain god: every last man.

All human transgressions are measured during those days, for it is said the time will come that they will mark the end of the world by earthquake, on the day 4-Movement, sometime in the unknowable future. Hence the need for a careful count of human crimes. To accomplish this task, the wise ones say, the gods molded a jar of tree-termite clay. And there they deposit every last tear wept for the evils we do in this world. When it is filled to the brim, everything ends.

Thus is Hurricane's lust for destruction sated, and the balance of chaos and creation maintained.

Feathered Serpent and the other gods looked down at the darkness and apprehension in the lives of human beings. They took council together: "Men and women will be quite sad if we do not craft something to make them rejoice so they take pleasure in living on this earth, praising us through song and dance."

And the lord of creation pondered for a time until he realized what was needed: a liquid that, being imbibed, would gladden the human heart. A plan unraveled in his mind. He thought of the perfect goddess to help him: the beautiful Mayahuel, jealously guarded by her fearsome grandmother, one of the tzitzimimeh.

Feathered Serpent winged his way immediately to the heaven of stars and found the goddesses asleep. He awakened Mayahuel and said to her:

"I have come to take you with me to the sea-ringed world."

She agreed at once, and the two descended, Mayahuel upon his plumed and scaly back. As soon as they arrived on earth, they transformed themselves into trees whose boughs lovingly intertwined: he an arroyo willow and she a wild olive.

When the grandmother of the young goddess awoke and could not find Mayahuel, she called out to the other tzitzimimeh. Together, the fierce harbingers of darkness rained upon the earth like splintered arrowheads and began to search for Feathered Serpent, whose trail they discovered spiraling downward from the sky.

As the tzitzimimeh neared, the two trees pulled away from their arboreal embrace, untangling their branches. The old skeletal star goddess recognized Mayahuel at once. Seizing her granddaughter, she uprooted and shattered her, handing limbs and roots and splinters to her celestial sisters. They tore away bark, devouring leaf and fruit and fleshy pulp.

None of them touched the arroyo willow. The lord of creation watched their frenzied feeding impassively. It was part of his design. He required raw, broken materials for his craft.

When the tzitzimimeh had returned to their starry realm, Feathered Serpent assumed again his accustomed form. Gathering up the bones left from the cannibalistic feast, he buried them deep. In time a new plant grew from Mayahuel's remains: the maguey, destined to be the source of pulque and mescal, potent liquors that enliven the spirit.

Resurrected within agave plants, Mayahuel became goddess of maguey and fertility. With Patecatl, god of medicine and discoverer of peyote, she brought scores and scores of sons into being: the Centzontotochtin or Four Hundred Rabbits, minor gods of drunkenness. Soon this family would help bring the double-edged sword of drink to humanity.

Lord Opossum Brings Fire to Humanity

Lord Yaushu, the Great Opossum, ruled the sea-ringed world in the early years of the Fifth Age, when animals still spoke and mankind had not yet usurped the earth. He was a kindly king who governed by virtue of his clever mind. Nothing pleased him more than to see his subjects happy.

Yaushu, in fact, once used his nimble hands to dig deep into a mature maguey plant and draw forth the delicious sap waiting within. Directed by the goddess Mayahuel, he stored this aguamiel in gourds and discovered fermentation. So the joy-bringing drink we call pulque was invented. Soon animals up and down his vast kingdom were producing the beverage. In celebration Lord Yaushu went on a binge, stumbling from tavern to tavern, leaving behind a meandering set of trails that eventually became the rivers of the sea-ringed world.

Most creatures were content with the quiet ebb and flow of the world, safe and at ease within Lord Yaushu's broad realm.

Except for men.

It was not enough that food aplenty was within Man's grasp: he wanted more.

It was not enough that prey surrendered themselves to Man according to the natural order: Man wanted to cook his prey.

Man had discovered fire when lightning struck and set a tree or two alight, but he was clumsy and greedy and stupid and could not keep the flame alive.

In vain Man rushed after the sun as it plunged each evening past the edge of the earth into Mictlan, the vast and daunting underworld. He hoped to catch a falling ray of heat to take back to his cave.

But all these foolish plans came to naught, so in desperation the Tabaosimoa—the most respected women and men on the sea-ringed earth—came before Lord Yaushu.

"We are cold and our food is raw. Please help us, clever and revered opossum!"

"What happened to the fire you got from that burning tree?" Yaushu asked.

"We fell asleep after drinking pulque and let the coals die out. Now we shiver and our stomachs ache."

Yaushu looked upon the Tabaosimoa and was moved to pity. He did not want a single one of his subjects to suffer or be unhappy. But obtaining fire was a terrifying task. He would be putting his very life at risk. Still, his heart yearned to bring Man joy, so he agreed.

"I'll bring you fire, but you must take better care of it this time." The Tabaosimoa bent their heads in shamed reverence and swore to keep the flame alive.

Yaushu first gathered his gourds of pulque and then set off toward the West, following the sun as it slipped down the sky. At the edge of the world, the brave lord of this land snuck quietly down the path the sun's passing had left, using his tail and nimble hands to navigate the narrowest patches, playing dead whenever a skeletal guardian of the Underworld happened to come along.

Soon he nearly caught up with the sun, but the flaming disk was accompanied by Xolotl, the massive, toothy hound of hell. Yaushu had no desire to confront that growling psychopomp, so he stayed out of sight, following the pair as they made their way deeper into the bowels of Mictlan.

Finally the sun reached the hearth of the fire god, Xiuhtecuhtli, and Xolotl left to guide more souls to their final abode. The fire god began to tend to the needs of the sun, feeding its heat with wood and coal, giving it some needed rest.

As if he had been invited, Yaushu scampered up to Xiuhtecuhtli and gave a little bow. "My lord," he intoned.

The fire god, who was also the patron of kings and brave warriors, looked surprised to see the opossum, but recognized him immediately.

"Yaushu! What brings you to the depths of the Underworld, O Lord of All Creatures? Did you suddenly die without my knowledge?"

"No, not at all! It's just that your last visit was several years ago. I decided to wait no longer, but to call upon you here in your own abode. I've brought you some pulque from my own royal stores. I think you'll find it quite tasty."

"Pulque? Let me try some."

And the two of them sat before the hearth and drank gourd after gourd. Soon Xiuhtecuhtli, unaccustomed to the power of fermented aguamiel, succumbed to its effects and fell into a deep sleep, snoring contentedly.

A smile on his face, Yaushu looked around for a bit of wood with which to carry fire back to Man. But the sun had devoured it all, so the clever opossum thought and thought until he realized what he would have to do.

Taking several more draughts of pulque to shore up his courage, he dipped his agile tail into the hearth, holding it still until the fur at its tip was blazing. Then, driven by pain and urgency, he rushed back up to the land of the living, passing the ascending sun and the spirits of warriors who guarded its rise to its zenith. He reached the dwelling place of mankind and thrust his burning tail into a pile of dry wood, rekindling for his neediest subjects the flame they so desired.

Man wept for joy at the sight. He immediately set to feasting the greatness of his lord, dancing and singing hymns of praise to the magnificent, resourceful opossum.

Lord Yaushu, nursing his now hairless tail, looked on the revelry with love and satisfaction. For now, Man was happy, and the loss of fur was a small price to pay to have brought that felicity to any creature.

The gods of the five suns soon discovered Yaushu's theft. In anger they rushed to the opossum's demesne, determined to end his meddlesome life.

But when they found him, he was already dead, stiff on his back, his bald tail cold as the grave.

Their anger spent, the gods muttered their mournful respects and returned to the heavens and the netherworld.

And Lord Yaushu, who had of course been playing dead the whole time, sat up and smiled at the sun.

Itzpapalotl and the Cloud Serpents

The beginning of the Fifth Age was a time of demigods, divine giants who roamed the earth, leaving primitive humans in awe of their wisdom and might. The first of these beings were the Centzon Mimixcoah, the Four Hundred Cloud Serpents.

The Cloud Serpents were born during a 1-Flint year to the earth goddess Mecihtli, she of the foam-flecked jade skirt. No sooner had these children emerged when their mother plunged into the ocean and slipped into a deep grotto. There she bore another five Cloud Serpents—Apantecuhtli, Camaxtli, Cuauhtliicoauh, Tlohtepetl, and their sister Cuetlachcihuatl.

These younger children left their mother's side to enter the water, where they spent four days alone. When they finally emerged onto dry land, Mecihtli drew them to her bosom and suckled them till they were strong.

Meanwhile, their father the sun watched his four hundred oldest scions rough-housing across the northern desert. Fiery Nanahuatzin, his blaze slackening some from a lack of divine energy, called down to the Cloud Serpents.

"O my daughters and sons! I thirst for sacrifice. You must slake my need by spilling blood in offering. Take these arrows, fletched with the lovely feathers of quetzals and egrets, orioles and herons, ibis and contingas. Your mother Tlaltecuhtli, source of teeming life, will provide you prey."

But the four hundred did not follow his commands. Instead, they shot birds out of the sky with those swift-flying shafts, stripping feathers from their wings to make themselves adornments. They felled a jaguar, but did not offer it to their father. They made a feast of its flesh, drank deeply of pulque, and then, thoroughly besotted, found themselves human women with whom to indulge their carnal desires.

Enraged, Nanahuatzin turned to the younger five. "My children, hearken unto me. Your four hundred brothers have shown no respect, have refused to worship their mother and father. Now it falls to you to destroy them."

The sun placed weapons in their hands—arrows barbed with vicious thorns, spirit shields to deflect any attack. Hiding in a copse of mesquite, the younger Cloud Serpents regarded their drunken siblings with awe.

"They're just like us," they muttered to each other. But all the same they fell on them in the midst of their stupor, and the two factions of Cloud Serpents waged war against each other.

The younger five were forced to withdraw, but they contrived to ambush the larger force. Cuauhtliicoauh hid himself within a tree. Camaxtli sank into the earth. Tlohtepetl slipped inside a hill. Apantecuhtli dove into a lagoon.

Cuetlachcihuatl, the Bear Woman, simply stood in the ball court and waited, baiting their surviving foes.

When the other Cloud Serpents arrived, surrounding her, a terrible groan came from the tree where Cuauhtliicoauh hid, and it burst apart, raining splinters and limbs on the attackers as Cuauhtliicoauh emerged. The earth began to shudder and split, releasing Camaxtli. The hill shattered and collapsed as Tlohtepetl came flying forth. The water of the lagoon churned violently and Apantecuhtli spun himself free.

This time there was no stopping the five younger Cloud Serpents. They slaughtered nearly all of their older siblings, tearing their hearts out as offerings to their father Nanahuatzin, slaking the sun's thirst with their blood. The five deposited the hearts in a cleft in a rock and burned them ritually. The souls of their brothers spiraled into the heavens, becoming the myriad stars of the northern skies.

The few survivors pled for mercy. "We have incensed our father, the sun. We have earned your wrath as well. Yet let your rage wane, brothers and sister. We yield to you our collective home, the vast caverns of Chicomoztoc. Dwell within them. We are content to live here, at the edge of your land, obedient to your will."

So it was pacted. The handful of Cloud Serpents abandoned the battlefield.

Then, as night fell thick across the land, an ambitious goddess descended to earth—Itzpapalotl, black-taloned butterfly, one of the tzitzimimeh. She perched among the bloody stones and devoured the remains of the dead.

Not long afterward, two of the surviving Cloud Serpents—Xiuhnel and Mimich—went hunting in the wastelands near Chicomoztoc. As they searched for prey, a loud groaning filled the sky, and a two-headed deer leapt toward them from above.

Seeing the brothers, the strange beast bolted. Xiuhnel and Mimich gave chase, shooting arrows that the deer easily avoided. All through the night they pursued it and then all the following day, until at last they collapsed as evening fell, their energy spent.

"Let the deer be damned," Mimich spat. "We need to rest. Build yourself a lean-to over there. I'll make a bed beneath yonder mesquite."

Soon they were both too asleep to notice a woman wander into their camp, bearing a clay pot. She ducked beneath the thatched rafters of Xiuhnel's shelter and sat beside him.

"Dearest Xiuhnel," she whispered. "Rouse yourself. I have brought delicious drink."

Xiuhnel opened his eyes, delighted at the unexpected sight. "Ah, welcome, Sister."

He reached out for her, but she slyly drew away. "Won't you take a draught?"

Leering, he took the pot from her hands and drank deeply. It was not pulque. It was not wine. It was human blood, hot and sweet. Xiuhnel consumed every last drop.

Then he pulled the woman down upon the ground and lay with her.

When they had consummated their passion, he asked, gasping, "Who are you?"

Climbing atop him, she smiled fiercely.

"I am Itzpapalotl, the Obsidian Butterfly. I have devoured the corpses of your late brothers, and now I hunger for yours as well!"

Leaning over him, she tore out his throat with her teeth and broke open his chest with her bare hands. Xiuhnel's terrifying howls of pain awakened Mimich, who rushed over just in time to see Itzpapalotl gnawing on the older Cloud Serpent's flesh.

"My brother!" he gasped.

"Ah, beloved Mimich!" the goddess cried. "Come, sweetling. Won't you join my feast?"

The younger Cloud Serpent did not reply, but took up his fire drill with shaking hands and sparked a blaze which he fed with fallen branches. Itzpapalotl stood, smeared with Xiuhnel's gore, and took a step forward.

Mimich did not hesitate—he drew a burning brand from the fire and began to run, setting the dry brush around them alight. As conflagration rose on every side, Mimich hurled himself through the blazing barrier, believing his brother's killer to be trapped within.

Itzpapalotl pursued him, however, through the flames and across the wastelands as he ran back to Chicomoztoc. Mimich was fleet of foot, but the goddess gained on him bit by bit.

Camaxtli happened to see them, approaching from afar. Intuiting the danger to his brother, the Cloud Serpent hid himself within a barrel cactus, waiting with bow in hand.

Mimich finally ran past, and Camaxtli burst forth in ambush, letting arrows fly in speedy succession into Itzpapalotl's flesh till she collapsed, defeated.

Mimich circled back and stood over the goddess.

"Mighty Mimich," she gasped, "and redoubtable Camaxtli, have mercy. I am Itzpapalotl, black-taloned tzitzimitl descended from Tamoanchan to fulfill a great purpose, to play an important role. Render me honor. Perform the proper rites. Let holy fires consume my divine flesh, and then bundle my ashes. Men are on the rise. Soon the Chichimecah will fill this wasteland, lost without a patron. You and I will guide them, puissant Cloud Serpents. We will teach them to sustain the cosmos."

"So will I do, Mother," Mimich swore. Removing the arrows from her flesh, he prepared her carefully, washing her corpse and then dusting it white with chalk. Then his remaining brothers and sister festooned the goddess with precious feathers.

Earthly fire does not suffice to immolate a god, so Camaxtli called on the four Lords of Fire—blue, yellow, white and red avatars of Xiuhtecuhtli. They brought with them flames from the great hearth in Mictlan where the sun is rekindled every night.

Itzpapalotl burned hot and fierce, until all that was left of her were ashes and a chunk of white flint. The Cloud Serpents dipped their fingers in those ashes and rubbed them on their faces, blackening the sockets of their eyes. Then Camaxtli packed the remaining ashes into two bamboo tubes, using leather cords to bind these and the flint up in the skin of an animal.

Thus was formed the first tlaquimilolli or holy bundle. Camaxtli would bear it for centuries as he roamed the sea-ringed world. From its depths Itzpapalotl whispered advice and commands. With her guidance, Camaxtli would assume his mantle as an aspect of the God of Chaos and bend the world to his will.

The Birth of Huitzilopochtli

At the heart of the sea-ringed world, near the future site of the city
of Tollan, the goddess Coatlicue lived on Mount Coatepec with her
daughter, Coyolxauhqui, and her sons, the Four Hundred Gods of the
South. Coatlicue—a fierce but loving deity whose nature encompassed
the duality of motherhood—wore a skirt of serpents and a necklace
of skulls as she diligently swept the mountaintop and cared for her
children. Her husband Camaxtli ranged far and wide across the earth,
only infrequently visiting Coatepec.

While sweeping one day, Coatlicue was struck by a ball of feathers. She
picked it up almost absent-mindedly and placed the downy object in her
bosom to continue her work. Once she was finished, she felt around for the
feathers in order to examine them more carefully, but she found nothing.

Coatlicue understood immediately that the plumes had penetrated
her flesh and made her pregnant. Sensing a cosmic plan beyond her ken,
she let the child grow in her womb.

Her sons, however, soon noticed her state and become wildly angry.
"Who made you pregnant? This shameful behavior impugns our honor!"

Their sister Coyolxauhqui was also indignant. She drew all four
hundred together to take council with them. "Brothers," she said, "we
must kill our mother. She dishonors us, the unfaithful wretch. There is
no telling who put that bastard in her belly."

Coyolxauhqui continued to fan the flame of her brothers' rage. The
four hundred sons felt as if their hearts had been ripped away by their
mother's betrayal of the family. Finally they agreed to their sister's plan.
They made ready, girding themselves as if for battle as Coyolxauhqui
supervised them. Like war captains they twisted and tied up their long hair.
They adorned themselves with the accoutrements of war: paper vestments,
reed and feather crowns, stinging nettles that hung from colorful ribbons.
They tied on their ankle bells and gathered their barbed arrows.

Then they began to march in military formation, Coyolxauhqui at the vanguard.

But one of the brothers, Cuahuitlicac, broke away from the group quietly, having rejected their goal. He hurried to his mother's side, handing over his shield as he told her what was happening.

When Coatlicue learned of the plot against her, she became fearful and sad. But then her unborn son, Huitzilopochtli, spoke to her from the womb:

"Do not be afraid, Mother. I know what I must do."

Having heard these words, Coatlicue felt at peace, her heart calm.

Next Huitzilopochtli spoke to Cuahuitlicac. "Be watchful, my brother. Look carefully. Which way do they approach?"

"They are near the skull rack."

After a few minutes, Huitzilopochtli asked again. "And now?"

"They are crossing the terrace at the foot of the mountain."

Once more the unborn god spoke. "Look carefully, brother. Now where are they?"

"On the mountainside."

Time passed. "And now?"

"They have just reached the summit. Here they come! Coyolxauhqui is out in front!"

In that instant, Huitzilopochtli was born onto his brother's shield, emerging fully formed from his mother's womb, whole and hale except for his left foot, withered as if in echo of Hurricane's ancient wound. Calmly, as his angry brothers spilled across the mountaintop, the god strapped on his gear, smeared paint across his face, crowned himself with a battle headdress, put in his earplugs. Taking up his shield, spears and spear-thrower, he slipped on sandals, the left one covered with feathers to disguise his weaker foot.

Finally, the newborn god lifted and brandished a twisted bit of wood carved into the shape of a serpent. One of the four hundred, Tochancalqui, laughed mockingly and notched a flaming arrow to his bowstring. Released, the fiery dart struck the serpent, setting it alight and bringing it to life. For this was none other than Xiuhcoatl, nahualli of the God of Fire.

Wielding the serpent, Huitzilopochtli hurled himself at his sister, striking her head from her shoulders and dismembering her, the limbs of the goddess tumbling down the mountainside to land in a jumble at the bottom.

Then proud Huitzilopochtli gave chase to the Four Hundred Gods of the South, driving them off of Mount Coatepec, down its slopes, across the plains at its foot. He pursued them as if they were mere rabbits, chasing them four times around the mountain. In vain they would stop and turn in order to attack, their ankle bells ringing as they banged their shields together. But to no avail: they could gain no ground against the new god, and they were defenseless against his blazing might.

Huitzilopochtli ran them down, singly and in groups. He humbled them. He defeated them utterly. He had no mercy, though they cried out, begging, "That is enough!"

In the end, he slaughtered them all. Stripping off their battle gear, he hurled their corpses into the sky, where they became the southern stars.

Though her son had defended her honor, Coatlicue wept in grief over the loss of her daughter. Not wanting his mother to be lonely and sad, Huitzilopochtli took Coyolxauhqui's head and tossed it into heaven, where it became the new moon, displacing the old forever. Now mother and daughter could look upon each other each night and learn to forgive, to trust, to love.

In time, the whole earth would marvel at Huitzilopochtli's prodigious feats and his miraculous birth. The product of feathers and the womb of his mother, this uncommon god would rise to prominence, embracing a bloody destiny.

For Huitzilopochtli was the god of war, and he yearned to stir up battle lust in the heart of every man.

Archer of the Sun

The nomadic tribes of the Chichimecah began to fill the northern wastelands, looking to the semi-divine Cloud Serpents for guidance. But many other groups flourished in Mexico as well, guided by the will of the gods.

Across the Isthmus of Tehuantepec, in the mist-shrouded mountains and hills of Oaxaca, live a people who call themselves the Ñuu Dzaui or People of the Rain. The Nahuas, when they came across this mighty nation, named them Mixteca—Cloud People. Their wise ones narrate a singular origin for this ancient tribe and its ancestral lands.

Ages ago in the land of Yuta Tnoho, within the cave from which the Achiutl River once flowed, two gigantic trees began to grow on either side of a fountainhead. These trees loved each other despite the chasm that separated them, and with the passing of the centuries their yearning overcame the divide: their roots and branches stretched over the river's source to intertwine as one.

The creator gods—revered by the Mixteca as Lady 1 Deer and Lord 1 Deer—found themselves moved by this improbable love. They granted the trees two special offspring: the first Mixteca woman and man. In time that primordial couple had children, who had children, on and on down the centuries until the multitude of Cloud People established the mythical city of Achiutla.

Generations passed, and Achiutla sprawled into a metropolis. One day, in one of its many homes, was born a boy who would become a hero to his people: Yacoñooy. As he grew, it was clear he would never reach the physical stature of other men, but what he lacked in height he made up for in tenacity, bravery, and skill. Soon his fellow warriors learned to respect and love him for his audacious feats in battle, and he rose to the rank of captain.

The leaders of the Achiutla faced a problem, however, that weapons could not solve.

"There is simply no more room upon this mountaintop for future generations of Cloud People," declared the toniñe, Achiutla's Lord of Blood, its divinely chosen king. "A new site for a sister city must be found, a beautiful place with great bounty where our nation may continue to expand."

The Cloud People were hesitant. Achiutla had always been their home. They had defended it against invaders for centuries untold. The trek to a new region would be harrowing enough. Who dared be the first to chart the way? To route enemies encamped nearby?

"By the leave of our Lord of Blood, I shall go," Yacoñooy declared. "I shall discover the ideal region for another settlement, brothers and sisters, uncles and aunts. You know my valor. Does anyone doubt that I can accomplish this task?"

No one gainsaid him. The king blessed the captain before the gods and all the people. Yacoñooy took up his bow and arrows, setting out to conquer new lands in the West, ready to vanquish any foe who stood in his way.

The warrior wandered for weeks and months, searching aimlessly. Entire days would pass without rest, despite the toll that exhaustion and heat would have taken on a lesser man. Yacoñooy went beyond the limits of human endurance, impelled by some mysterious force to continue his quest as long as necessary.

At last the brave captain came to a vast, uninhabited expanse. No one appeared to stand in his way as he explored that lovely and fertile land— only the sun accompanied his every step, shining with brilliant heat upon his head and back.

Finding no man with whom to prove his mettle, Yacoñooy lifted his eyes to the heavens. Not a single cloud appeared to cover the unrelenting sun. As thirst and fatigue threatened to overwhelm him, Yacoñooy felt sunrays hit him, biting into his flesh like arrows from above.

Realization dawned. No man or woman ruled those lands. This

was the Evening Kingdom of the Sun. The solar god himself was their sovereign lord!

This knowledge would have stopped a lesser man. Iya Ndicandii—Lord Sun—had initiated the Age of Light, ending the Age of Darkness when he had emerged for the first time millennia ago. The clarity of daylight, the elders taught, allowed the Cloud People to see, understand, reason, establish social order. That first morning was the beginning of time itself, of human history. Before that dawn, unimaginable and unending sacred night had filled the cosmos.

In the Age of Darkness, the wise ones said, lived the Stone People. Lord Sun had not appeared: only Lady Moon—Ñuhu Yoo—glimmered faintly in the sky. When Iya Ndicandii crossed the horizon at last, the Stone People were terrified, thinking the world was about to end, consumed by fire. They tried to kill themselves, leaping into caves, hiding under boulders, slipping down ravines, tumbling from mountaintops.

Yes, the ruler of these lands was fiercesome indeed. But Yacoñooy was undaunted. He cried out in defiance:

"Iya Ndicandii, Lord Sun who rules these lands with awesome force—I challenge you. Let us see who is greater, who can give greater glory to this unequaled paradise!"

The sun laughed, confident in his own power, ignoring the small being that defied him from the ground below.

Yacoñooy cried out again:

"I am not frightened by the strength of your light. I have time as a weapon, aging slow within my heart!"

He notched an arrow and pulled his bow taut, aiming for the center of the haughty sun.

The sun laughed again, reaching his zenith and pouring from his belt of fire a hail of sunbeams at the upstart, thinking to roast him alive.

Dropping his weapons, Yacoñooy lifted his shield and stood firm, heat passing around him in waves, until noon gave way to afternoon.

The regal solar god watched his strength begin to wane as time progressed. There below, however, the small warrior had not budged—he resisted still beneath his ample shield, waiting for an opening.

Afternoon waned. The sky began to gloam. The sun grew weaker as the wheels of time spun ever onward. Yacoñooy tossed aside his shield and took up his bow once more. Quickly notching and loosing, the captain sent seven arrows winging their deadly way toward the glowing orb even as Iya Ndicandii rushed toward the refuge of some distant peaks.

Twilight fell. The sky went blood red as the sun dropped down the sky.

Impassive, Yacoñooy watched his opponent sink behind the mountains. The mist that wreathed them was stained scarlet at the god's passing. The valient warrior waited in silence, his heart thundering in his ears. At any moment, a last glowing missile might come arcing over the peaks, a surprise attack from a dying enemy.

But Lord Sun was gone. He did not reappear, clambering up over the horizon to face his human foe.

The warrior lifted his weapons and bellowed in triumph.

"I have defeated you, Lord Sun! The prowess of my arm has dealt you a mortal blow! Beyond those peaks you cower, wounded—never again will you reign in these lands. My one regret is that I cannot watch you writhe in pools of your own blood! What I would not give to see you die before me!"

Thrusting an arrow into the starlit soil, Yacoñooy claimed those lands in the name of his Lord of Blood, in the name of the Cloud People themselves.

In due time, he led his people to the vast expanse he had ripped from the hands of a god. There, upon sands blackened into glass by the sun's attack, they built the city the Nahuas would call Tilantongo.

Its Mixtec name was Ñuu Tnoo—Huahi Andehui.

Black Town—Temple of Heaven.

The Toltecs and the Rise of Civilization

Convocation

Do you see the blur of history, time flowing past like a rapid river, allowing only glimpses of moments caught within its currents?

Dive in with me. Let us navigate that racing tide.

The Fifth Age is well under way. Decades become centuries—centuries, millennia. All across the world, women and men band together in tribes, cities, nations. The wild complexity of woods and plains is tamed into cultivated symmetry. Bit by gradual bit, rising above the trees as if to touch the gods, come the mighty statues and temples, the ziggurats and pyramids.

Among all the mighty peoples who work their will upon the world, there is one whose name will go whispered down the years in awe, the very epitome of our collective potential.

The Toltecs, noble nation for whom creativity is philosophy—

And their home, that fabled city, shrouded in mists, glimpsed through tall reeds at the water's edge, glittering and haughty beneath a proud sun—

Tollan, jewel of Mexico, height of civilization, cradle of the arts.

This majestic realm is ruled for centuries by wise kings and queens until at last, in its waning years, Tollan places a crown on the brow of Feathered Serpent made flesh.

His reign cannot last. Chaos will not abide the perfection that Order seeks to realize in this earthly kingdom.

So once more Hurricane plots the downfall of his brother Feathered Serpent. Born as mortal men upon the sea-ringed world, they assume names that echo down the centuries:

Tezcatlipoca.

Quetzalcoatl.

Tragedy follows.

We can piece together the vast sweep of the tale from the old manuscripts—*Popol Vuh, Historia Chichimeca,* the *Florentine Codex,* the *Codex Chimalpopoca.* We can fill in narrative gaps with the words of Conquerors and priests—Torquemada, Herrera, Landa.

Listen. You can almost hear our ancestors, moaning their loss.

This fifth and final sun will die, like every sun before—but for a moment we laughed in its light, like wind-blown petals sparkling near an exile's campfire before the flames take them.

If you can bear it, friends, sing with me the song of Quetzalcoatl and his beloved Toltecs. Let us remember the dream of our Feathered Lord and weep to know ourselves fallen.

Tollan and the Toltec Queens

The Rise of Civilization

The gods guided humanity little by little: from Opochtli, men and women learned to fish; from Camaxtli, to hunt. Divinities of staple foods—like Xochipilli and Centeotl—taught the myriad tribes to gather tubers, grains, legumes and fruit. Xochiquetzal showed them how to weave sturdy clothing to stave off the cold. People lived simple, short lives centered on basic needs. They loved, they fought, they died. But they never forgot their covenant with their creators. Worship and thanksgiving were part and parcel of every daily act. Blood-letting and animal sacrifices were common, and when the need arose, a man or woman would be selected to lay down his or her life for the good of the people.

Then Chicomecoatl—wife of that smoking mirror, Hurricane—taught humanity the basics of agriculture, and everything changed. No longer needing to move from place to place, following migrations and seasons, the tribes built more permanent shelters and temples. Before long other gods came among them, like Toxipeuhca, patron of metalworking and stonemasonry. Over time, nations arose with their great cities and ziggurats, teeming with people needing to be fed. The providence of the gods became a much more crucial matter.

It was during this epoch that Camaxtli, last of the Four Hundred Cloud Serpents and incarnation of Hurricane's red aspect, rose to prominence in the kingdoms of the sea-ringed world. Understanding the dire need of urban centers and their potential in terms of sustenance for the gods, Camaxtli encouraged greater bloodshed to call down rain from Tlalocan and to ensure the vitality of precious crops. He was called Yohuallahuan, "Nightdrinker," because of the midnight showers he brought. But most enduring of his titles was Xipe Totec, Lord of Husking and Flensing. To symbolize the cycle of life, death and rebirth—sloughing away of old skin, bursting forth of shoots from seeds, shucking of shells to get at kernels—his priests flayed sacrificial victims before the spring rains, wearing those bloody husks until they rotted away to reveal the healthy flesh within.

And so, down the millennia, the great empires arose. Along the Gulf coast, the Olmecs spread their divine wisdom, lifting great pyramids to honor the mountains and volcanoes on which their ancestors had begged the gods for bounty. The Olmecs were a civilization of firsts— the ballgame that would become ubiquitous in Mesoamerica, the dual calendar that governed lives, a system of writing, the mysterious number zero. For centuries those ancients flourished, carving enormous heads with the features of their rulers, spreading their knowledge of the cosmos and shape-shifting magic through breathtaking art that has endured long after their fall.

Farther south, the Olmec mother culture came in contact with the peoples we now call Maya. A few centuries later, new urban centers sprawled in the jungles, massive monuments to humanity's skill and power when guided by the gods. Vast trade networks connected the city states of the lowlands, and the Maya refined their Mesoamerican cultural heritage into one of the greatest civilizations our world has ever seen, a society teeming with life and wisdom and vision. Its kings became gods. Its priests could reach into the future through complex calculations and stunning divination.

None foresaw the price such size required—Mother Earth herself appeared to turn from the Maya as drought and plagues and hunger swept across the southern lowlands. Those who survived fled into the highlands or north toward the Gulf, abandoning their vast cities to the whims of nature, which gradually swallowed the gleaming stone back into the jungles.

On a distant plateau, near Lake Xaltocan, a people often allied with the Maya had built a city that would come to be known as Teotihuacan— the place where people become gods, an earthly reflection of the capital of heaven. Covering eight square miles, housing some 125,000 souls, Teotihuacan evolved into the most important religious center in what is now called the Valley of Mexico. Supplying obsidian to allied armies throughout Mesoamerica, Teotihuacan helped decide the course of progress for many societies. Its rulers adored above all other gods the Sun, his father the Feathered Serpent, and the Great Goddess, Mother of All. The temples they erected to these deities would inspire utter awe in newcomers to the area for more than a thousand years after their descendents had abandoned life along the city's broad avenues.

The Arrival of the First Nahuas

Well to the north of Teotihuacan, there existed a land now lost in the mists of time. Aztlan it was called: Place of Whiteness. Fleeing their oppressors in a vast exodus, seven tribes escaped Aztlan and shrugged themselves free of their ethnic name, Aztecs. Calling themselves Nahuas, clear-talking folk, the tribes made their way to the mountain of Chicomoztoc, finding refuge in its vast network of caves, long abandoned by the Cloud Serpents.

Compared to the luxurious paradise of Aztlan, the new home of the Nahuas was austere and unforgiving, replete with thorny plants, wild maguey, cacti, xihuallacatl squash, and wild rye. Yet, though life was difficult, the earth yielded her bounty to their hard work, and the Nahuas thrived.

As centuries passed, some of the tribes felt the tug of destiny and emigrated, heading east and south. Many became eternal nomads, restless hunters who nourished themselves upon agave sap, mesquite beans, cactus blooms. They called themselves Chichimecah, people from the land of maguey milk.

Others wended their long way to a highlands plateau, settling over the years in a great basin or valley whose ample lakes made a more sedentary existence possible. Among these tribes were the women and men who would come to be known as Toltecs. Guided by Camaxtli, now called Mixcoatl, *the* Cloud Serpent, for having vanquished his four hundred sinful brothers, the Toltecs founded the mighty city of Tollan and forged an empire that would become legendary.

Tollan Established

From within her sacred bundle, the goddess Itzpapalotl whispered to Mixcoatl. "It is time you left these Chichimecah, time they had a human ruler. I choose Huactli, chief among them. Tell them their goddess says to travel to Necuameyocan there in the wilderness and build a house of thorns and maguey in which to lay the mats of power."

Her people carried out these commands and others. Travelling to all four cardinal directions, they hunted for animals of all four sacred colors: blue, yellow, white, and red. Once they had gathered an eagle, jaguar, snake, rabbit, and deer of each hue, Itzapapalotl had them build a fire to honor Xiuhtecuhtli, Lord of Time.

"Consign your catch to these flames," the goddess instructed, "but first place three hearthstones amidst the blaze. These symbolize Mixcoatl, Tozpan, and Ihuitl, the mighty demigods who have traveled with you across vast deserts, the three keepers of the holy fire, guardians of time itself. They leave you now, but forever shall you honor and remember them thus, until the wheels of time grind away to nothing."

Then their first ruler, Chichimec prince Huactli, fasted for four days within the house of thorn and maguey. His people made him a banner of egret feathers that he carried wherever they might go, a startling white sign for all to rally around in battle, for all to settle around in peace.

And so they set forth, travelling from nation to nation, bearing the bundled remains of Itzapapalotl and the three sacred hearthstones. When they began, they did not know how to plant corn or to weave tilmas for clothes. They still draped animal hides across their backs and hunted wild game. Homeless, they followed plants and seasons, awaiting the divine sign that would tell them they had finally reached their promised land. In every kingdom they visited, they learned a new skill, preparing themselves for their destiny.

Leadership of the tribe passed from man to man until, at last, among the reeds that bordered a broad river in the valley of Tollantzinco, Itzapapalotl told her people to build a city.

Tollan grew in fits and starts, its inhabitants slowly abandoning their barbaric ways. A king was selected from among the wise and valiant elders—Chalchiuhtlonac, whose communion with the goddess allowed him to craft the first laws. He was succeeded by his son Mixcoamazatzin, who founded a dynasty that would lead the city to cultural greatness. King after king fostered the arts in Tollan until kingdoms throughout the central highlands and beyond vyed for trade alliances with the Toltecs. Over time a new concept evolved among the Nahuas: toltecayotl, the inimitable artistry of that vital civilization.

The Queens of Tollan

Not all of the city's sovereigns were kings, of course. Many women guided the Toltecs—as Tollan's citizens were now called—through peace and war. Early on, the wife of Chief Huactli became ruler. Lady Xiuhtlahcuilolxochitzin—"Flower Painted Emerald Green"—ruled from a house of straw beside the city square. She knew how to invoke the goddess Itzapapalotl, a holy connection that served her well in the twelve years of her reign.

Death also brought another queen to the throne a century later. When King Nauhyotl fell victim of age, Tollan unanimously selected his wife Xiuhtlaltzin as his successor. During four peaceful years, the queen managed public affairs with a wisdom and strength that rivaled her husband's statecraft. Upon her passing, the Toltecs mourned like children bereft.

Of course, not all of Tollan's queens were widows continuing the work of their husbands. In the 11th century, a noble named Itztacxilotzin—

"White Maize"—was crowned sovereign. After establishing a palace beside the Izquitlan River, she governed in Tollan with a council of women at her side until her death eleven years later.

During their wandering, the Toltecs had forgotten the gift of pulque given to humanity by Lord Opossum so many millennia before. But not long after Itztacxilotzin's reign, a sixteen-year-old girl rediscovered the recipe while helping her father Papatzin to store agave nectar harvested from his fields. When her family realized the value of this miraculous drink, they brought her before the new king, the young and handsome Tepalcatzin.

The ruler was fascinated by the beverage, but even more so by Xochitl's beauty.

"Loyal Papatzin," he said to her father, "please permit your daughter to remain in the palace so she may teach the women on my staff to prepare this delightful brew."

Papatzin reluctantly agreed. Tepalcatzin was already married, but Queen Maxio had only given him daughters. It was not unusual in such cases for a king to take a second wife, but Papatzin worried about his daughter's treatment by the older woman. She was so lovely and so intelligent—just the combination to enrage a first wife whose husband has lost interest in her.

While living on the royal estate, Xochitl found herself surrounded by bright green maguey plants and rows of huisaches and rose bushes whose gold and scarlet flowers spread sweet perfume throughout her room. In the midst of such sensory delight, the king approached her with rich gifts and words of love.

"Xochitl, all this beauty fades alongside you. The artisanship for which Tollan is known has found its maximum expression in your dark hair and eyes. Such ineffable qualities belong on a mat of power at my side. Will you consent to be my queen?"

"But you have a queen, my lord."

"Ah, but this last pregnancy has left her weak and ill. I fear her time in this illusory world draws to an end."

Over the days and weeks, Tepalcatzin wooed Xochitl without ceasing. She at last relented. Her parents, worried at so long a stay, called upon the king, who announced their betrothal. The two were married, and in time a son was born. The king, wanting to pay homage to the beverage that had brought his love to his side, named the boy Meconetzin—child of the maguey.

When Maxio finally succumbed, Xochitl was proclaimed queen of Tollan. Wise and compassionate beyond measure, she ruled at her husband's side for decades, a peaceful reign until civil war broke out among the Toltecs.

As warriors loyal to the king were decimated and Tepalcatzin deposed, an aging Xochitl called on the mothers and daughters of Tollan to fight by her side.

"We are the heart of the sea-ringed world! We are the citadel amidst the reeds! We are the skilled hands that reshape the cosmos! Tollan shall not fall! Take up those spears, dear sisters, once brandished by your husbands and brothers and sons! Take up their bucklers, their feathered helms! Today we abandon the hearth, rush beyond these walls—today we fight!"

Queen Xochitl led the furious battallion of women during the king's last stand near the town of Xochitlalpan. There she hacked and slew many rebel warriors before falling at last under the obsidian blades of the enemy.

Her fierce Toltec sisters carried the body of their beloved queen from the field, laying it beside her husband's broken corpse, taking a moment to entrust her to the Lady of Death.

Then, screaming her name, they flung themselves back into the fray.

The Brothers Incarnated

Such was the cycle as the Fifth Age progressed—kingdoms rose and fell down the long count of years, often due to struggles between factions of gods. At last, the Feathered Serpent saw that it was time for him to descend into the world as a man, to more directly guide his beloved creation toward a path of enlightenment and beauty.

His brother, learning of this plan, decided in secret to do the same.

In those distant, hazy years of the legendary past, there existed a town known to us as Michatlauhco. On its outskirts lived a woman that had once loved a god: Chimalman, who had snatched from the air swift arrows shot by the hunter god Mixcoatl. He had found the woman warrior lovely, so he had slept with her. Nine months later she bore him a daughter, Quetzalpetlatl.

Not many years afterward, Chimalman was sweeping the temple of Quilaztli when she discovered a piece of green jade. On impulse, nudged by forces she could not comprehend, she placed the stone on her tongue and swallowed it. Soon she realized she was pregnant, clearly by the will of the Divine Mother.

At the end of the thirteenth year of that calendar cycle, Chimalman went into labor. For four days she struggled to bring her child into the world, aided by midwives and priestesses. Early on the morning of the last named day of the year, 1-Reed, her pain ended: a baby boy emerged into the world.

But the next five days were the nemontemi or uncounted days, perilous times for human beings. Chimalman was beset by all manner of evils. Before the Lord of Time had been renewed by sacrifice, she was dead.

The newborn and his toddler sister were sent to live with their grandparents, who at first called the boy Ce Acatl—One Reed—for the day of his birth. Soon, however, the boy's horoscope was drawn up and his baptism performed, at which point he was given the name Quetzalcoatl in honor of the Feathered Serpent.

When Ce Acatl Quetzalcoatl reached the age of nine, he began to wonder about his heritage, especially his father's identity.

"What is my father like?" he asked his sister.

"I do not know, Brother. He left when I was very little."

"Can I see my father?" he then asked his grandparents. "I wish to look upon his face."

Though his mother's family did not know the whereabouts of Mixcoatl, they called out to him in prayer, tipping out libations of blood and wine. When the hunter god finally came, he was presented with Quetzalpetlatl, his daughter, and Ce Acatl Quetzalcoatl, who was believed by all to be his son. Mixcoatl could see teotl glowing brightly in them both, but he was drawn especially to the boy. Though inwardly he knew Ce Acatl Quetzalcoatl could not be his son, he agreed to take him for a time.

For the entire year of 10-Flint, the boy learned to hunt and fight at his erstwhile father's side in the land of Xihuacan. But Mixcoatl's three surviving brothers—the last of the Cenzton Mimixcoah or Four Hundred Cloud Serpents whom the hunter god had slaughtered and thrown as stars into the northern sky—were jealous of the boy and decided to kill him. Apantecuhtli, Tlohtepetl and Cuauhtliicoauh conferred for a good while before coming up with a wily plan.

First they tricked their nephew into visiting Tlachinoltepec, a massive boulder around which inexplicable flames raged at certain times of day. Leaving him at its base, they hurried away to watch. But Ce Acatl Quetzalcoatl sensed the coming of the fire and slipped into a tunnel in the rock. His uncles left, believing him burned alive.

After a time, the boy emerged unscathed. Taking up his bow and arrow, he killed some game. He hurried home, the kill thrown across his shoulders, and arrived at his father's side before his uncles, who were dumbfounded when they saw him.

Next the three villains took him to a great tree and had him climb up into its highest boughs to better shoot at the birds that winged their way through the sky. Once he was installed in those branches, the three began to loose bolts at him. Discretely, Ce Acatl Quetzalcoatl let himself fall to the ground and pretended to be dead. His uncles imagined him shot and killed, so they immediately left.

The boy then got to his feet and slew a rabbit, which he took to his father before the uncles arrived. Mixcoatl at this point suspected that his brothers meant to murder his adopted son, so he asked Ce Acatl Quetzalcoatl where his uncles were.

"Oh, they are on their way, Father."

"I see. Son, I have an errand for you." And he sent the boy to a nearby house, meaning to confront his brothers alone.

When they arrived, he asked them without hesitation:

"Why are trying to kill my son? Do you not remember the fate of our other brothers?"

The three, expecting just such a query, had prepared themselves. Before he could react, they fell on Mixcoatl and killed him, dragging his corpse off toward the desert and burying him in the sand.

When Ce Acatl Quetzalcoatl returned from his errand, he found his father gone. The boy went about, asking everyone he saw, "Where's my father?"

Finally Cozcacuauhtli, the king vulture, answered him:

"Your uncles have killed your father. He lies over yonder, buried in the sand. I'll show you."

His hands shaking, the boy soon dug up the corpse of Mixcoatl, bundled it properly, and took it to his father's temple, Mixcoateopan. His uncles learned of the funeral rites and approached him. "The Northern Stars will be enraged if you do not dedicate this temple correctly. You cannot sacrifice a simple rabbit or snake, boy. This requires an eagle, a wolf, a jaguar."

"Very well," Ce Acatl Quetzalcoatl responded. Going into the wilderness, he called to the eagle, the wolf, the jaguar. "My true uncles," he said to them formally, "come. They say I must dedicate my father's temple with your blood. But you will not die. Instead, you will dine on the flesh of the men I shall use to sanctify Mixcoateopan: my human uncles themselves!"

Tying leads around their necks for appearances' sake, the boy conducted the three animals to the temple. His uncles seized the ropes, laughing. "Thank you, knave. Now we will be the ones to drill fire upon the temple platform and sacrifice them!"

Though his uncles barred him from entering, Ce Acatl summoned gophers to his aid. "Uncles, come! Help me dig my way into the temple." The creatures made short work of it, and soon the boy had slipped inside and made his way to the platform.

Apantecuhtli, Tlohtepetl, and Cuauhtliicoauh had been rejoicing and making merry. By the time they regained their senses and emerged onto the platform, their nephew was already drilling the fire for the sacrifice. They rushed at the boy, Apantecuhtli in the lead, but Ce Acatl Quetzalcoatl smashed a metal pot into his uncle's head, sending him tumbling. The animals seized the other two. As the fire blazed bright, they tore out the hearts of the last Mimixcoa and consigned their bodies to the flames.

Ce Acatl Quetzalcoatl returned to his grandparents then and resumed the life of a noble boy his age. He attended school in the temple, learned to adore the gods and mortify the flesh, studied the lore and paintings of his people, acquired greater skill in the use of spear and shield and bow. As a young man he fought campaigns in Ayotlan and Chalco, Xicco and Cuixcoc, Zacanco and Tzonmolco. He rose quickly through the ranks, becoming captain and then general before finally serving as adviser to the king.

But a deeper longing filled his soul, a thirst for knowledge that warfare and sacrifice could not acquire. So at the age of twenty-eight, Ce Acatl Quetzacoatl took leave of his men and his king and left for Tollantzinco, a land of fertile valleys and volcanic peaks. There he built a hermitage in the mountains and spent four years fasting and meditating.

News of his turquoise and timber cabin spread throughout the land. He was consulted by the shamans of Tollantzinco, who were awed by the depth of his wisdom. Soon word of this philosopher reached the ears of Ihuitimal, ailing and heirless king of Tollan. He had Ce Acatl Quetzalcoatl brought before him, and they talked long and intently about the cosmos and humanity's role in it.

The king was greatly impressed. At his urging, the council of Tollan offered the physical and spiritual leadership of the city to Quetzalcoatl, who accepted, filled with visions of the transformations he would work on the kingdom and in the hearts of its inhabitants. He sent for his sister Quetzalpetlatl, who lived alone now that their grandparents had died, and she joined him in Tollan.

When King Ihuitimal of Tollan finally passed into the House of the Sun, Quetzalcoatl was enthroned at the age of thirty-one. His people called him Topiltzin, "our beloved prince." He brought a decade of great peace, prosperity, and artistic flowering to mighty Tollan. He introduced great wealth to the city—precious stones like jade and turquoise, precious metals like gold and silver, precious gifts of the sea like coral and pearl, precious feathers from cotingas, ibis, herons, and orioles. He himself was a great artisan, producing beautiful earthenware and textiles, inspiring his subjects to rise to greater and greater heights until, across the sea-ringed world, the word Toltec, citizen of Tollan, became a synonym for master craftsman.

Spiritual enlightenment, however, was still the primary objective of Topiltzin Ce Acatl Quetzalcoatl. He built four houses of fasting, prayer, penance, and praise throughout the city: one of turquoise beams, one faced in coral, one inlaid with whiteshell, one festooned with quetzal plumes. After spending his evenings in one of these special houses, he would go down to a shrine at the water's edge, amongst the reeds, to draw blood from his flesh with penitential thorns and spines he crafted from jade and quetzal quills. From time to time he took sabbaticals in the mountains, burning incense there atop the craggy peaks of Xicolotl, Huitzco, Tzincoc, Nonoalco.

And ever at his side was his older sister Quetzalpetlatl. Their ecstatic prayers echoed in the skies. They cried out to all the doubled gods—Citlalinicue and Citlalantoc, Tonacacihuatl and Tonacatecuhtli, Tecolliquenqui and Eztlaquenqui, Tlallamanac and Tlalichcatl. They strove to pierce the heavens with their hearts and peer into Omeyocan, the place of duality from which our grandparents wing our souls to the sea-ringed world. Those two, source of all, looked down contentedly on their beloved son, pleased with his prayers, his humility, his contrition.

And in the silence of his penance, they whispered to the philosopher-king of Tollan:

"Remember."

Rising in Topiltzin Ce Acatl Quetzalcoatl was a surety that the world could be better. His own blood offerings were merely snakes, birds, butterflies. Gradually he eradicated human sacrifice from Tollan, driving out the priests and sorcerers who refused to accept his new vision.

Among these exiled necromancers was Tezcatlipoca, a powerful priest who had torn many hearts from the chests of many warriors to ensure sun, rain, crops. He despised the weakness he perceived in his king, and he worked in secret to turn the city against the new laws. But the Toltecs loved Topiltzin Ce Acatl Quetzalcoatl with too great a fealty to be swayed. Even as their ruler became more and more of a recluse, rarely leaving his houses of penance or mountaintop retreats to walk the streets of Tollan, his subjects would find no fault in his leadership in that year of 2-Reed, a decade after he had been enthroned.

Long black hair clotted with blood, robes filthy and tattered, Tezcatlipoca took up his staff and searched for his colleagues: Ihuimecatl and Tlacahuepan, powerful sorcerers and shape-shifters, both.

"We must torment this weak-hearted fool," he told them, "and force him to abandon the city. Then Tollan will be returned unto our hands. We will grease the wheels of time with glorious gore."

"He has exchanged the human payment for his strange sacraments," Tlacahuepan said. "So let us brew pulque and make him drink. He will become besotted and forget his penance, his fasting, his prayers. His shame will then drive him hence."

Ihuimecatl had another stratagem in mind. "We should undermine his lauded humility by appealing to his sense of vanity. Let him adorn himself in the full regalia of a god, let an effigy of him be placed in the temple, and he will abandon his cowardly ways."

Tezcatlipoca nodded. "Yes. Yes. But first let us give him the means to see his own form for what it really is."

The other two agreed, so Tezcatlipoca began. Wrapping up a small obsidian mirror, he altered his appearance to seem a young man and approached the house of fasting where Ce Acatl Quetzalcoatl was doing penance.

"Please inform the High Priest," he said to the guards, "that young Telpochtli has arrived to show him, to deliver unto him, his true form."

The guards did as Tezcatlipoca bid. The king asked, "What does he mean, venerable guards? What is my 'true form?' Go, examine what he has brought and then we shall let him enter."

But Tezcatlipoca would not permit them. "I myself must show him."

When Quetzalcoatl heard this, he nodded. "Then let him enter, august ones."

Tezcatlipoca was ushered in. He greeted the sovereign of Tollan. "Our beloved prince and high priest Ce Acatl Quetzalcoatl, I salute your Highness. I have come to show you your true form."

"Ah, venerable friend, you have wearied yourself. Whence came you? What is this 'true form' of which you speak? Show it to me."

"Your Majesty, I am but a humble subject of yours from the foot of Mount Nonohualco. As for your true form, you will behold it here."

Tezcatlipoca unwrapped the mirror, from which wisps of smoke curled at his touch. He placed it in Quetzalcoatl's hands.

"Look within this polished glass, dear Prince, and know yourself."

Quetzalcoatl peered at his reflection and stifled a scream. Dedicated to worship and penance alone, he had come to conceive of himself as a being of pure teotl, a spirit spun from Omeyocan, eternal and formless. So he was overcome with horror to see the aging flesh of his human face, wrinkled and scarred, eyes sunken and dark, brows furrowed and brooding. The dark magic of that smoking mirror went further, burrowing into his mind so he imagined the vivid passing of years, hair thinning, skin sagging and melting away to reveal bones that crumbled to powder dispersed by the indifferent winds of time.

"I am mortal," he whispered, appalled. "Ugly and decaying, bound to be bundled and burned like every king before me. How can I inspire my subjects like this? I tell them that we can be one with the Dual God, but we are but ephemeral and crude pictures scratched into sand. One look at me and they will know the truth!"

The mirror shaking in his hands, Quetzalcoatl began to weep. "My subjects can never again see me. I shall remain here, hidden from Tollan."

Tezcatlipoca bowed and left. Returning to his comrades, he called to Ihuimecatl.

"I have been successful," he explained. "Now we need to further disgrace the fool."

"Good. The chief feather worker, Coyotlinahual, has agreed to help. I shall send him to turn this shame into vanity."

Coyotlinahual entreated the guards for an audience with the king, and he was permitted to enter. He found Quetzalcoatl despondent and despairing, gazing wretchedly into the obsidian mirror.

"Beloved Prince," said the feather worker, "it is time you left your house of fasting and let your subjects gaze upon you."

"Never," the king replied, gesturing at his reflection. "I am no unfolding of divinity, no holy fragment of the source. One look at me, and the common man will turn his back on my laws."

"Then permit me to array you in immortal beauty so they are inspired by the sight."

Hope lit sparks in Quetzalcoatl's eyes. "A mask! Yes, revered brother, fashion me a disguise. Let me see what you can do to hide this ugliness."

Coyotlinahual set to work. First he crafted his conical jaguar cap, plumed like quetzal tails. Then he fashioned a mask inlaid with turquoise, its beak red, yellow striping forehead, and eyes. He affixed the serpent teeth and a beard-like fringe of ibis and cotinga feathers. Then the feather worker tailored a bone-ribbed jacket, a jaguar-skin cape, anklets with bells, and sandals of soft cotton.

The king looked upon the costume with approval. Coyotlinahual helped him get dressed. Then he handed Quetzalcoatl the mirror.

"I look…"

"Exactly like your namesake, dear Prince. The very image of the Feathered Serpent himself."

Pleased at his reflection, Quetzalcoatl agreed to visit his city. Accompanied by his guards, he walked along the broad streets of Tollan until he came to the unfinished temple he had begun to erect in honor of the god whose name he bore.

His subjects, elated, fashioned an effigy of their king in his divine garb. The manikin was set up in the temple, and people prayed to it as they would at a statue of the god Quetzalcoatl.

In the meanwhile, Ihuimecatl called to Tlacahuepan. "We have done our part. Now go: bring what is needed."

Tlacahuepan made his way to the fields of Xonacapacoyan, where he stayed with a farmer by the name of Maxtlaton, the lord of Mount Toltec. Together they prepared a stew for the king, replete with greens, chilis, tomatoes, fresh corn, and beans. There were also magueys on the farm. With Maxtlaton's permission, Tlacahuepan drew forth the aguamiel and fermented it in just four days, mulling the resulting pulque with honey from hives he found in nearby trees.

Tlacahuepan then returned to Tollan and met with Tezcatlipoca, who immediately visited Quetzalcoatl's palace, bearing the stew and the pulque. At first the king's guards would not admit the sorcerer. Twice, three times he tried to get in, only to be turned away.

Finally, the king had his men ask Tezcatlipoca where his home was.

"On the Peak of Priests, near Mount Toltec. I have brought a peace offering from those who opposed him."

Hearing this, Quetzalcoatl said, "Let him enter. I have awaited this meeting for some time."

Tezcatlipoca greeted the masked king with great deference and offered him the stew, explaining that the adherents of human sacrifice had realized the error of their way, enlightened by the wisdom of Tollan's ruler. Quetzalcoatl accepted the food with great generosity.

After the king had eaten from it, Tezcatlipoca drew forth a jar of pulque. "My august lord, how is your Majesty's health? I hear your Majesty is plagued with the aches and pains of encroaching age. Behold a potion that I have brought. Will you not drink it?"

Quetzalcoatl considered the older priest. "Come closer, wise brother. Your energy is clearly spent. You have exhausted yourself traveling. But I am glad you have come. Long have I wanted to heal the rift between us."

"As have I," Tezcatlipoca replied. "But tell me truly: how is your Majesty's health?"

"The truth is that all parts of me feel heavy and ill, from my limbs to my very soul. Though this costume and my subjects' praise fills me with pleasure, it is fleeting. When I return to this throne room, I feel as if I have been undone."

"And here is the remedy, Beloved Prince: a good, soothing and intoxicating potion. If you drink of it, it will relieve and heal your body. As for your soul...at first you will weep. Your heart will be even more troubled. You will think upon your mortality and despair. But then you will see where you must one day go, your sacred destination."

"My destination? What might that be, august one?"

"My vision is not clear, but you will travel to a land of red and black. There a wizened sage stands as sentinel. From him you will learn many things. When you return, you will have been made once more a youth."

Quetzalcoatl was moved by the prophecy. But when Tezcatlipoca urged him to drink the pulque, the king refused. "I cannot. It would be folly to risk my life on an unknown potion. I have a responsibility to my people."

"Come, Beloved Prince. You are in sore need. Drink. Rather, let me serve a small portion for you to have on hand should the urge arise. At the very least taste it. You will see that it is good, if a little strong."

Quetzalcoatl tasted a little and then took a hearty draught. "What is this drink? It is indeed quite good. My pain and despair subside. How can I feel better so soon?"

"Drink some more, your Majesty. You will soon find yourself stronger, healthier."

In a short space of time, Quetzalcoatl had imbibed five jars of pulque and was thoroughly drunk. Tezcatlipoca smiled cruelly and said:

"Beloved Prince, a song will lift your spirits even more. Let me teach you one and we can sing together."

And the sorcerer began to recite:

"I must leave my house of plumes,
My house of quetzal feathers,
Quetzal feathers, oriole plumes,
My house of lovely coral!"

The king joined in, and they sang in rounds till Quetzalcoatl was quite jubilant. Calling out to his men, he cried, "Go and fetch my sister Quetzalpetlatl—I want her to feel this joy at my side!"

The guards went to Mount Nonoalco, where the king's elder sibling was doing penance. "Princess Quetzalpetlatl, noble fasting lady, we have come for you at the high priest's command. Topiltzin Ce Acatl Quetzalcoatl awaits you. Will you not accompany us and join him?"

She readily agreed. Upon arriving, she sat down on her reed mat at her younger brother's side. Tezcatlipoca served her pulque, and she drank five portions as well.

When both siblings were thoroughly besotted with alcohol, Tezcatlipoca had them intone again the song. Then he taught them a second verse:

"Sister dear, dear elder sister mine,
Where will you go? Where can you abide?
Ah, sweet Quetzalpetlatl,
Let us drink ourselves blind!"

Drunk as they were, they no longer urged each other to keep the sacraments. They neither visited their riverside shrine nor pierced their flesh to draw blood as penance. As dawn set the sky to glowing, they did not perform their accustomed rites.

Finally, the sun's light and heat awakened them. They were overcome with sadness, almost bereft with remorse.

"Woe is me!" cried Quetzalcoatl, for in that moment of anguish he heard the sun calling: *You are not that flesh, father, nor did you come to rule. Remember your purpose, the reason you descended. Know who you are, and come to the land of the red and the black.*

Quetzalcoatl understood that he was indeed a holy unfolding from on high, and he despaired at his weakness, the ease with which he had been fooled. Sinking to the floor of his throne room, the divine king lifted his voice and sang the lament of his exile:

"No longer will the days
Be counted in my house—
This one is the last,
And forever it endures.
Let it be so in this place."

Then he sang a second stanza:

"Alas! I weep to think of her shame,
The one who formed and shaped me—
The mother I never knew,
That noble woman, that goddess."

When he ended his song, his sister and guards and attendants were devastated with grief, sobbing openly. They raised a hymn of praise to their beloved prince:

"Hail Quetzalcoatl, our jade-bright king!
Broken are his timbers,
His feathered house of prayer.
We look upon him one last time
And wail with lamentation!"

When they all fell silent, he ordered a sarcophagus of stone be carved and brought to the palace. Once it was ready, he closed himself within, seeking to cleanse himself of sin.

"Four days," he told his sister. "You must leave me to lie undisturbed for a span of four days."

But while Quetzalcoatl lay in penance, the three sorcerers set out to punish the men and women of Tollan for abandoning the human price and following their philosopher-king.

Tezcatlipoca adorned himself with feathers to resemble Quetzalcoatl and called the high priest's closest disciples to Texcalpan, a rugged canyon rimmed by crags. When all the youths and maidens had gathered, the sorcerer began to sing and beat his drum. As if compelled, the people started dancing wildly and chanting along with raucous joy. Night fell and deepened. At midnight, the music ceased, and the false Quetzalcoatl disappeared. Stumbling, dazed, lost, the disciples fell from the craggy cliffs into the raging river below. A few regained enough composure to reach the stone bridge that spanned the canyon, only to find it destroyed.

Meanwhile, Ihuimecatl took the form of a brave captain of Tollan and had the city crier announce to priests and noblemen that they were to meet in Xochitlan, the floating garden of Quetzalcoatl, in order to harvest flowers for their king. When the aristocracy of Tollan was gathered there, however, Ihuimecatl turned on them, smiting the backs of their heads, slaughtering hundreds while scores more trampled each other attempting to escape.

In the market place, Tlacahuepan appeared with a strange child-like golem, making it dance intricate steps as he held its hand. The Toltecs, mesmerized, gathered close, crushing and smothering some in the press. Soon Tlacahuepan released the unnatural being to continue its complex, jerking dance. The sorcerer faded into the crowd and called out, "This is an evil omen, friends! How can we permit such black magic? We must stone the creature!" The dancing thing fell beneath a hail of stones. But then it began to stink, and the stench was so powerful that the common folk of Tollan collapsed lifeless when that odor wafted past. Attempts were made to drag the body away with ropes, but these snapped, sending people tumbling together, dead amidst the stench.

Other omens came to pass. The dormant volcano Cacateptl erupted with a horrifying croak, sending flame and ash into the heavens. The people of Tollan were seized by panic. "The gods have forsaken us!" they cried. "If our city is consumed, where will we go?"

Stones rained down, some of them enormous. In the woods near Chapultepec fell a large sacrificial stone. An old woman who lived there began to pass out paper flags to likely victims.

She was, of course, Tezcatlipoca in disguise.

The old woman toasted corn, drawing the Toltecs to her with that tantalizing aroma. From near and far they came, heedless of the omens. She gave each a flag.

When they were gathered near the sacrificial stone, Tezcatlipoca revealed his true form and slaughtered them upon the stone, tearing their hearts from their chests.

Then, on the fourth day of Quetzalcoatl's penance, Tezcatlipoca—Hurricane incarnate—transformed into his nahualli, the fearsome jaguar Mountainheart, prowling the streets of Tollan, frightening its citizens. Upon reaching the incomplete temple of Quetzalcoatl, the sorcerer ripped the king's effigy to shreds and harried the acolytes from the inner sanctum.

Finally, weak and ill, the king emerged from his sarcophagus. Confronted by the destruction and death the sorcerers had wreaked on the city, Quetzalcoatl felt his will break. At the same time, divine teotl surged within him, making him capable of wondrous deeds. But he could not bear to remain in Tollan. The voice of the sun echoed in his soul. He called together his guards, his sister and his few remaining aides.

"Let us depart, my friends. Gather up all our riches and go down to the shrine at the river's edge."

As they exited the city, Quetzalcoatl set his houses of prayer alight. Gesturing at cocoa trees, he transformed them into mesquites. He called to the quetzals, the blue cotingas, the scarlet ibis—with a whistle he sent them winging their way south.

His companions buried the bulk of his wealth in the loamy banks of the river, taking only works of art and learned codices. Then they set forth across the sea-ringed world in search of that fabled land of red and black.

Following the road, the company came to Cuauhtitlan, Place of Trees. Resting against the thick bole of a tree there, Quetzalcoatl asked for the smoking mirror. Seeing his craggy features and unruly beard in his reflection, he sighed. "I am truly an old man now. Let this region be known as Huehuehcuauhtitlan, Place of the Old Tree."

Seizing a handful of rocks, he hurled them at the tree's trunk, where they stuck fast and remain to this day, embedded from the roots to the highest branches.

The company soon continued its travels, playing softly on flutes to lift the spirits of their beloved prince. Once again they stopped to rest. Quetzalcoatl leaned against a stone slab, tears running down his nose and falling like hail or acid against the marbled rock, leaving pockmarks. Where his hands had pressed against the stone, his palms left deep impressions as if the rock were merely clay. Hence the name of that site—*Temacpalco*, Place of His Palms.

After a time they moved on, coming to a wide and long river that could not easily be forded. Quetzalcoatl used his divine abilities to lift stones and fit them together, forming a bridge the likes of which had never existed. He and his followers crossed over on it, thus giving it the name Tepanohuayan, Stone Bridge River.

Later in their journey they came upon a bubbling spring. There a group of priests awaited the king, men whom he had exiled when they refused to stop their sacrifices. They blocked his way and asked:

"Where are you going? What is your destination? Why are you leaving the city? To whom have you left it? Who performs your sacraments?"

Quetzalcoatl responded, "Out of my way. I must continue."

"Answer us! Where are you bound?"

"The land of red and black. That is what I seek. That is my destination."

"What will you do there?"

"I have been summoned by the sun."

They seemed satisfied at this answer. "Very well. Go, but leave us all the Toltec arts."

And so he did. Quetzalcoatl left them the casting of gold, the cutting of jewels, the carving of wood, the sculpting of stone, the writing of books, the working of feathers. They made him abandon it all, taking it by force.

All that was left him was a handful of jewels which he scattered in the spring. He named it Cozcahapan, Place of the Jewel Spring. Over time this became *Coahapan*, Place of the Serpent Spring.

Now freed from all earthly entanglements, Quetzalcoatl fasted and prayed until another epiphany stole over him. All was revealed: his true origin, his purpose on earth, the nature of the priests who had so cleverly deceived him.

He gathered his retinue around him and spoke. "We are exiles from Tollan, but the sacraments we taught the Toltecs must be revealed to all the sea-ringed world. So, as we search for the place of my ultimate destiny, we will teach the peoples we meet the value of penance and fasting and prayer, mighty enough to move the wheels of time without requiring the human price."

And so they set out in earnest on a trek that lasted nearly a dozen years. First they passed through Acallan, Tzapotlan, and Mazatzonco, sharing the wisdom of the king. Then they crossed the Sierra Nevada: many of the travelers died upon those glaciers, but Quetzalcoatl revived them with weeping and singing.

In the great basin of the highlands, Quetzalcoatl made the rounds of all the villages, performing miracles and leaving behind signs that exist to this day. In one place he built a stone ball court. Elsewhere he pierced a cotton tree horizontally with another. He balanced an enormous rock on a smaller one: though it seems to sway with the wind, no one can budge it. He rested on a reed mat beside Metztli Iapan—that broad Lake of the Moon, which future generations would call Texcoco—infusing those fibers with power that would one day help a wandering tribe called the Mexica find at last their home.

Quetzalcoatl spent long months in the walled city of Tenayuca. He taught wisdom to the shamans of Colhuacan. In Cuauhquecholan, the people revered him as the god he was and erected a temple and altar during the few years he lived there, instructing them on the proper rites. The rulers of Cholula also bid him remain for several turns of the sacred calendar, and they erected a temple to the Feathered Serpent in which to fast and pray.

Cempoalatl begged him to rule. He tarried long in that kingdom, even meeting with the leaders of an exodus of Maya from the distant shores of the Eastern sea. A great temple to the sun was built alongside two temples for Quetzalcoatl: a ziggurat for his role as creator and sustainer, a round structure for his role as the wind that prepares the way for essential rain.

It was here that Tezcatlipoca arrived, driven from Tollan, hunting for his hated twin. Quetzalcoatl fled, leading the sorcerer on a chase into the wastelands until reaching a mighty ceiba, sapling of the World Tree. After loosing a magical arrow to open a cleft in its broad trunk, the divine king used the smoking mirror to trick Tezcatlipoca into the hole, where he sealed the dark mage away for the remainder of his earthly existence.

Then Quetzalcoatl, now known across the sea-ringed world as Nacxitl, the Wayfarer, saw that his time on earth was coming to an end. In his heart he understood the nature of the land of the red and the black. One last mission remained before him, and then he would meet his destiny at last.

Gathering up his companions, he journeyed to Poyauhtecatl, that white peak formed in ages past by the giant eagle Orizaba. One last time he laughed and played with his sister and friends, sliding down those slopes on foot, bouncing along to its base. Then he made his stately way to the sea.

"My friends, Quetzalpetlatl and I must leave you now. But weep not, for I shall return one day to lead you once more. Until then, keep my memory alive. Remember my teachings. Hew close to the Toltec way, the path of creation. May the Divine Mother bless you all."

Then, with his sister by his side, Quetzalcoatl stood upon that beach and gave a haunting whistle. Across the foam-topped waves came streaming a raft of feathered serpents. The holy siblings stepped onto the writhing backs and were borne away, disappearing over the eastern horizon.

The living raft deposited them in a distant land, a peninsula that thrust out into the rough blue of the sea. It was the Mayab, land of jungles and hills, ziggurats and cenotes.

The siblings trekked for a time through the broken hills of Puuc until they came across the small city of Uc Yabnal, recently conquered by the Itza—"Water Witches"—a mighty tribe that had traveled great distances looking for a new homeland. They had been drawn to Uc Yabnal due to the two massive cenotes or sinkholes that provided vital water in such an arid landscape.

Quetzalcoatl helped mediate between the natives and the newcomers, forging a long-lasting peace during which he led the expansion of the city. Called Kukulkan—a literal translation of "feathered serpent" into the Itza tongue—the incarnate god of creation worked with his new people to establish beneficial laws and technological advancements. The city he renamed *Chichen Itza*—"at the mouth of the well of the Water Witches."

Through the wonders he worked, Kukulkan's divine nature became clear to the Itza, and they began to renovate one of their pyramids in his honor, increasing its size and splendor. As this work was underway, the Feathered Serpent incarnate took his sister and a group of Itza to a spot some eight leagues distant, close to present-day Merida, some sixteen leagues from the sea. There they lifted a great circular wall with two principal gates, and they built temples and other edifices at the heart of the enclosed space.

"I name this city Mayapan," Kukulkan declared upon its completion, "fusing your native tongue with mine. It means 'banner of the Maya,' and I intend for it to stand as a symbol of your greatness, my wise adopted people. My time on Earth nears an end. Remember what we have learned together. Live in peace and goodness, creating lovely works to please the heavens. It has been an honor to walk among you."

Amid great weeping and outpourings of love, the siblings departed from that land, walking hand in hand toward the sea. A small retinue followed them—priests and healers and a scattering of aluxes. The mood was somber and restrained.

"The secret of the land of the black and the red," Quetzalcoatl told his sister, "is that *we choose* where it lies and when we arrive. It is the final bundling and burning, the fulfillment of our purpose, our returning to the source."

Quetzalpetlatl, though bereft at his words, knew great joy as well. Her lord was bound for his throne on high. They say that when Quetzalcoatl arrived at the water, the edge of the sea, he stopped and wept, arranged his clothes, strapped on his shield, his turquoise mask. And when he was fully prepared, he set himself ablaze, let fire eat his flesh. Hence the name of that land, Tlatlayan, "Place of the Burning," where Quetzalcoatl self-immolated.

They say that when he was burning, his ashes lifted up into the air. In that cloud appeared many rare birds, spinning upwards through the sky: fire-red ibis, blue cotingas, tzinizcans, Great White Herons, yellow-headed parakeets, scarlet macaws, white-bellied parrots, and other precious birds.

Finally the wind had blown his ashes far, and behold! The heart of Quetzalcoatl leapt up from the ground and hurtled to the sky. The elders say it became the Morning Star: Venus appeared for the first time in years after the death of the Wayfarer. Tlahuizcalpantecuhtli they called him—Lord of the Dawn.

But first, they say, when he died, he disappeared for four whole days, slipping down to the Land of the Dead, shadowy Mictlan. During another four whole days he made himself many arrows with which to punish sin.

At the end of those eight days, a magnificent star began to gleam. The people named it Quetzalcoatl, sure that their earthly king had returned to his heavenly throne.

Tales of the Maya

Convocation

Shall we journey like Kukulkan to the dense jungles of southern Mesoamerica? Shall we wonder at the mighty cities, festooned with vines, imperial histories carved in glyphs upon towering steles?

Here are crumbling observatories where the ancients studied the stars. Here are complex notations of time, calendrical calculations that gave birth to zero.

Although the Maya have retreated from their failing kingdoms, nestling in towns amidst the verdant vegetation, they return to these sacred sites to pay tribute to the gods.

Can you feel their wonder, their awe? Does your pulse quicken with the same desire? Do you ache to wield the power that set stone upon stone in those inscrutable temples?

Ah, but look! The Feathered Serpent travels with his sister through the Mayab—the Yucatan and neighboring regions. His love of creation and order, beauty and complexity—they are contagious, snagging in the hearts of his followers.

So there, in the northern lowlands of the peninsula, the last kingdoms—guided by the example of Kukulkan—enjoy a fleeting period of glory and wealth, erecting sprawling religious and government complexes near holy cenotes: sinkholes whose waters sustain and sanctify the people.

But power and wealth open the mind to tyranny and greed, and Chaos was not long in swirling its black tendrils through the Mayab.

Tales of those conflicts were nearly effaced. Bishop Diego de Landa himself set the old books to burning, a vast auto-da-fe that darkened the land. Only three codices survived.

Oh, but take heart, my friends—the mind and heart endure. The people remember.

Can you hear the Maya priests, whispering those venerable words to their acolytes? Can you see the unbroken chain of holy memory, century after century?

Look now as Chilam Balam, sage priest of legend, takes up a quill and uses the alphabet of the Conquerors to record his people's lore. Others will soon follow his example. We will have access to knowledge long thought erased.

Through the pages of the *Books of Chilam Balam* and the oral traditions of the Yucatec Maya themselves, we can peer into that mythic moment a thousand years past, a time when humans lived alongside elfin kin and sought to reclaim a glorious birthright.

We find ourselves at the beginning of the end.

The Dwarf King of Uxmal

During the Maya renaissance inspired by Kukulkan, in the city of
Kabah, there lived a young x'men or witch who set out to find a sastun,
that enchanted stone from which the powers of a shaman flow. She
traveled into the Puuc Hills where lived the aluxes—mystic elfish beings
descended from the sky bearers, protectors of nature and wielders of
great magic. The aluxes, seeing goodness in her heart, appeared to the
witch and guided her to the right sastun for her natural talents.

To her surprise, however, the aluxes also gifted her with a small
tunkul drum and a soot rattle. "In the right hands," they explained, "these
instruments will announce the rightful king of Uxmal."

Now, the witch knew there had not been a king in Uxmal for more
than a hundred years, but she said nothing. One simply accepts the gifts
of the aluxes. To question them is to court great danger.

Returning to her people, the witch became a valuable member of the
community, interceding with the rain gods to ensure bountiful harvests
in that area, which lacked the precious cenotes with which so much of
Maya lands are dotted. She also worked many other spells for the good
of men, women, and children as year cycled into year.

Time passed. A king rose up in Uxmal, establishing a regional
state. The new sovereign had a white limestone road, a sakbe, built
across the eighteen kilometers that separated the capital from the
city of Kabah, setting an arch at either end of the long highway.
Down the sakbe flowed goods, rules, and priests—the witch and other
practitioners of magic gradually found themselves replaced by the
sorcerers of the new state.

The witch grew old and lonely, childless and increasingly shunned.
As she wandered the Puuc Hills one day, however, she found an unusual
egg in her path. Wrapping it in her shawl, she took it back to her

humble home and placed it near the hearth where she had long ago
hidden the gifts of the aluxes. Every day she watched for signs of its
hatching, but she was not prepared for what finally emerged when the
shell cracked open: a little boy, already able to walk and talk.

"Who are you?" he asked.

"Why, I'm your grandmother, little one!" exclaimed the witch,
embracing him and laughing delightedly.

For years she doted on the boy. He grew normally at first, but then
stopped, though as time went on his voice began to deepen and his limbs
thickened. The witch realized he was a dwarf of some sort, perhaps even
an alux. Regardless of his true nature, she taught him the green magicks
of leaf, tree, and root, the sacred prayers and rites that call down gentle
showers in spring. She imagined he might become a great h'men one
day, a wizard who could keep his community safe and healthy.

The dwarf loved his grandmother, but he was very curious and
examined her every move for clues about himself. He noticed that each
day, before starting a fire in the hearth, she would spend an unusual
amount of time sweeping and adjusting the clay bricks and stones.
Certain that the old woman was hiding something from him, the dwarf
thought and thought about how to keep his grandmother away long
enough for him to investigate.

Finally he hit on a plan: he made a small hole in the water jug she
carried each day to their rain cistern. As the witch tried unsuccessfully
to fill the clay container, the dwarf swept away the ashes and pried up
several stones till he discovered the drum and rattle that had lain hidden
for decades. Smiling, he struck the drum with the rattle.

The booming sound that thundered forth nearly knocked him to the
ground. Its echoes reverberated throughout Kabah, into the Puuc Hills,
along the white road, and all the way to the palace of the aging king in
Uxmal, whose sorcerers had long ago prophesied that their ruler could
only be usurped by one who could produce such an awesome noise.

Trembling with rage, he called to his guards. "Find the man who has made that sound, and bring him before me at once!"

Back in Kabah, the witch, who had just discovered the hole and patched it with a bit of mud and a quick spell, felt her heart soar as the hollow boom thrummed through the air. She rushed back to her humble home and found the dwarf staring at his hands in astonishment.

"That couldn't have been me, Grandmother," he whispered. "Such little instruments can't possibly make such a big noise."

"Oh, but it was you, my boy! And now you are destined to be king."

The dwarf looked at her with solemn eyes. "King? Isn't there already a king?"

The witch took the drum and rattle, replacing them in their hiding place. "Yes, and I'm sure his men will be here soon. We must get ready."

"Ready? To do what?"

"To challenge him."

Indeed, it did not take long for the guards to interview people along the sakbe until they had found the epicenter of the sound. They beat with their spears on the door until the witch opened.

"Yes?"

"We're searching for the man who sounded that infernal drum. The king wishes to see him immediately."

"Well, there is just me here. And my grandson."

The dwarf stepped from behind her. "I sounded the drum, uncles. I'll accompany you if my grandmother can come with us. She is old and should not be left alone."

"Fine. Let's move."

They marched up the white road all day, arriving at sunset before the king, who demanded that the dwarf immediately hand over the drum he had played.

"Your Highness, I'm afraid I can't. The prophecy, as we both know, is quite clear—you have the right to challenge me to three tests. If I complete them successfully, then you have to abdicate, and I become king."

The king's council and his sorcerers confirmed this point, so the king, though boiling with anger, had to agree.

"Very well. But if you fail, your life is forfeit, dwarf. Here is your first test. Do you see that ceiba tree in the courtyard? By morning you must tell me how many leaves are on its branches. Now be gone!"

Once they had emerged into the moonlit night, the dwarf groaned to his grandmother, "How am I supposed to count every leaf on that tree? It's impossible."

"Don't you fret, my boy. We have friends aplenty that will help us. Use a summoning spell and call to the ants."

The dwarf did as she instructed, and soon the ground was swarming.

"Go, little ones," murmured the witch. "Climb into that ceiba and taste each lovely leaf. Then tell us how many there are, and I promise they will all be yours."

The tiny insects agreed.

When the sun rose, a mass of spectators had already gathered in the courtyard to watch the tests. The old king had the dwarf and the witch brought before him.

"Tell me, then, how many leaves are on this tree."

"There are exactly 121,919 of them," replied the dwarf with a confident smile. The king had not quite expected such a response. To verify the number, he had a team of vassals pluck each leaf and deposit it in a stone receptacle, counting as they went. The task took three days, and in the end they confirmed the dwarf's answer.

The king was livid. "Time for the next test," he growled once the dwarf stood before him again. "You and I will both fashion figures and place them in the fire. Whichever of us crafts a figure that withstands the fire undamaged wins the throne."

"Agreed."

The king went off and had his artisans make him a figure of dense wood soaked in water and a figure of sturdy bronze. The witch, meanwhile, told her grandson to mold his of clay. They met in the plaza, where a blazing bonfire raged. The people of Uxmal had gathered once again.

When the king unfairly placed two small statues in the flames, the dwarf did not protest. He simply thrust his clay manikin alongside them.

Soon the wooden figure began hissing before blackening and burning up. The iron glowed red, then white, and finally melted. But the clay figure appeared unharmed when the flames died down to pale ashes.

Snatching up the dwarf's handiwork, the king exclaimed, "A-ha! This figurine is *not* undamaged. You placed a soft clay object in the fire, and now it is as hard as a rock!"

The dwarf knew this was unfair, but he held his tongue.

"So neither of us wins," the king continues. "On to the final test. My guards will now go gather *cocoyoles,* the hard fruit of those palm trees. They will then proceed to break three of the *cocoyoles* on your head, one at a time."

The dwarf felt his stomach drop. There would be no surviving such a test.

"Excuse me," said his grandmother, "but will you first agree that, if the boy passes your test, three cocoyoles will be smashed upon your head as well?"

"Yes, yes," said the king impatiently.

"Then we will be ready for the test momentarily."

The witch motioned for her frightened grandson to follow her. They walked a short distance away while the guards gathered the fruit.

"Don't worry. You won't be hurt." She reached into her pouch of herbs and withdrew her sastun. Acting as if she were simply rubbing the dwarf's head, she slid the stone amidst the dense thicket of his black hair and whispered a sticking spell.

The trial began. First one, then another, then a third hard fruit was cracked upon the dwarf's head. He staggered a little under each impact, but he was otherwise unharmed.

The king's council and sorcerers now turned to their ruler. The guards approached, carrying the cocoyoles.

"Wait!" he cried. "I command you to wait!"

But the crowd hissed and howled in protest. Their ruler was seized and made to obey his oath. The first fruit came slamming down, but it did not crack. Instead, the king's skull burst wide open, and he collapsed dead on the spot.

The dwarf was immediately crowned king to the joy of the spectators, who cheered his ascension. He became a very popular figure, adored by his subjects for his wisdom, goodness, and humility, not to mention his ever-increasing control of magicks that benefited his realm.

During the early years of his reign, he built his grandmother a wondrous palace that would come to be known as the Witch's Pyramid or the House of the Old Woman. The dwarf king also added a new layer to the temple of the rain god that he and the witch so faithfully served: the temple was known everywhere as the Wizard's Pyramid or the House of the Dwarf.

After a decade or so, the witch passed away, insisting with her last breath that the king respect the gods and rule justly. And so he did, for the better part of a century. It was a time of peace and enchantment in that small kingdom at the edge of the sea-ringed world. The aluxes descended from their hills and greeted the king, establishing treaties and trade. No drought ever touched the fields of Uxmal, and disease and blight seemed distant memories.

The common folk of the region took to fashioning figurines in the shape of their beloved king, clay statues they would fire till resistant and hard as stone. Even after the dwarf died and other nations controlled Uxmal, the tradition continued for generations.

Today, in the loose tropical soil of Yucatan, you can still find these clay dwarves, testimony to a people's enduring love for their very unusual king.

The Rise of Hunak Keel

After the death of the Dwarf King, Uxmal was ruled by the Tutul-Xiu dynasty. Their king, Ah Mekat Tutul Xiu, was a visionary. Using economic and religious pressures, he allied Uxmal with Chichen Itza and the burgeoning city-state of Mayapan to form the League of Mayapan. Together, the three kingdoms began to absorb other communities through diplomacy or battle: Zama, Ichpatun, Izamal. At last the League controlled nearly the entire Yucatan Peninsula, and a new period of peace began.

Over time, of course, the ties among nations began to fray as each vied for supremacy within the League. Squabbles broke out here and there. Rebellions were quickly squashed by the alliance, though these rebellions came with greater and greater frequency.

Two hundred years after the founding of the League, the pivot of change arrived. In the city of Mayapan, a child was born to the Cauich, an aristocratic family of the Kokom tribe. As he was prone to shivering at the slightest breeze, his parents named him Ah Keel—"the cold one." The name would prove prophetic.

As he grew older, Ah Keel Cauich began to chafe at the dominance of the Itza. It was true that those arrogant Water Witches had founded Mayapan as an outgrowth of Chichen Itza centuries ago under Kukulkan's direction. Now, however, the Kokom people had become the majority in the city. Ah Keel found himself drawn to other disaffected young Kokom warriors wanting to assert their tribe's ascendence.

Because of his eloquence and cold, implacable nature, Ah Keel became the leader of this insurgent group. They attacked the Itza strongholds in Mayapan, killing many. But in the end, the superior military forces of the Itza defeated them.

Ah Keel Cauich, along with his men, was taken to Chichen Itza to stand before the four leaders of the city, who spoke together with the authority of a king. Each of them bore as title the name of a powerful elemental: *Chak Xib Chaak*, Red Rain God of the East. *Sak Xib Chaak*, White Rain God of the North. *Ek Xib Chaak*, Black Rain God of the West. *Kan Xib Chaak*, Yellow Rain God of the South.

Speaking for this council was Ah Mex Kuuk, the given name of the Red Rain God of the East. He would declare their collective will as to judgment and penalty.

"Valiant Kokom!" Ah Mex Kuuk cried. "Though rebels, you have acquitted yourselves well in battle. Therefore will you be permitted a great honor as sacrificial victims, plunged into the Sacred Cenote as an offering to Chaak, mighty Lord of Rain! Your commanders will look on in awe as the men they led slake the thirst of the god."

Ah Keel Cauich raised his voice in protest.

"My lord, it is not proper that my men should leap to their deaths while I am allowed to live. I prefer to join them in this glorious destiny."

Ah Mex Kuuk, impressed at his opponent's valor, nodded. "So be it, Cauich."

Not long after, the captives stood at the rim of a massive sinkhole at the heart of Chichen Itza, their hands bound behind them. The murky water glinted jade green sixty-five feet below, its 200-foot diameter ringed by a steep, jagged wall of rock.

The rain priest took his place nearby on a stone platform and intoned the Cha Chaak, a ritual prayer required by the god.

"O puissant lords of mist and storm, of wind and thunder, look upon us now with mercy. Intercede for us with your volatile king, there upon his mountain fortress in that verdant paradise, ever-jeweled with holy dew. Stream your heavy clouds across our scorching skies, crack your lightning bolts down rocky slopes. Open the sluice gates of heaven, and let our sustenance flow once more. We remand into your power these men, hearty and proud, blood teeming with divine power. Accept them as a willing token of our debt to Chaak, sacred source of all life."

Prodded by the spears of many guards, Ah Keel Cauich and his warriors leapt into the abyss, most smashing to an instant death against the flat green surface of the cenote.

Ah Keel struck the water feet first, dropping immediately into the blackest of blacks. As he sank, he struggled with his bonds to no avail. He was pulled deeper and deeper, his lungs burning until he could bear the effort no more and opened his mouth to breathe in the cold water that would surely end his life.

Before he could drown, however, Ah Keel slipped from the sinkhole, falling to his knees in a thick, luxurious glade. Shaking water from his eyes, he peered around at an impossible scene—a paradise stretched on every side, green trees resplendent with flowers of every hue to which millions of birds flocked, flitting through the air, and calling to each other in the most harmonious and breath-taking tones.

His reverie was snapped as lightning cracked behind him. He felt a quick burning sensation on his wrists and realized that his bonds had been cut. Turning at once, he saw a group of four unearthly beings floating in the air—forged of wind and rain and veined through and through with thunderbolts, the creatures encircled him as their voices pealed like distant claps.

"Ah Keel Cauich, you have been chosen to stand before Chaak himself, yonder in his chamber of storms."

They gestured as one at the mountain that loomed impossibly large at the heart of the paradise. Wreathed in clouds at its summit was a glittering pyramid of jade and gold.

Ah Keel understood at last that he was in Chaak's heaven, that southern afterlife called Tlalocan by the Nahuas. These beings were the true chaakob—elementals in service to the rain god, carrying out his will on Earth. The Water Witches of Chichen Itza had usurped their names for titles, but their might could not be rivalled.

Without another word, they spun a whirlwind around Ah Keel that lifted the warrior into the air. Then with nudges from their staffs, he was carried up the teeming slopes to Chaak's palace on high.

Ah Keel was deposited before a massive throne shrouded in fog and mist. A towering figure leaned out of the haze to contemplate the visitor.

Chaak's body was like that of a gigantic man, though tinged green and covered in amphibian scales. His head, however, was not human at all—strange eyes goggled from an amphibian face with a long, pendulous nose. The god sneered at Ah Keel, and dagger-like fangs jutted below his lower lip. Turtle shells dangled from his ears, dancing as he made menacing gestures with his awe-inspiring lightning-axe.

"I have a purpose for you, mortal," that voice rumbled, the sound of mudslides and tornadoes and thunder combined. "Thus do you still live. The Itza and their simpering cult of Kukulkan displease me. Yet none of you within the League have sufficient might to break them. I shall give you what you require, Ah Keel. You will emerge from my realm and prophesy to those you hate. You will win their trust—they will lift you up, put power in your hands. Bide your time. Let them not see what is in your heart. The moment will come that I will send a messenger, one who will help you bring about the destruction of Chichen Itza itself."

Ah Keel Cauich, kneeling in dread obeisance, listened and smiled.

The acolytes sweeping the edges of the Sacred Cenote could hardly credit their eyes when the man pulled himself over the lip of that sinkhole and stood dripping in the light of dawn.

"Tell your leaders," he gasped, "that Cauich has a message for them from Beyond." It did not take long for guards to guide the survivor to the house of governance. There Ah Mex Kuuk and the other elders of the city stared at him in naked disbelief.

"How is it you stand here," Ah Mex Kuuk asked, "alive and breathing?"

"By the will of the god, my lord. He preserved me so that I might prophesy before you today. The rains will come late this year. We must wait two additional weeks before planting our next batch of crops. Chaak himself told me so, there at the heart of his watery realm."

The leaders of Chichen Itza consulted with their diviners and priests, but the signs were inconclusive. Finally Ah Mex Kuuk declared to all assembled:

"We will heed the prophesy the Kokom commander has made. But he will stay with us through harvest time. If his predictions prove truthful, then we will know he has the favor of the god."

So Ah Keel spent the better part of the season in the midst of his enemies, treated with respect but watched by wary eyes.

The rains were indeed late. The crops, having been planted on the new schedule, grew hardy and plentiful. Ah Keel was celebrated throughout the city of the Water Witches.

Ah Mex Kuuk, impressed with this spokesman of the god, threw his support behind Ah Keel.

"You will enjoy the goodwill of the Itza," he declared. "We will see to it you are given titles and great responsibility, that you serve on the council of Mayapan's king. You are our representative in our sister city, Ah Keel Cauich."

The commander inclined his head. "In everything I do, I will exalt the name of Ah Mex Kuuk, chief among his peers. Though the Water Witches claim no sovereign, I pledge my allegiance to you, my lord, with Chaak as my witness."

But as he was escorted back to Mayapan with much pomp and circumstance, the Kokom warrior felt the divine path of vengeance freezing his heart. By the time he presented himself before his king, he had selected a new name as a reminder of that secret purpose: Hunak Keel, "the forever cold."

Years went by. Hunak Keel rose to prominence in Mayapan. He

married the haughty princess, Ix Taakin Ek, who bore him a lovely daughter. Sak Nikte, they named her—"snow-white blossom."

When the old king finally died, Chaak's chosen one was asked to sit on the throne.

And there in his great palace, Hunak Keel plotted and planned, waiting for the promised messenger to arrive and herald the destruction of Chichen Itza and all its vaunted Water Witches.

Sak Nikte and the Fall of Chichen Itza

To this day those who live in the Mayab speak the sweet name of the princess Sak Nikte, pale flower of the ancient Maya. She was like the moon, peaceful and distant, looking upon the world with tranquil love—a moon adrift upon the still waters, fluid light that all may drink. She was like the ringdove that, when it sings, causes the woods to shudder and sigh.

Like the dew that beads on leaves, filling them with coolness and clarity.

Like silvered cotton drifting on the wind, adorning the air.

Like the shining of the sun, renewing every life.

To her people, Sak Nikte was the flower that blooms in the month of Muwan: joy and perfume of the fields, soft to the touch, joy to the ears, love in their hearts.

That was Sak Nikte during that long peace of the three nations, that pinnacle of glory. She was born early one morning as the sun climbed the sky beside Venus, the smoking star. Her father was Hunak Keel, king of Mayapan, warrior and prophet. Her mother was Ix Taakin Ek—"the golden star"—wise and fierce, of haughty mein.

Under Hunak Keel, Mayapan—the banner and crown of the Mayab— had risen to dominate the League. Uxmal and Chichen Itza had spent their time glittering in the sun: now their sister city lifted a proud head above them.

The rulers of the three nations still showed one another deference and love. Those living within the Mayab traveled freely from community to community without obstacles or armies. Peace reigned and people were content.

But all things come to their end at last.

Hunak Keel looked out upon his city from a vantage point in his stone palace. Twenty years had passed since he had clambered from the

Sacred Cenote of Chichen Itza with a word of prophecy from the god Chaak. He had been promised revenge for the sacrifice of his men, for the usurpation of his city. His long, cold patience had reached its limit.

"Lord of Rain," he muttered through gritted teeth, "today is the last day I wait for your messenger. Then I take matters into my own hands."

"Then it is fortunate that I have arrived today," came a strange voice from behind him. The king spun about to find a diminutive figure sitting cross-legged on his throne. Though Hunak Keel had never seen such a being in person, he recognized it from sculptures and paintings throughout the Mayab.

It was an alux, one of the Little Folk.

"I believed your people gone from the Earth forever," Hunak Keel replied, his nerves as calm and cold as always.

"Indeed. For the most part we are. Myself, I serve at Chaak's command. He has sent me to you. Together, we will bring the Water Witches to their knees and remove their collective head."

Then Hunak Keel, his heart brimming at last with hot hate, sat like an eager student at the feet of that magical elf and listened to its plan.

In Chichen Itza, the great Ah Mex Kuuk had died not long after Hunak Keel's coronation, vacating the title of Chak Xib Chaak, Red Rain God of the East. But he had left behind his son, Kaan Ek—the obsidian serpent of the Water Witches, handsome and noble like his father, destined to lead his people.

Kaan Ek was a dreamer. He was also deadly cruel. When he was but seven years old, he killed a butterfly and shredded its wings between his fingers, staining them with brilliant color. That night, he dreamt he became a black caterpillar, fat and blotchy.

When he was fourteen, he found a small deer caught in a hunter's noose. With his obsidian blade he gutted the fawn, which cried out weakly for its mother, and tore out its heart to offer it to the dark gods that grant sorcerous skills to their followers. His hands were covered in blood. That night he dreamt he was a ravenous jaguar. When he awoke, the vision stayed with him all day, dimpling his smooth cheeks with a strange smile.

When Kaan Ek turned twenty-one, he was selected for the position of Chak Xib Chaak, Red Rain God of the East, one of the four leaders of Chichen Itza. Rulers of every nation in the League of Mayapan attended the ceremony, including Hanuk Keel, whom Kaan Ek revered as an uncle because of his father's debt to the man. But there was no love in his heart for the sovereign of Mayapan—their ties were political, expedient, tenuous.

"Lord Kaan Ek," the king said after the ceremony had ended, "my congratulations on your well-deserved position. You do remember my wife, Queen Ix Taakin Ek? And this is our daughter Sak Nikte. You have not seen her since she was a child, I believe."

Kaan Ek greeted the princess with the formality and deference that custom demanded. But that night he did not dream. He did not sleep at all. He wept till morning, the first tears his cruel eyes had ever shed.

That morning he knew sadness. Desire. Despair.

Determination.

When Sak Nikte was five years old, she gave a weary traveler fresh water to drink. As she handed him a clay bowl, the water reflected the compassion in her features. A flower blossomed in the bowl.

When she was ten, the princess took a stroll amidst the cornfields. A dove spiraled down and perched upon her shoulder. Sak Nikte fed the bird grains of maize from her hand before kissing it upon the beak and loosing it to fly away free.

When she was fifteen, she met Kaan Ek, newly selected leader of the Itza.

Her heart burned like flames from a nascent sun. All night she slept with a smile upon her lips. She awakened joyous as if her soul had been lit up by some marvelous light.

She knew her moment had arrived. For the hidden flower the sunny days of Muwan arrive, helping it bloom, making it blush with lovely hues. Then the clear breeze of dawn brushes those petals, spreading their aroma throughout the countryside.

So did the heart of Sak Nikte blossom that fateful day in the land of Mayab, stirred by the inscrutable will of the gods.

Hunak Keel suspected nothing.

That morning, Kaan Ek had his aides arrange for Sak Nikte to spend some time alone in the sacred gardens near the temple of Ixchel. As she hummed lovely little tunes to the hummingbirds and quetzals, the young Itza approached unannounced.

"You fit perfectly, dear Princess, among the birds and blossoms of the goddess."

Sak Nikte turned slowly, her eyes wide in surprise and joy.

"My lord Chak Xib Chaak," she breathed, making a small gesture of obeisance.

"Please call me Kaan Ek, my dearest bloom."

As he stepped closer, her honey skin glowed with blush.

"Such an unexpected pleasure," she remarked, regaining her composure, "coming across you in these gardens. But you, too, seem a part of the natural beauty…like a stealthy predator emerging from the shade of some tree."

Her tone was teasing. Kaan Ek's smile broadened.

"If so, just a mewling cub, Princess. Yesterday I was born at last," he murmured, taking her hand in his. "The twenty-one solar years before were merely gestation, two decades spent within a darkened cocoon, insensible to the glow of the sun. Your smile cracked open my chrysalis, Sak Nikte. See me now, spreading tremulous wings, nervous as I taste your perfume on the air."

Her heart fluttered like the hummingbirds that flitted about them. "When my parents stood beside me as your eyes locked with mine, they could not see the invisible dart that flew from the heavens to pierce my heart."

"That arrow plunged into mine as well, Sak Nikte, pinning our souls together. Such is the will of the gods, that we be united in love's sharp yet sweet embrace."

The princess sighed, drawing closer to him. "Never had I thought that Chichen Itza, White House of the Sacred Sun, held within her mighty ziggurats a resplendent light that would make all my former days gloomy in hindsight."

"It was the destiny that Itzamna and Ixchel, our divine parents on high, inscribed for us at the dawn of time, my dear, a love that only the ineffable hieroglyphs of heaven could adequately express."

And bending his face to hers, Kaan Ek kissed Sak Nikte amidst the bowers of that garden, sealing not only their fate, but that of the League of Mayapan itself.

The Itza lord swore to his beloved princess that, once fully installed in his new position, wielding his stately power, he would travel to Mayapan to petition her father the king for her hand in marriage.

But upon their return to the royal palace, Hunak Keel set the god's plan in motion, shattering Sak Nikte's joy.

While she had dreamt of Kaan Ek, had encountered him in that glorious garden, her father had been meeting with Ah Ulil, king of Izamal. Their negotiations had lasted the better part of a day, but in the end, the two kings had reached an agreement.

Standing together on the steps of the temple of Kukulkan, the kings announced the news.

San Nikte was bethrothed to Ah Ulil. Their marriage would take place in thirty-nine days, heralding a renewed and tighter bond between the two nations.

While Sak Nikte wept, Kaan Ek went mad with rage. He understood precisely what this alliance meant—Mayapan and Izamal intended to seize control of the Mayab, cutting Chichen Itza out of the League altogether.

Then, of course, there was the matter of Kaan Ek's freshly awakened heart. Seeing the object of his affections stripped from him in such a brutal fashion, the cruel stoniness of his childhood returned. When the four leaders of Chichen Itza came together to debate a course of action, Kaan Ek spoke with cold and calculated calm.

"Even Mayapan and Izamal together have not the military might to move against us. Let Hunak Keel forge his foolish alliances. If conflict arises, we will break them, gut them, rip out their hearts."

Messengers from Mayapan were not long in arriving before Kaan Ek. "Our lord Hunak Keel invites his dear friend and ally to the wedding of his daughter, a feast like none the Mayab has ever seen."

Eyes ablaze, Kaan Ek replied, "Tell your king that I shall be present."

Messengers from Izamal arrived soon afterward. "Our king Ah Ulil begs your lordship's presence at the celebration of his eternal union with Princess Sak Nikte. Stay as brother and associate there in the royal palace."

Sweat beading on his brown, hands twisted tight into fists, Kaan Ek sneered, "Tell your lord he will see me that day."

Night fell, deepening the darkness that reigned in Kaan Ek's heart. As he stood at a window, lonely and aching, watching the stars flicker on the surface of the Sacred Cenote, the Itza ruler heard footsteps behind him.

Standing in his chambers was an elfin being, an alux like those in the stories his mother had once told him.

"And so, Kaan Ek, Chak Xib Chaak of Chichen Itza, breaker of butterflies and fawns, mewling little jaguar cub, is this the extent of your manly rage? That white flower trembles to be cupped in your hands— are you truly going to allow another to pluck her for himself? Come, sir. Tell me it is not so."

"Of course not, you damnable dwarf. I plot my revenge even now."

"Revenge? Oh, you will need to act before the wedding if you hope to shatter this alliance."

Kaan Ek scoffed. "What, do you expect me to march up to the walls of Mayapan? Hunak Keel could easily withstand a siege, and Ah Ulil would then attack me on both flanks."

The magical being slapped his bare feet against the stone dais. "There exist other paths into human cities, Kaan Ek. I myself used such a hidden way to enter your chambers without a single guard's noticing. If you can assemble—with great care and secrecy—a select group of warriors, I shall take you at the right moment into my people's tunnels, which run beneath the broken hills of Puuc. Then I shall guide you and your men into the royal palace of Hunak Keel, where you can wreak such havoc as you will."

Once Sak Nikte's sorrow had abated, her indignation began. She poured out prayers to Ixchel, begging for aid. When no answer came, when no servant hurried to her with news that her father had recanted, she considered petitioning her mother, though the attempt be in vain.

As the princess fretted over her limited options, a child-like creature emerged from the shadows of her room, bowing deeply. Its skin was golden and it wore only a white loincloth and a crown of quetzal feathers on its bald head.

"An alux!" she cried, backing up with a start.

"Fear not, Sak Nikte," the being said, its voice chiming with alien joy. "I have just come from Chichen Itza, from the residence of your beloved. Even now he prepares to effect your rescue, to whisk you off with him before this ill-starred wedding can take place."

Sak Nikte sat heavily upon her bed, pensive. "He means to abduct me? I should think that such a rash plan will break the League of Mayapan and plunge us into war."

The alux crossed its arms over its thin chest. "Do you not see? Your father already intends to shatter the peace. Even now he awaits the arrival of foreign mercenaries. Once you are married to King Ah Ulil, the two nations and their hired thugs will attack Chichen Itza, killing Kaan Ek and every other Water Witch in the Mayab."

The news overwhelmed the princess. That her father might do such a monstruous thing—it was unthinkable. But had he not betrothed her to a man twice her age without even a word of notice? The minds of men loomed unscrutable to her.

"What...what would you have me do?"

"Await my word. Show patience. The preparations for your wedding procession will provide ample distraction and cover, so we cannot act until then. Do not betray your true feelings. Obey your parents in everything they command. Soon you will be free of them."

But the loving couple had been deceived, for the alux sought only to rupture the alliance of men by inciting violence between Mayapan and Chichen Itza. It had first appeared to Hunak Keel, promising the ruler dominion over the Mayab if he heeded its counsel. Everything had been part of the plan they concocted together, the betrothal, the alliance.

And now the mercenaries.

Twenty-six days after the king's announcement, the foreign captains arrived under cover of darkness. There were seven of them— Cinteotl, Tzontecome, Tlaxcalli, Pantemitl, Xochihuehuetl, Itzcoatl, and Cacaltecatl. Tall and rangy, lighter-complexioned than most Maya, they called themselves Mexica and promised an army of five thousand were waiting in the hills for their signal.

Hanuk Keel assured them that the time would come soon. In the meantime he gave them many gifts and sent his most trusted men back with them, bearing food and other supplies.

He had done as the alux had instructed him. All that was left was the inciting incident, which the elfin being had alluded to in vague terms, assuring the king that the moment would be clear to him when it came.

In the interim, the preparations. At the heart of Izamal, on those great stellae where time is inscribed, the figure of Sak Nikte was carved and painted, never to be forgotten in the land of the Maya. At her side King Ah Ulil was placed, her eternal husband, and beneath them a series of glyphs reading, "From these comes the greatness of the Mayab. In these we find peace and earthly abundance."

Sak Nikte waited and waited, but no further word came from her beloved. The alux never returned. Preparations ended, and the day of the procession arrived. The princess fell into a deep, despondent trance of despair. She obeyed commands, but moved like one dead in life.

In Chichen Itza, Kaan Ek screamed at the alux, who had returned to tell him the way into Mayapan was blocked by sorcery.

"Be calm, Chak Xib Chaak. Another route is open to us. When the bride and groom sit at their feast, then will you arrive with your men to steal her away."

Though this approach was riskier by far, Kaan Ek had no choice but to agree.

On the thirty-eighth day, from Mayapan came the princess with all the Kokom lords and her parents the king and queen. The brilliant procession stretched along the sakbe between their city and Izamal, filling it with lovely songs and laughter.

As the stream of people approached Izamal, King Ah Ulil emerged with his nobles and warriors to receive his bride. When he caught sight of her, he saw she wept, though he imagined those were tears of joy.

Everyone else danced and sang through the streets and plazas, happy. None of them knew what was about to happen. The streets were festooned with feathers and ribbons, with flowers and painted poles. It was time for the wedding feast, a full day of riotous celebration before the stern and serious ceremony of the following morning.

There was food and drink aplenty. As night fell, the goddess drew a full moon over the trees that shone nearly as bright as the sun. Sumptuous gifts were given by the guests, who had come from afar at the groom's invitation: the kings or governors of Uxmal, Zama, Ichpatun, T'Ho, Copan, Motul, Chakan Putum.

But the chieftains of Chichen Itza were late in arriving. When they came, it was without Kaan Ek. None could give a satisfactory explanation for his absence. He had been delayed, they said. They knew nothing more.

King Ah Ulil waited for the final dance until well past nightfall, praying that Chak Xib Chaak would make an appearance. Even scouts sent toward Chichen Itza returned with no news of him or his entourage. It seemed strange. The hearts of the leaders of the League were troubled.

Sak Nikte, however, smiled for the first time that evening. Ah Ulil felt sure she was thrilled at the coming ceremony. In truth, she was the only one present who knew what was about to occur.

By midnight, most of the guests were thoroughly besotted. Many had slipped from their seats to slumber on the ground or stumble off to their chambers. Musicians struck up the final song, and the princess stood before her parents and future husband to dance her last dance as a maiden.

Of course, what has not happened in a thousand years may yet happen in a blink of an eye. All that is required is for a god to breathe, and the wind can change its course. As Sak Nikte moved her limbs, she thought of her freshly born beloved, of the variegated wings of his wakened soul.

In that instant, Kaan Ek arrived at last.

He burst from the sand at the center of the feast, emerging from a gaping hole in the ground with three dozen of his most faithful warriors. Pushing musicians and priests aside, he rushed toward the dancing princess. He was garbed as a warrior, the insignia of the Itza emblazoned on his breast.

His men, roaring a battle cry, leapt onto tables and brandished their obsidian swords. Those warriors of Mayapan and Izamal not overcome by drink stumbled to call the sentries from the gates, but by the time these could return, the deed was done.

Rushing to Sak Nikte like a blazing wind, Kaan Ek seized the princess and lifted her in his arms. Everyone looked on in dumbfounded horror. Nothing could be done to stop him. On such an auspicious day, what man dared bear arms?

Extinguishing the lamps, the Itza slipped into the dark. When the kings began to bellow orders, to demand the invaders be stopped, Kaan Ek and his men were gone. The gaping tunnel had sealed itself up as if never there.

Ah Ulil had the other three leaders of the Itza seized. One by one he dragged them up the ten levels of the great pyramid and beheaded them beneath the glowing smear of the Milky Way, kicking their lifeless skulls back down those many steps.

The magic of the alux shortened the return trip. Kaan Ek and Sak Nikte stood embracing in the chambers of the Chak Xib Chaak long before dawn. Their love was forbidden, of course, dangerous to everyone. But for the span of a few hours, they contrived to forget the rest of the world. As the stars wheeled slowly overhead, the gods blessed them with the solitude of young love.

Perhaps it was a curse.

The city itself drifted into dreams. For a moment, every inhabitant felt perfect, untrammeled peace.

It would be the last restful night for many months to come.

The abduction was the rain god's sign. Hunak Keel sent runners to the hills. By morning the Mexica mercenaries had joined the warriors of both Mayapan and Izamal. The force marched toward Chichen Itza, a city whose final hour had come at last.

Hatred boiled in Hunak Keel's heart. He cursed the alux. He cursed Chaak almighty. They had given him his vengeance, but imperiled the life of his only daughter in the process.

Dust rose in clouds from the gleaming sakbe. Shouts and battle cries joined the shrill of rattles and cymbals, the thunder of war drums, the blast of the conch.

Chichen Itza, drowsy in the dream of its young chief, was unprepared for the onslaught. The invaders burst through the defenses, slaughtering every man, woman, and child they encountered.

For the first time since their ancestors had arrived in the Mayab and learned the wonders of Kukulkan, the Itza abandoned their homeland, fleeing death at the hand of the Kokom and the Mexica. They went weeping, single file, with what divine statues and codices they could carry.

Bringing up the rear, ensuring the safety of the people they had put in danger, came Kaan Ek and Sak Nikte. From a vantage point upon a ziggurat, Hanuk Keel caught sight of them, notched an arrow, and sent it whistling through the morning light.

The obsidian tip found its mark, tearing through the young man's back and piercing his heart. Kaan Ek, last ruler of Chichen Itza, tumbled into the dust, his eyes closed forever.

Sak Nikte stifled a scream, dropping to her knees to embrace the cooling body of her beloved—her true husband, bound to her by the gods themselves.

Ahead of her stretched his tribe, thousands of Itza robbed of their homes.

Behind her stood the warriors of her nation, weapons at the ready, willing to mow the innocents down.

The choice was clear.

The princess pulled her beloved's white mantle from his unmoving shoulders, draped it across her own. She took the insignia from his breast, lifting it over her head as she made her way down the line of weeping men, children and women till she stood at their head.

"Follow me, revered Itza," she cried, "for I loved Kaan Ek as did you all. In his name I will lead you to a better home!"

With the insignia she bore she pointed the way, and every soul followed in her wake.

Their journey was long and arduous, but at the end they reached a green and tranquil place beside a still lagoon. It was the first day of the month of Muwan. Sak Nikte looked down from a hill into those waters, holding the baby that had been born to her during the difficult trek, the true son of Kaan Ek.

As she smiled at her reflection on the surface of the lagoon, flowers began to bloom.

With their new queen to guide them, the Itza lifted homes and temples and pyramids, far from other nations. Peten, they named the city. It would be the very last to one day fall beneath the Spanish steel.

Hunak Keel and Ah Ulil, enraged at the loss of Sak Nikte, had stood in the deathly silence of the empty streets of Chichen Itza and ordered the destruction of every altar, every wooden structure, every stela lifted to revere the Water Witches.

Thus did Chichen Itza meet its end.

But that was not all. The events of that day had repercussions down the years. Discontent flowered in Izamal and Mayapan. An aging Hunak Keel watched as seven noblemen of the Tutul-Xiu tribe led a revolt within the walls of his city that razed it to the ground.

As they stretched the king out for sacrifice, he swore he could hear mocking laughter from the dark thunderclouds that had begun to pile high upon the horizon.

The Tale of Xtabay

As the last kingdoms of the Mayab fell, people moved to smaller villages. These were nestled among the wooded hills near the empty cities that nature had already begun to reclaim. Here the people lived simple lives in obedience to the gods, tending to their milpas and families with care.

But families can be so very diverse, even in the smallest, most united of communities, and those who do not conform to their assigned social roles often come in conflict with those who do. In one village of the northern Maya lowlands, two girls were born who would forever be remembered for the lessons their differences teach us.

Xtabay, a hunter's daughter, was named in honor of the noose-wielding goddess of the hunt. A free spirit from an early age, she was encouraged by her family to be loving toward all and generous in giving of herself. For Xtabay, this generosity would come to include her very flesh. She was devoted to the Protector in her aspect of Ixchel, midwife, and fertility goddess, and she learned from the priestesses that her body could be a tool of worship and fellowship.

Her many lovers regaled her with jewels and feathers, costly blouses and skirts. Xtabay enjoyed these gifts for a time, but she invariably gave them away to women less fortunate than she or sold them to help the poor and infirm. Despite the attentions she received from men of power, she remained humble and simple, never looking down her nose at others, treating everyone with dignity and respect.

Yet Xtabay was despised all the same.

The name of her nemesis has been lost to us. Likely she was called as a child by her day sign, as was the custom in those times. But after years of piety, of rectitude, of virginal purity, she earned herself the moniker Utz Kolel—virtuous woman.

Ironically, Utz Kolel—while superficially chaste and good—harbored evil of every kind in her heart. She despised the people in her town, saw those in poverty and sickness as beneath her, envied the good fortune of those above her. Cold and proud, she could not stand to hear her neighbors extol the virtues of Xtabay.

"She is well-named," Utz Kolel observed. "She ensnares men with her wiles like the goddess does her forest prey. Still, there is something sacrilegious about her bearing such a holy name. Better we should call her Xkeban—for she is indeed a 'shameless tart.' My sisters, how long will you continue to allow her to frolic sinfully with your brothers and husbands and fathers? When will you see past her sweet façade to the rot that lies within?"

So began a campaign of lies and character destruction. One by one the women of the village were swayed by the attacks of Utz Kolel. Xtabay made no public outcry, leaving her fate in the hands of the gods. Instead, she continued to live her life as she believed she should. Her ongoing charity kept the poorest members of her community loyal to her.

Still, most people turned on her, convinced that an upstanding woman like Utz Kolel must be trusted. Gradually Xtabay's name faded, replaced by the hurtful epithet, until even the leaders of the village referred to her as Xkeban. Her once gentle lovers were cruel and rough, withholding further gifts.

Saddened but undaunted, Xtabay began to spend her days in the wild, finding comfort in the bounty of the earth, plants and animals that did not judge, that accepted her as part and parcel of the sprawl of creation. Her nights she spent alone in her humble nah, sleeping peacefully despite the ill will of her neighbors.

One day Xtabay did not emerge from her home. No one saw her slip the margins of the town to walk among the ceibas, calling to the quetzals and hummingbirds as was her custom.

Days passed. Her absence was ignored at first, but it soon troubled the minds of those loyal to her. Gradually, a lovely and delicate scent began to spread throughout the village, like flowers shaken out from the depths of heaven itself. Searching for its source, a crowd found itself thronging before the entrance to Xtabay's abode.

Inside, they found her lifeless body, uncorrupted and beautiful.

"Lies!" snarled Utz Kolel when she heard the news. "Or at the very least, black magic. Impossible that a woman so marred by sin could naturally smell so sweet. It's her vile spirit, rejected by the Underworld, lingering on earth to inveigle men once more! Ah, imagine, sisters—if the corpse of such a tart can release this perfume, when *I* die, the aroma will be utterly divine."

Somber and filled with pity, a handful of family members and friends buried Xtabay, knowing this to be their obligation. The next day, inexplicably, the grave was crisscrossed by vines bearing delicate white blossoms whose enticing scent had attracted hundreds of bees. Xtabentun, that species of morning glory was called—snakeplant. Honey from those flowers had been used for centuries to ferment a mead as intoxicating as the passionate love of Xtabay herself.

The message of the gods seemed clear. The villagers regretted their awful treatment of the lovely soul that had now slipped forever Beyond.

Not Utz Kolel, of course. Growing more and more bitter at her rival's miraculous end, the pious woman withdrew from the world, dedicating herself to sanctimonious blood-letting and exhausting prayer, working to outdo Xtabay's renewed reputation for blamelessness. Her heart curdled with hate and her cold beauty wasted to nothing.

One day, her mother found her dead, sprawled on the floor of her room. There was much public outpouring of grief at the news of her passing. Her family plunged into mourning as they prepared her body for its journey to Xibalba, placing maize and jade in her mouth as food and currency, laying carved whistles in her hands to help her find her way, wrapping her flesh with a cotton mantle and then sprinkling the bundle with holy cinnabar.

The entire village attended her funeral. The priests openly wept at the loss of such an exemplary woman. There was talk of building a shrine above her tomb. People spoke until very late about her many virtues, though a few whispered ugly truths about Utz Kolel had emerged over the years.

In the depth of the night, a rotten stench began to float along the limestone streets.

The next morning, all were shocked to find the grave of Utz Kolel covered with a patch of brutally spiny cactus known as tzakam. The normally odorless blood-red petals nestled amid the thorns now curdled the air like putrid human flesh.

Again it appeared the gods had rendered judgment.

Sensing the shocked comments of her community, the soul of Utz Kolel strayed from the path to Xibalba, lingering furious near her grave. Envious beyond words of her rival even in death, the twisted revenant reached a foolish conclusion—Xtabay's sins of passion had somehow brought her rewards in the afterlife, so Utz Kolel would have to imitate her to escape the miasma of corruption that enveloped her soul.

So it was that—aided by dark forces that rejoice in chaos—Utz Kolel took up residence in an ancient ceiba and learned how to return to the physical world at whim, assuming the form and name of Xtabay. Drunken men stumble across her, deep in the wood, combing her long black hair with cactus spines. She calls to them, seduces them, hungry for the pleasures that she mocked and condemned when alive.

The man who approaches her is lost forever. When his townsfolk or family search for him, they will discover his corpse, abandoned amid the ceiba's gnarled roots, his flesh gashed by fingernails and tzakam needles, his chest ripped open, his heart devoured.

Lingering on the air is a strange scent—sweet at first, but quickly fading into rot.

Aztecs Ascendant

Convocation

Think on the name of this land: *Mexico.* Consider the millions who whispered those syllables in awe, bending knees and bowing heads. *Place of the Mexica.* A small, scrubby island with two meager towns—destined to spread its might and glory to every corner of Mesoamerica before it fell.

Consider carefully: Who were the Mexica?

Regard the distant past of this Fifth Age, the slow and steady surge of humanity across the sea-ringed world.

Seven tribes there were that fled ancient Aztlan—the Nahuas, clear-talking folk, shrugging off oppression and striking out on their own. They made their way to Chicomoztoc, the mountain of seven caves once ruled by the Cloud Serpents.

But life in that harsh northern desert was difficult. One by one the tribes began to leave, heading south into the central highlands. Thus the Chichimecah and Toltecs came to be, and many other Nahua nations as well.

Stand with me upon the mountain. Look down upon its darkling caves. The last of these peoples is about to emerge. They will begin as nomads, yes. Then mercenaries and slaves.

But watch closely. The Mexica are on the rise. From humble beginnings they will achieve hegemony over the sea-ringed world.

Centuries hence, we will no longer call them by their tribal name.

We will use a word that resonated with tyranny to Nahua ears.

Aztecs. The ancient title of the rules of Aztlan.

To understand them, let us consult their own official histories, a handful of codices that survive to this day.

But let us also weave in the accounts of the men who crossed the ocean to conquer them.

And let us pray the truth lies somewhere in this weft of words.

The Mexica Exodus

Leaving Chicomoztoc

The population of Chicomoztoc dwindled till only one tribe remained. Ruled by Mexitli Chalchiuhtlatonac, jade-rich jackrabbit of the maguey, these Nahuas were fierce and proud. Their ancestors had escaped Aztlan to carve out a home in the wilderness. None of them was eager to follow the example of their sister tribes.

The rites and sacraments of this people were overseen by the high priest Huitziltzin, "beloved hummingbird," and his sister, the shaman Malinalxochitl, "wild rye flower." The siblings guided their community well: everyone venerated their ancestors, prayed to sun and moon and earth, spilled blood to bring the rain.

One day, however, a voice whispered to Huitziltzin in dreams. "I am the sun and the blood spilled to feed its might. I am the knife that cuts the flesh and the hand that wields the blade. The Terrible One. The Prodigy. Born upon my shield at the battle cry. I am Huitzilopochtli, your god. It is my command that my people leave this arid land and travel south to their destiny, spreading news of my greatness as you go, leaving temples for the benighted fools of the sea-ringed world to come and worship and die for my greater glory. Tell your king. Your long trek is at hand."

When Huitziltzin first went before Mexitli Chalchiuhtlatonac, the ruler was dubious. But night after night the god of war returned to the dreams of the high priest, giving him messages and portents that finally persuaded the king that a divinity spoke through his most trusted advisor.

First, Huitziltzin told him the new name of his tribe. "We long ago abandoned the name Aztecs. The god is greatly pleased. Now our people will carry your name, O King: they will be called the Mexitin."

When the king expressed his willingness to comply, the priest continued:

"Venerable Chalchiuhtlatonac, you must begin to plan with care, devising a method to travel across the wastelands with such a mass of followers. Organize them well, in seven calpoltin or houses according to the great clans, setting as calpoleh or leader of each the strongest, ablest of the Mexitin. For in truth I tell you that we must set ourselves against the indigenous people of many regions, against the Chichimecah and others, because we are destined to establish ourselves in distant lands, where we will abide and spread out to conquer every thinking being in the sea-ringed world. Thus does the god through me declare that he will make us lords, kings of all throughout the earth. And as kings our vassals will be without count, never-ending, infinite, who will render tribute to us: numberless precious stones, gold, emeralds, coral, amethysts, gorgeous plumes of every hue, cotton dyed with myriad color. And I, your priest, will ensure this comes to pass. For that reason have I been sent by the god."

And so Mexitli gave his people their new ethnonym, establishing the houses, calling upon the calpoleh who stewarded the lore of the clans, their bundles, their gods. Together they established a plan for their travels. For seven years the Mexitin worked arduously to gather goods, to prepare clothing and other necessities, to fashion bows and arrows and spears, to make themselves ready for the long years of walking.

Some, however, looked with doubt upon the guidance of the high priest, including his very sister. A shaman and acolyte of the Protector— known to this tribe as the earth goddess Quilaztli—Malinalxochitl urged Huitziltzin to consider carefully the counsel he had given the king.

"Here in the caves of Chicomoztoc," she said, "we are close to the womb of the earth from which all life springs. Our Mother and Protector provides for our every need. Why should we set out to rule? Do we not fulfill our destiny by the spilling of our own blood and that of animals? Why trek for long generations through hazards just to spill more? You promise us emerald and jade, but do those precious stones truly endure? Only the divine song, drifting down from Omeyocan, outlasts human life and earthly age. All else is but a dream, dear brother."

But the words of Malinalxochitl went unheeded by the tribal leaders, though men and women close to her shared her many concerns. Her brother's power grew with each dreamed command of their chief god. He harnessed strange magic and learned to call forth his own nahualli, transforming into an eagle or hummingbird when the need arose. The people were in awe. Many began to suspect that Huitziltzin was more than just a divine mouthpiece.

Finally, at the close of the seventh solar circuit, the long trek began. It was the year 12-Reed, nearly one thousand years ago. At the head of the mass of Mexitin went the four godbearers, venerable priests and priestessesv who carried the effigy of Huitzilopochtli. With them walked Huitziltzin, guided by the voice of the god.

Schisms

The nation would travel, eating beans and corn, tomatoes and chilis as they went. When their stores of food ran low, they would stop for a few years, planting crops, hunting, replenishing the tribal bounty. Then they would move on, normally at the god's urging, but often because of conflicts with the various Chichimecah people they encountered.

One of the first of these stopping sites was Lake Patzcuaro in Michhuacan, "Land of Fishers." When the time came to depart those lovely shores, a group of Mexitin expressed reluctance. They had developed a fondness for fishing and swimming, and the lush abundance reminded them of the tales of ancient Aztlan. The high priest, guided by the god of war, looked upon them as they played in the water. Then he approached the king.

"The Terrible One says we are to leave these behind. Now, while they are bathing, he commands us to take their clothes and depart."

So the Mexitin did, though Malinxochitl protested. The bathers emerged to find themselves abandoned and naked. There they established a kingdom, mixing with natives of the place. They would become the Purepecha, and that land is still called Michoacan.

The journey continued, but so did the schism between Malinalxochitl and Huitziltzin. At the very first Binding of the Years since their emergence from Chicomoztoc, the sacrifice demanded by the god was not simply some captured Chichimec warrior, but one of the Mexitin. Malinxochitl and her followers, the tlatlahuihpochtin or illuminated children, were vocal in their opposition.

"Enough," Huitziltzin commanded. "This is the will of the god. If you will not bend to his will, you will suffer the consequences."

"We will not relent, dear brother. Quilaztli's will must also be considered. As earth goddess, she eases our way through hostile lands."

"So be it. Sister, as chief tlahuihpochtli, purportedly the most illuminated of your little band, you are forever cursed. You abhor the forced spilling of blood, but now you will have to drink the blood of innocent children to survive. Detaching your legs, you will fly through the night, glowing with your erstwhile illumination, transformed into a turkey or buzzard, seeking once a month your horrible sustenance. This curse is upon you and all of your descendants.

"Now sleep, all of you."

Malinalxochitl and her followers dropped into a deep trance. Then the high priest addressed his king and the godbearers and the leaders of the houses:

"Fathers, the magic worked by my sister is not the same as mine. She is a drinker of blood who bewitches people into following her blindly. She makes her band spill the cold blood of snakes and toads, burn scorpions and spiders, whisper arcane spells to centipedes and slugs. Malinalxochitl represents all the rot and weakness in the sea-ringed world. We must leave her behind, her and her followers. Understand—I have come with arrows and a shield, for battle is my work! With guts and heart and mind, I will lay siege to cities everywhere! I will lay in ambush for people from every corner of the earth and confront them in noble battle! I will provide for you all. We shall conquer every nation, bringing men, women and children together under a single banner! So gather up our provisions, and let us go. We abandon these traitors here, asleep in the dust. Leave them nothing!"

When Malinalxochitl awakened at last, she stood and looked round at her followers. "Ah, sweet illuminated children of Mother Quilaztli! Where shall we go? My brother has tricked me. That evil man has abandoned us here with no food or supplies. Let us search, then, for the land we will call home, the nearest place with a settlement."

Soon they came across Mount Texcaltepetl. There they established themselves after being granted permission by the native Texcaltepecans. Malinalxochitl married one of the nobles of that nation, Chimalcuauhtli, and together they founded the great kingdom of Malinalco. Within time Malinalxochitl became big with child, and soon a son was born: Copil.

On Mount Coatepec

As the rest of the Mexitin continued on their way, King Mexitli Chalchiuhtlatonac reached the end of his earthly days. Upon his death, the king had a jadestone placed in his mouth to serve as his heart in the afterlife. His body was bound and bedecked with feathers and jewels. His faithful servants prepared him food and drink before readying themselves to follow their sovereign into the next world. All Mexitli's weapons and shields, capes and quilted armor were piled high around him. A yellow dog was tied by its lead to the pyre, a faithful hound that could carry its master across treacherous nether rivers. Then the whole assemblage was set alight. When it had all burned down to coals, the priests quenched the heat with water and buried the resulting slush. The king's most trusted servants were sacrificed and buried, unburnt, nearby.

Afterward the godbearer Cuauhtlequetzqui was installed as teyacanani or military governor by the calpoleh and the priests: the high priest had received a revelation that there would be no new king until they reached their promised land. The governor, following the instructions received by Huitziltzin, led his people to Mount Coatepec, where they shocked the natives of that place, the fearsome Otomies, who declared to one another: "Who are these people? Where did they come from? What city was their home? They cannot be simply human: there is something godlike about them!"

There on the mountaintop, the Mexitin erected a temple to Huitzilopochtli. Inside, they set up the cuauhxicalli, that holy receptacle for the hearts of the sacrificed, as well as the effigy of the Terrible One. Beside him were arrayed the gods of each house.

Huitziltzin immediately had a ball court constructed. Nearby he set up a skull rack to display the bones of the Mexitin's defeated enemies and sacrificial victims. The king's engineers worked to dam the river that wound its way down the mountain. Soon there was a reservoir that could divert water for irrigation.

The high priest then spoke to his people. "O beloved fathers, now that we have water aplenty, it is time for planting trees and reeds, flowers and grain. Let fish and frog, worm and fly gather in this lake. May ducks and mallards, thrushes and swans gather at its shores."

Then, inspired by the god, he taught the Mexitin a song: "Tecuilhuicuicatl," the Hymn of the Lords of the Fields. Together they sang and danced and praised the spirits of maize, bean, squash. Then the people settled in and began to plant, to build more permanent housing, to spread round the mountain like an actual nation.

The years passed. The Mexitin grew content. A contingent of citizens led by priests from the House of Huitznahuac came before Huitziltzin at the start of the nameless days, hoping to intercede:

"Mouthpiece of the god, high priest and general, let here end the task for which you came—to rule, to confront the peoples of the four corners of the world, to urge our tribe forward and exercise power over us. Here we can find all you promised us—the diverse jewels, precious stones, gold, quetzal plumes, multicolored feathers from every bird, rainbow-dyed cotton, all the fruits and flowers and riches one could dream. Truly have you founded a nation here on Mount Coatepec, gathering together your fathers, your vassals, once Aztecs, now Mexitin."

The high priest became furious, replying, "What is this you say? Do you know more than I? Are you my rivals? My betters? I understand what I must do, fools. Do not think to question my leadership."

The potential for rebellion chafed at Huitziltzin's mind. He knew definitive action was required to quash the movement to remain at Coatepec. Before going to the king with his concerns, the high priest slept, hoping for revelation from the Terrible One.

When it came, the knowledge was wholly unexpected, horrifying yet glorious. In the darkness of early morning Huitziltzin awakened and went to the temple. There he armed himself as if for war, staining his face a filthy yellow-brown, drawing blue lines down his cheeks.

The priests of the House of Huitznahuac were asleep in the sacred enclosure beside the ball court when he descended upon them like a funnel of destruction. When the sun rose glowering in the eastern sky, the Mexitin awoke to find the rebels sprawled lifeless in the bloody dirt, their chests ripped open.

Beside the dead stood Huitziltzin, devouring the last of their hearts. He had been transformed into something fearsome and powerful. He was no longer just a divine mouthpiece: the high priest had *become* the god of war.

The Mexitin were horrified. Like the rebels, many had secretly hoped that the tribe would remain upon those verdant slopes, that this would be their kingdom, but Huitzilopochtli-made-flesh had other ideas.

With a single blow of his fiery serpent, he smashed the dam to pieces, sending floodwaters rushing down the mountainside, carving a great canyon in its wake. Another gesture withered the willows and reeds, killed the frogs and flies, sent storks and mallards beating the air in frenzied escape.

"Ready yourselves," he thundered to his cowering people. "We depart as soon as the New Fire Ceremony is complete! For I, your god, declare to you that no mere mountain will suffice to bear the name *Mexico*, land of the Mexitin—no, only the entire sea-ringed world itself can come close to the scope I envision for our realm!"

The Mexitin, trembling, spent the final days of the year storing food, gathering belongings, preparing to restart their trek. When the new fire blossomed in the chest of the sacrificial victim, Huitzilopochtli ordered the torches of each house lit immediately. Beneath the glittering stars and gleaming eyes of tzitzimimeh, the tribe abandoned Mount Coatepec and threaded into the darkness.

Arrival in the Promised Land

For twenty more years the Mexitin wandered with the avatar of their god. Their governor died and was replaced by Acacihtli. Beneath his standard, the nomads harried again and again the Chichimec tribes and other indigenous peoples, emerging victorious every time. Battle and sacrifice became regular parts of daily life for the nomads. In awe they offered a new epithet to Huitzilopochtli: Tepanquizqui, He Who Towers over All. The god was well pleased.

At last he led them to the abandoned city of Tollan. They picked through its ruins, amazed by the glory that had been brought low by the hand of Tezcatlipoca. They added effigies of that dark lord and his feathered twin to their pantheon. Humbled by the artisanship evident everywhere about them, the Mexitin began to call such skill toltecayotl, contrasting with the barbarism of their greatest foes of the time, which they labeled chichimecayotl. When they visited other great cities, they would append Tollan to the name of each.

After conflicts with the Chichimecah that cost them in rapid succession the lives of three military governors, the nomads moved on to the fertile, water-rich land they named Atlicalaquian. There between the roots of trees at the water's edge they established chinampas, little island gardens of tomato and squash, beans and maize, chili and amaranth.

The Mexitin were honored and loved by the neighboring nation of Atenco, whose king—Tlahuizcalpotonqui, fragrant dawn—venerated Huitzilopochtli and allowed a skull rack or tzompantli to be erected in the god's honor. For that reason, the city-state became known as Tzompanco, place of the skull rack. The king gave the newest Mexitin governor his youngest daughter, Tlaquilxochitzin, in marriage. She would bear Lord Tozcuecuextli three children, including the future leader of the nation, Huitzilihuitl the First.

The Mexitin set out once more. Soon they saw spreading before them broad Lake Xaltocan and the whole vast basin of the high plains.

"This is the land I promised, this watery, fertile valley. Here we will face many challenges and obstacles, but we will also find the home from which to rule Mexico, land of Mexitli, land of his people."

For decades more they skirted the lakes, making allies and enemies, hiring out their warriors to fight the wars of others, never backing down from confrontations. They befriended their fellow Nahuas of Cuauhtitlan, but annoyed the Tepanecas, who had also emigrated from Chicomoztoc centuries before and now controlled a large region along the western shore of Lake Texcoco.

At the foot of Chapultepec Hill, at a place they called Tepepanco, against the mountain, the Mexitin stopped at the command of their god. It was time to bind the years. The crags of that ancient tor were soon glistening with blood.

As the new calendar round began, Huitzilopochtli called together Governor Tozcuecuextli, his high priest Axolohua, General Ococaltzin, all the calpoleh and the god-bearers, including Cuauhtlequetzqui the Second.

"O fathers of the Mexica, people of Mexico, wait but a little longer for what must come to pass, for soon you will see the fruit of your long journeying. Have patience, for I know what comes. Work diligently, be brave, build yourselves up, and make yourselves ready. This is not yet our home. First we must entrench ourselves upon this hill, anticipating those who come to destroy us. Two classes of enemies will array themselves against us, but we will prove the worth and might of the Mexica. In the end we will make slaves of them all and rule forever!"

Conflicts at Chapultepec Hill
By this time, word of the Mexica's passage through Tepanecapan had reached the ears of Copil, wizard king of Malinalco, a city-state to the southwest of Lake Xochimilco established by Malinalxochitl, sister of the mortal man who had since become Huitzilopochtli.

The sorcerer, seeking information, approached the ancient crone who had given him life. "Mother, you once told me you had an older brother, the living avatar of a god."

"Yes, indeed. You have an uncle, Huitzilopochtli, patron of the Mexitin. He abandoned me on the long trek out of Chicomoztoc, but then I chanced to meet your father, and we established this kingdom that you now rule."

Copil nodded savagely. "Very good. Know this, Mother: I intend to go confront my uncle in this place your former people have settled. I go to destroy him and devour his heart, to batter and conquer the ones he has led to the valley, his nobles and vassals. I will drag from the bosom of that tribe booty of varied riches, from gold to precious plumes, cocoa and rainbow cotton, diverse flowers and fruit. Yet do not lament, Mother. I tell you I am off to find my fiend of an uncle. His very existence chafes my soul."

Copil rounded up a battalion of warriors. With his shaman daughter Azcalxochitzin, he set out to confront the god of the Mexica, conferring with various nations as he went, forging alliances against his mother's native tribe.

Huitzilopochtli immediately sensed his coming. He called again to the tribal leaders, "O Fathers, gird yourselves, take up arms! My wicked nephew approaches. I will destroy him, bring death down upon his head, but you must face his army!"

In a flash Huitzilopochtli transported himself and King Copil to Tepetzinco, a barren rocky isle in the midst of Lake Texcoco.

"So you are the pup my sister Malinalxochitl bore, are you?"

"Yes, you monster. I have come to trap and destroy you for having abandoned my mother so many years ago."

The god of war laughed. "Not if I kill you first, knave."

"We will see," Copil growled, readying his weapons and his magic. "Come and try, ancient hummingbird!"

They circled each other cautiously, then they unleashed arrows and spells, fire and magic. The rock of Tepentzinco was blasted and burned. The wizard wounded the god, rending his human flesh, but the Terrible One simply howled in rage and ripped Copil's head from his shoulders with a single blow. It landed a great distance away. To this time that spot by the lake is known as Acopilco, water of Copil.

Prising open his nephew's chest, Huitzilopochtli lifted out the heart and returned in a blink of an eye to the foot of Chapultepec Hill, where the Mexica were routing the Malinalcans and their allies. Collapsing onto the sandy earth, his mortal wounds signaling the end of his incarnation, Huitzilopochtli summoned the godbearer Cuauhtlequetzqui to his side.

"O Fearsome Lord," cried the priest, "what has happened to you?"

"My time on the sea-ringed world draws to a close,

Cuauhtlequetzqui. Take this: it is the heart of the fiend Copil, whom I have killed. Run to the lakeshore, amongst the reeds of the marshes. There you will find a mat, left by Quetzacoatl during his long exile. Stand upon it till its power fills your limbs, then hurl this bloody heart as far as you can."

So the godbearer did, marveling at the strength of his own arm. Then he raced back to his dying god, whom he found surrounded by the king, the priests and scores of weeping nobles.

"I leave you," spoke Huitzilopochtli, "with a final prophecy. When you have reached the lowest point, the very nadir of your history, when all seems lost, then you will discover the place where Copil's heart has fallen. There, upon a rock, a cactus will have sprung, and perched on that cactus you will encounter me again in eagle form. I will speak to you in words that curl like serpents through the air, and your journey will have reached its end. Upon that spot you will build a city from which to rule the sea-ringed world."

Then the god abandoned his flesh, leaving the corpse of Huitziltzin lifeless in the dirt. The Mexica paid him extravagant honors and burned him till only bones were left. These they wrapped in most sacred bundles and delivered them into the hands of the godbearers, who truly earned their title as they carried Huitzilopochtli's remains during the many trials and tribulations awaiting them.

Azcalxochitzin, daughter of Copil, was soon given in marriage to Cuauhtlequetzqui, and the great-niece of the Terrible One bore him a beloved son, Coatzontli. Not long afterward, Cuauhtlequetzqui passed into the east forever, to accompany the sun at his lord's side, winging his bright way through the heavens.

For many years afterward, the Mexica harried the cities near Chapultepec Hill: Acuezcomac, Huehuetlan, Atlixocan, Teocolhuacan, Tepetocan, Huitzilac, Colhuacan, Huixachtla, Cahualtepec, Tetlacuixomac, and Tlapitzahuayan. During this long campaign of aggression, the nomads earned the hatred of Tepaneca, Xochimilca, and Colhua alike. Only the Chalcans managed to rout them from their lands.

When Tozcuecuextli, governor of the Mexica, fell at last in battle, the god of war sent a vision to the high priest. It was time the Mexica had once more a tlatoani or king. Once Huitzilihuitl the First was unanimously selected by the council of priests and generals, he led his people back to Chapultepec Hill, where they erected a monumental temple to Huitzilopochtli. For nearly twenty years the Mexica tended their chinampas, making occasional forays into enemy territory to capture sacrificial victims for the altar of their god.

So disgusted and angry did the neighboring peoples become that an alliance was born. Tepaneca and Colhua, Xochimilca and Chalca: all four Nahua tribes united against the Mexica. Appealing to the tribe's mercenary fervor, the Tepaneca hired the warriors to make an initial attack against Colhuacan, promising them many war captives. As soon as the bulk of the Mexica army had marched off to the sham battle, however, the alliance laid siege to Chapultepec Hill and its environs. Against such a massive host, the people of Mexitli had no chance: they were broken, scattered, ground down, taken captive. Women were raped, children enslaved. Some few escaped into Tepanecan lands, others made for Xochimilco. Those who laid down their arms were generally allowed to stay. They became exiles from a homeland that did not yet exist.

The Mexica warriors, Huitzilihuitl at their head, were ambushed on the way to battle, taken into bondage by the Colhuas and marched forcibly into the kingdom of Colhuacan. There King Coxcoxtli ordered the public sacrifice of Huitzilihuitl and his daughter Chimalaxoch to that nation's patron goddess Cihuacoatl. The Mexica warriors looked on in impotent fury, a thirst for vengeance rising within them.

Captivity

The Colhuas settled their captives in the borough of Contitlan, where they lived and worked for four long, arduous years. Then came the war between Colhuacan and Xochimilco. The Colhua king sent the Mexica into battle, restoring to them their spear throwers, their bows, their macanas edged with obsidian razors. Unable to bear captives back for ritual sacrifice, the warriors sliced off an ear from each of their kills as proof of their prowess. When in the end they stood victorious before Coxcoxtli, each man bore a bag full of these trophies.

"Your Majesty," the Mexica generals called out, "we have served you well, and we will continue in your service. We know this is your kingdom, and we are merely the lowest of your subjects. But we are hated in your city. Is there no meager plot of land somewhere in your demesne where we might go to live in peace, awaiting your pleasure?"

"Very well," replied Coxcoxtli. He called together his council, asking them to advise him on a suitable place for the mercenary nomads.

"O King!" they responded. "Let them settle in Tizaapan, that dangerous lava flow there beside the mountain."

"Perfect," Coxcoxtli said. "That barren land is wholly apt. These are not people, after all. They are monstrous and evil. With luck, the many snakes of Tizaapan will finish them off."

But the Mexica rejoiced when they saw all the serpents. They killed and spitted them, roasting and devouring all. When his messengers informed him of this turn of events, Coxcoxtli was unperturbed. "You see what savages they clearly are. We have broken their designs on civilized behavior. Just leave them be for now."

So the Mexica warriors remained in Tizaapan, and they took as wives the daughters of the Colhua, who saw them as viable sons-in-law for their fierceness and might. Within a generation, they referred to themselves as the Colhua-Mexica, proud of the Toltec blood being intermingled with their own (for Colhuacan had been founded by refugees fleeing the destruction of Tollan).

Nevertheless, while the people of Colhuacan mostly accepted the captives and their children as part of society, the behavior of the Mexica was often seen as barbaric, and many conflicts arose. To bring rain to the arid wilderness of Tizaapan, the warrior tribe would sacrifice children to Tlaloc from time to time. The meager temple they erected there near a mountain was often red with blood spilled in the name of Huitzilopochtli. Some Colhua, deriding the Mexica's patron god, once entered the temple and smeared it with excrement and straw.

As long as the Mexica helped win battles for him, King Coxcoxtli was willing to tolerate their Chichimec ways. When he finally died, his son Acamapichtli the First ruled over a Colhuacan in which the captives had become thoroughly intertwined with the native Colhua. Even the noble bloodlines of each tribe had begun to blend: Copil's grandson Coatzontli married Nazohuatl, daughter of a great chief. Opochtli Iztahuatzin, who had risen as one of the greatest Mexica warriors, won the hand of Princess Atotoztli, youngest child of Cocoxtli.

Mexica living in exile throughout the great basin began to immigrate to Colhuacan, to Tizaapan, bringing their children and mixing with the Colhua. Many believed their long exodus was finally at an end.

But on a rocky isle in the midst of the lake, a cactus had begun to grow from Copil's stony heart. Huitzilopoctli's prophecy would soon be fulfilled.

Hapunda and the Lake

The Mexica had abandoned a group of their own in the lush, verdant lands of Michoacan. With time, these strangers to the Land of Fishers blended with the native Purepecha people. Down the years, they grew into a mighty nation led by the warrior priest Tariacuari.

It is impossible, perhaps, to think of the Purepecha without thinking of the broad expanse of Lake Patzcuaro, teeming with white cranes. More than simple beauty, those waters sparkle with magic. With divine energy.

You see, in the dimness of the distant past, a massive ball of fire lit up the night skies above Michoacan, looming like a second sun before smashing into a fertile valley nestled among the mountains. The ground thrummed and trembled at the impact. Those men and women living nearby were terrified to behold what they believed was the end of the world.

What was the flaming force that fell from heaven that night? We might say a meteor, confident in our reasoned understanding of the cosmos. But to those ancient folk, it was clear that a god had been expelled from paradise to crash into our world.

Gradually, the crater left by the impact of this being was filled by water rushing up from a hidden spring. So Lake Patzcuaro was born, its blue expanse dotted by lush islands.

It was to this lake that the great Tariacuari led his people, establishing the Purepecha Empire on its reedy bank, a nation that would repel both Aztecs and Spanish before it finally fell.

Despite all the momentous events that took place at their margins, only one person ever learned the true nature of those vital waters.

Her name was Hapunda.

At the heart of Lake Patzcuaro curves a half-moon of land, the isle of Yunuen. Long before the Spanish came, its pride and joy was the

Princess Hapunda, a young woman gifted with great beauty and grace from the moment of her birth. Her gentleness and affection toward the inhabitants of Yunuen—both the royal family and their subjects—exerted such a positive influence that islanders strove to be as proper, well spoken, and good as possible whenever she was near.

Even the animals of the island and the waters around it felt joy at her presence. No sooner would the princess approach than they would show off their loveliest songs, their most complex flights, their most daring leaps into the air from the wind-driven waves. It was as if something greater than the people and beasts of the island, something that subsumed them all, was responding to the basic goodness and beauty of Hapunda.

A hint of the deeper truth was revealed whenever the princess waded into the water or rowed herself away from the shore. At such times, the waves took on a life of their own, flowing in strange rhythms, flashing brighter beneath the sunlight, twirling aquatic plants and foam in a mesmerizing ballet.

"It's as if the lake itself were smitten with her," the islanders whispered. "And look how she laughs and claps her hands with delight!"

Their comments were made half in jest. They could not realize how close they had come to understanding a magical secret!

For Hapunda had been adrift on the lake one evening, watching the sun slip down the sky, when Lake Patzcuaro had spoken to her.

"The sunset is lovely, dear girl, but not half as lovely as you."

Searching about for the source of the voice, Hapunda had asked, "Who are you? Where are you?"

"I am here, all around you. Patzcuaro, your people call me."

"The lake? How can this be?"

Patzcuaro explained. "I was once a star, glittering in the darkness of night, placed there by the gods. I despised fading each morning. So one day I decided to keep burning bright. But Cuerauáperi, swift-blowing goddess of wind and moon and sky, became angry at my insolence and spun me from the heavens with a mighty gale. I fell to Earth and made this lake. With the passing of eons, I have merged with it, Hapunda, delighting in its simple beauty. But you, dear princess, you have taught me to love."

Thus began their courtship. Hapunda thrilled to the vast knowledge of the lake, his intricate tales about beasts and men and gods. She found him beautiful, and before she knew it, she had fallen in love with him as well.

The fame of the young princess and her exceptional beauty spread throughout the region, as unrestrained as the wind. A group of Chichimec warriors, celebrating their victory in some border village, overheard their Purepecha host extol Hapunda's virtues.

"We should visit this little isle," they murmured among themselves, "and abduct their beautiful princess. Why should she be wasted on fishermen and ducks? Let's take her back to our chieftain to be his wife!"

Their journey into Purepecha lands was fraught with conflict and combat. Word came to the aging king of Yunuen that a small army of barbarians was headed toward the lake, terrorizing people in the countryside, robbing their precious goods. The king consulted with his sons, who disguised themselves as fishermen and went among the villages on the far bank to learn what news they could.

One evening, the Chichimec warriors arrived in a certain town, demanding food and drink. As they got thoroughly drunk, they began to brag about their conquests. They babbled openly about their purpose when a villager mentioned the king and his unparalleled daughter.

"If this perfect princess you folks keep mentioning actually exists," one of the Chichimec invaders slurred, "it's not this land she should rule over, but our desert stronghold, at the side of our chieftain!"

Once the warriors had made their camp and set their guards, the princes slipped back to their canoe and returned with stealth to the palace on Yunuen. They immediately warned Hapunda, who listened to their tale with deepening despair.

"There are hundreds of them," her brothers exclaimed. "Though we shall send word to the other Purepecha kings, our messengers may not get through, as the barbarians are watching every road. Even if we managed to convey our need, our allies may not arrive in time or even suffice to fend off the invasion."

"Then we must hide!" the princess exclaimed. "The palace is not safe."

"But where? Our island is small. We could, of course, place you in the home of some islander family..."

"And risk their lives?" Hapunda shuddered. "No."

As her brothers continued to weigh the options, the princess grew sadder and sadder. There would be no escape, she realized. All was truly lost. No matter where she went, the Chichimec army would discover her.

Her kind, compassionate heart kept her from worrying her brothers though.

"Let us go to bed," she said with a smile. "I am certain a restful sleep will bring new options to our muddled heads. The enemy is camped, you said. We shall be safe for the night."

Her brothers agreed. "Till morning, then."

"Good night!"

As they kissed her cheeks and left, the princess felt guilt twist in her guts. Hapunda, for the first time in her life, had lied.

She waited a while, till her father and brothers were fast asleep, then she slipped on a simple white skirt and blouse, sneaking out of the palace without a sound and heading toward her beloved, the lake.

Patzcuaro would know what to do.

As she made her way down the gentle slopes of the hill, she glanced at the humble houses where her subjects rested peacefully. Realizing that this might be the last time she would see them, Hapunda could not help but spill a few tears. Not wanting to worry her beloved, she blotted at her eyes, struggling to remain calm the rest of the way.

Still, when she reached the water's edge, Patzcuaro roiled his waters in agitation and spoke with great concern.

"What ails you, my love? I can see that tears have dampened those lovely cheeks. Why? Is it that...you have come to confess that your love for me has curdled in your heart, that no longer can a simple lake command your affections?"

"Do not say such things, beloved!" Hapunda cried. "I have never considered abandoning you. I never shall. I am blessed and happy to be yours forever. No, you perceive quite another pain in my heart."

The lake stilled in suspense, starlight flooding its clear depths as if in breathless anticipation. "I am eager to hear from your lips what pain this might be and then to work the impossible to free you from it. Speak, my darling."

Hapunda spoke, telling Patzcuaro of the invading warriors and their plan to abduct her for their barbaric chieftain.

The lake seethed with whitecapped waves as if a gale were roaring over its surface.

"Never!" Patzcuaro cried. "Let them come, Princess. Let them attempt to cross my waters. I shall seize their boats with fists of foam and plunge them to their deaths!"

"Wait!" Hapunda pleaded. "I cannot bear to see you thus, beloved. And think—the deaths of these barbarians would only bring more!"

Whirlpools spun like cyclones of rage there beneath the blinking stars.

"Let them come! I shall drown them all!"

"And fill your breast with death and corruption? No, Patzcuaro. There must be another course of action."

Bit by bit, the tide receded. The waves grew calm. The eddies stilled, and Patzcuaro spoke:

"I am going to suggest something quite extreme, my love. You may not agree, may not be prepared to take this step. It may strike you as rather mad."

"You know how much I respect and admire you, not just for your beauty, but for your wisdom, beloved Patzcuaro. Tell me your plan."

"Then," the lake began, its currents halted, all life trembling within its vast expanse, "you should get in your canoe, row out to my very center, and wait for the moon to rise. When the goddess has left the horizon...leap into my waters. I shall draw you into me, and no one will ever separate us from each other."

Hapunda stared into her beloved's formless face for long moments, thinking. It was a gentle way to die, in the sweet embrace of a lover. She would be free from the threat of abduction and forced marriage. Her family and people would be safe from the Chichimec menace.

"Very well, beloved. So be it. United forever."

Slowly she rowed, watching the eastern sky as the faint lunar glow smeared the distant mountains. As the moon fully entered the night sky, Hapunda said goodbye to her life without regret and dove into the lake, letting her lover draw her deeper and deeper into his heart.

The palace was frantic. Morning had come, and the princess was nowhere to be found. Her brothers and the islanders started to search, scouring the isle, but no one discovered her. The king, overcoming the weakness of old age, travelled to the far bank to confront the Chichimec captain and demand his daughter's return.

But the barbarians had not seen her either. Each side suspected a plot, but as the day wore on, it became clear that Hapunda had simply disappeared.

Then a frightened fisherman came forward with a harrowing tale. He had been casting his net late the previous night when he saw a young woman leap into the center of the lake.

She had never emerged again.

"My daughter!" the king exclaimed, weeping piteously.

The news of Hapunda's suicide threatened to burst her brothers' hearts. They, along with dozens of islanders, sailed out to where her little canoe floated aimlessly upon the gentle waves. Moans of anguish came from the lips of all her subjects.

Ah, but Lake Patzcuaro had more magic than you could know. He had never planned to see his beloved die.

There in his watery heart, that fallen star worked a miracle.

Bursting from the surface in a flash of downy white came the most beautiful crane Yunuen had ever beheld. She spread her wings upon the thrumming wind and wheeled around the boats, skimming over her brothers' head, mussing their dampened hair.

It was Hapunda, transformed by love and faith into pure white perfection.

Ever since, Lake Patzcuaro has protected his princess, his bride, feeding her fish and keeping her content with the dance of his waves.

The princess skims the surface of those waters, calling out in keen delight, showing her beloved, her husband, her love and eternal thanks.

And the people of Yunuen, they all affirm this wonder—as long as white cranes teem like stars upon that lake, their miraculous love endures.

The Volcanoes

While the Mexica integrated themselves into the social fabric of Colhuacan, exiles from that tribe attained positions of prominence in other highland kingdoms. In the Tepanec city-state of Azcapotzalco, King Acolnahuacatl allowed the greatest Mexica warriors to rise through the ranks, becoming captains of his mighty army through their valorous deeds.

One day, a runner arrived with a message from the ruler of Huexotzinco, an ally of Azcapotzalco that sat cradled in the roots of the eastern mountains. That city-state requested military aid, as it found itself harried again and again by fearsome Chichimecah who had come from the North a generation ago and now lived in the mountains, descending to wage war against their neighbors.

King Acolnahuacatl called together his advisers. "These are the same barbarians who crushed the Colhua and others on the plains of Poyauhtlan. We cannot allow them to conquer Huexotzinco. If they gain a foothold in the East, they will soon turn their eyes westward, to Chalco and Colhuacan...and finally to us."

The council objected. Huexotzinco lay at a considerable distance from Tepanec lands. Coming to its aid meant marching an army across the marshlands and wilderness, through enemy territory and without much hope for reinforcements should the battle go poorly.

The king dismissed these concerns. "With the right man at its head, an army of Tepaneca could cross the entire sea-ringed world from lip to lip and still have the strength to swing macanas and hurl spears. Yet I will make the reward even more enticing than mere honor and patriotism: I will give my youngest daughter, Iztaccihuatl, in marriage to the general who leads our troops to victory."

Once the king declared his intentions to the warriors of the city, two great captains offered to lead the army of Azcapotzalco:

Xinantecatl, a proud and fierce Tepanec from an illustrious family, and Popocatzin, a handsome and likeable Mexica youth descended from exiled nobles. The choice of tlacochcalcatl or general was put to a vote, and the leadership of the army threw their support overwhelmingly behind the popular Popocatzin.

Many in Azcapotzalco were relieved at the result, but none so much as Princess Iztaccihuatl herself. For the better part of a year, she had been meeting with Popocatzin in secret, their rendezvous arranged by loyal and discrete handmaidens of the Mexica tribe. The bond of the young lovers, at first merely the irresistible pull of attraction and chemistry, had blossomed into an earnest, deep devotion.

The evening before the army was set to march, the couple met beneath the silvery glow of a waxing moon.

"Ah, Iztaccihuatl, my fragrant popcorn blossom. I go to battle, to win honor for Azcapotzalco and to win your hand."

"My days will stretch endlessly until your return," the princess replied. "Be valiant, my love. Slay our enemies, gather victims for sacrifice, but keep yourself safe as well. Your future awaits you here, by my side."

"Yes," the warrior promised. "By your side. Forever."

The following morning, Iztaccihuatl watched from the balcony of her father's palace as Popocatzin—resplendent in his war gear, feathered cape and headdress ruffled by the wind—led his pinioned battalions away along the gradual curve of Lake Texcoco's shoreline. He looked to her eyes like a god, invulnerable and mighty.

Among the troops at his back, however, were those who felt not love but great antipathy for the newly appointed commanding officer. Xinantecatl, though raised to rank of achcauhtli or lieutenant-general, was furious that a barbaric Mexica boy stood at the head of the army in a position that ought to have been his. What gnawed at the Tepanecan even more was the thought of the princess' marriage to Popocatzin. For long years Xinantecatl had watched the pale beauty grow and bloom into womanhood, coveting her flesh with an almost ravenous hunger. He could not bear to see her possessed by another.

So for days he had spoken, quietly and in private, to key military leaders and outstanding warriors, revealing his concerns and plans to men he knew he could trust. "We cannot let this mongrel bed the king's daughter, comrades. Think of the precedent it would set! Do we really want one of these filthy, snake-eating nomads sitting on the mat of power in Azcapotzalco one day?"

The answer was a resounding *no*.

"Indeed not. So I need to enlist your help. The battle will be furious and chaotic. Generals have been known to fall under such circumstances. Should Popocatzin be mortally wounded, well, then his second-in-command would be required to step in and ensure our victory. The king would undoubtedly, in such a case, give his young daughter's hand in marriage to the warrior who had accomplished that which the mongrel pup could not."

When the army of Azcapotzalco finally reached the mountains— imposing peaks and craggy volcanoes believed to be the bones of ancient giants—the Chichimecs boiled from the heights in swirling waves. Combat was indeed fierce, arrows and spears raining thick all around, clubs and macanas thudding against shields and flesh, ripping and snapping.

No matter how they tried, however, the traitors could not arrange Popocatzin's death. It was as if some god protected him from their schemes. As the days progressed, Huexotzinco and Azcapotzalco turned the tide against the Chichimec invaders. Victory under the command of the young general seemed guaranteed.

"Come, brothers," Xinantecatl said at last to his fellow conspirators. "We will peel off a squadron of soldiers and rush back to Azcapotzalco. I have a plan that will undermine the Mexica dog before he has a chance to celebrate his victory."

They returned with great haste to the city and were ushered in before the king. Xinantecatl made a convincing show of wild grief. "O Acolnahuacatl, Tepanec king! There at the heart of the battlefield, amidst divine blooms and shield dust, our brother Popocatzin was shorn of the flesh, his blood feeding the fires of the Lord of Time! He has winged his way to paradise, reunited with all heroes. In his stead, I have commanded your great army, my king, leading them to victory against the encroaching hordes. The better part of my men have remained behind to bundle and burn the dead, to help Huexotzinco clear its streets and repair its walls.

"The death of my dear brother, however, is news that my heart could not bear in silence. Forgive me, Majesty. Life is a short and brutal dream. Nothing lasts, not friendship or jade. But Popocatzin was a man among men, and I keenly feel his loss."

King Acolnahuacatl was moved by these eloquent words. He summoned his cihuahtlanqui or priestess of marriage. "Wise mother," he began. "Call together the diviners: have them consult the *Book of Days*. Find the most propitious and speedy moment for my daughter Iztaccihuatl to be joined in marriage to Xinantecatl."

When the various viable options were revealed, the military advisers who had returned with the traitor used their wiles to argue that a small wedding held very soon would be more appropriate than a huge spectacle upon the army's return. The death of one as loved as Popocatzin required a period of serious mourning. The whole city would be bereft by the news.

King Acolnahuacatl agreed. He called his daughter before him and, with the cihuahtlanqui at his side, gave her the news. "Sadly," he said, "our valiant son Popocatzin has fallen in battle, giving his life for the glory of his nation. But Xinanatecatl, his second-in-command, has ensured our victory. By my troth, you are now to become his wife. To avoid unseemly pomp and gaiety in this dark time, you will be wed the day after tomorrow, an auspicious date for joyful marriage."

Iztaccihuatl said nothing, but her heart quailed within her breast. Her beloved was dead, and she was to have her huipilli blouse tied to the inferior cape of the cruel and bigoted warrior who had ogled her for years. It was not an existence she wished to experience. Better to give her life in sacrifice to Mictecacihuatl, Queen of Death, and to Itzpapalotl, the Taloned Butterfly, mistress of women slain in metaphorical battle.

Her handmaidens discovered her in the morning, hanging from the rafters, a rough agave-fiber mecatl twisted 'round her neck.

When the last of the Chichimec invaders had been routed, Popocatzin took stock of his men. It was then that he realized the absence of his lieutenant-general and that man's staff, along with several dozen warriors. A horrible suspicion rose in him then. He rounded up his captains to give the word: they would be returning double time to Azcapotzalco.

After a few days of grueling march, the host swept into the city. There, before the great temple, the priests were bundling the lifeless form of Iztaccihuatl. Standing nearby were the grieving king and Xinantecatl, whose eyes fell with impassive coldness on the returning troops.

One of Iztaccihuatl's Mexica handmaidens rushed to Popocatzin. "General! O beloved son of my tribe! They said you had fallen in battle." Breathlessly, she explained Xinantecatl's claim, the marriage plans, the suicide of the princess.

Rage surged in Popocatzin, a fury that dwarfed any lust for war he had ever felt. Seizing his macana, he raced up the temple steps and beheaded Xinantecatl with a single, mighty swing. He turned to his beloved's corpse and loosed a bereaved howl that shook the heavens. Then he scooped Iztaccihuatl up in his arms and fled the city without a word.

Trekking back across the wilderness, Popocatzin came at last to the Sierra Nevada and climbed up onto the vast glaciers till he had reached the highest point on the sea-ringed world. Then he turned his face to the heavens and roared, "Mighty gods, hear my plea! Do not take Iztaccihuatl from me, Mothers and Fathers! Send her soul winging back to this cold body! Let these limbs move once more! Let me embrace the woman I love and find her living and warm! Do you not comprehend? I swore I would be by her side forever!"

There was no response. The gods either would not or could not respond. Popocatzin laid the corpse of Iztaccihuatl down and knelt at her side, weeping and raving against the cosmos.

Finally the gods had mercy. They did not revive the princess. Rather, they fused Popocatzin's soul with the ancient volcano and melded Iztaccihuatl's supine body with the mountain range, reshaping peaks till they resembled a sleeping woman. Now the brave warrior could keep his vow—the two lovers will remain there, together, as long as this age is permitted to endure.

King Acolnahuacatl, devastated himself by the clear betrayal, at first gave his general time to grieve while he dealt with the remaining conspirators. But when Popocatzin did not return, he sent his men out to track the warrior down. His trail led them to the Sierra Nevada, where, dumbstruck, they beheld the snowy silhouette of their sovereign's youngest daughter rising above the city of Huexotzinco.

Smoke was curling from the larger neighboring volcano, and suddenly a groaning howl thrummed the earth, ending in an explosion of fire and ash that lifted toward the heavens like an angry supplication.

The men of Azcapotalco understood what had transpired. They returned and told their king. The story of the two lovers slowly spread. The people of the highlands renamed the volcanoes in honor of their undying love: the dormant one became Iztaccihuatl, the white woman, and the active one was named Popocatepetl, smoking mountain.

To this day, the soul of the warrior remembers his loss from time to time. His raging grief darkens the skies and sets the world to trembling.

Tenochtitlan

Generations passed in Colhuacan as Popocatepetl wreathed dark smoke over the highlands and Iztaccihuatl slumbered beneath her mantle of snow. The Mexica who lived among the Colhuas had thrived and grown, becoming an integral part of the community. Some two centuries after abandoning Chicomoztoc at their god's command, the tribe bound the years for a fifth time, electing as governor Tenoch, a highly respected general.

Around this time, a Colhua nobleman named Achitometl decided to wrest control of Colhuacan from King Acamapichtli the First. He arranged for the king's assassination, installing himself as regent in the aftermath.

Then did Huitzilopochtli appear to Tenoch in a dream, saying, "O, my son, listen! It is time for Yaocihuatl, War Woman, my grandmother the Protector, to come and shield my people. The moment has come to leave this place. You will lead your nation to the seat of its power at long last. It is my will you dominate and enslave, not be dominated and enslaved! We will not bother with friendly overtures and requests of the Colhuas. No. We will incite war, bloody war. Dress yourself in your greatest finery, Tenochtzin. Go before the regent and ask for his daughter's hand in marriage. She will be given unto you, that I swear. And then I will reveal my plan."

Tenoch approached Achitometl with an extravagance and elegance of speech to rival the Toltecs themselves, explaining the value of uniting their bloodlines and creating a broader base of political support for the regent. After some deliberation, Achitometl agreed.

The Mexica arranged a splendid wedding in Tizaapan, a rite of such pomp and circumstance as Colhuacan had never seen. But Huitzilopochtli spoke again to Tenoch, explaining his terrible purpose. "O my son, you must kill and flay this Colhua princess, and then your high priest must don her skin and come before Achitometl."

As attendants worked to prepare the princess, Mexica warriors burst into the room and killed her. The high priest Cuauhcoatl then carefully flensed her skin away from the meat and slid his limbs into the bloody garment of flesh.

"Come," called Tenoch to the regent, his council and his guards. "Look upon the goddess Cihuacoatl made flesh!"

Achitometl and his retinue drew closer, and Cuauhcoatl emerged. It was dark, so the regent could not make out the figure standing before him. As the incense he lit flared up, Achitometl cried out in despair:

"They have flayed my daughter! O Colhua lords, we will rout these evil bastards, killing all we can!"

They rushed off to rouse their batallions. Tenoch gathered his people and without delay led them hurrying from that land. The Colhuas were soon chasing at their heels. After repeated skirmishes, the Mexica reached the reedy swamps that divided Lake Texcoco from Lake Xochimilco. There they plunged into the shallow, briny water.

There was no escape. The cities that dotted the lakeshore were either allies of the Colhuas or enemies who had no love at all for the Mexica. Their pursuers rushed into the marshlands after them.

To survive, the tribe needed a miracle.

Tenoch had led his people out of bondage, but now the Mexica found themselves floundering in the marshes along the edge of Lake Texcoco. The Colhua warriors who had harried them retreated a bit, waiting. The Mexica could go nowhere. Water was to their north and west. Their enemy camped to the east and south.

Looking around at the thousands of his fellow tribesmen struggling to stay alive in the pestilent swamps, Tenochca had a flash of inspiration. He moved his people into the lake proper. Women and children were seated in the curved inner surfaces of shields. Warriors began to swim, gripping the edges to propel the makeshift boats toward the northwest.

Others set about lashing spears and arrows together to make rafts. Several trips were needed, but Tenoch moved his people to the rocky, uninhabited island in the middle of the lake. The Colhua returned to their homeland, leaving a garrison to watch the shore.

"Surely the Mexica will perish," the commanders said. "No one can survive on that blasted isle."

As the Mexica reached the relative safety of the island, the women began to search about for food along the reedy shoreline, finding fish aplenty. They urged the men to build a temazcal or sweat lodge with which to wash away impurities and bad luck. This was done. Cleansed search parties discovered water fowl and fresh springs hidden within the reedy depths of the island.

That evening a palpable sense of excitement settled over the Mexica. With little more than their weapons and clothes, they gathered round fires on the sand and rock and marsh, staring up at the stars and singing ancient songs.

When sleep and silence finally reigned, High Priest Cuauhcoatl heard a voice in his dreams:

"O faithful servant! Your people have discovered the bounty I have prepared for you upon this uncharted isle. Heed closely, however, for there is something more for you to see. Do you recall my prophecy? Head north from here, and you will soon discover the eagle, waiting joyfully on a cactus that grows upon the stone, the tenochtli of legend. Copil's heart enriched that meager soil till my sign could rise. There will you establish yourselves, you will wait, you will encounter diverse peoples, ours in heart and head. With arrow and shield you will confront the neighboring nations and conquer them, make them vassals.

"There upon that spot my kingdom is born: Tenochtitlan, jewel of Mexico, domain of the Mexica, where the eagle screams and wings the skies and seizes prey, where the myriad fish swim, where the serpent is ripped open. Tenochtitlan, where wonders will surely be wrought!"

Instantly awake, the high priest roused the governor and his council, telling them of the vision. The search began at dawn. Within hours, Tenoch and his men came to the place, a stony field beside a cave. A single cactus stood in that rocky soil. Upon it perched an eagle, tearing at the flesh of a serpent with its beak. It lifted its head as they approached, then bent again to its task. All around were scattered feathers of every hue and type: blue cotinga, scarlet ibis, emerald quetzal. Strewn amongst these were the skulls of hundreds of precious birds, along with bones and claws.

Huitzilopochtli spoke then for every man, woman and child to hear, "O Mexica, you are home at last!"

And they all wept for joy, crying out, "The promised land! The dream of generations, finally realized! Let us gather up the others. Then we build his temple and our city."

It was the year 2-House: 1325 anno domini in the reckoning of the men beyond the sea.

The first order of business was the resting place of Huitzilopochtli. Gathering dirt from all parts of the island, the Mexica raised a platform, building upon it a tlalmomoztli, an altar of clayey earth. Though the holy site was miserable and poor, there they set the image of their god, there they laid his bundled bones to rest. On that reedy isle, what else could they offer? Where was there wood or proper stone for masonry? These were disputed lands, claimed by the Tepaneca and the Colhua alike, but neither nation had fought that hard for the barren bit of water-logged land. There was nothing of value within its meager swamps.

"Perhaps we could throw ourselves on the mercy of Azcapotzalco," some suggested.

"King Acolnahuacatl would simply become enraged," Tenoch countered. "No, we must have something to trade for the materials we need."

Other leaders had an idea. "We could barter the plentiful life teeming among the reeds: fish, crayfish, tadpoles, frogs, dragonflies and their larvae, ducks and mallards."

Tenoch agreed. They set about catching and hunting as much as they could. In small towns along the shore, they traded for wood and stone. Then there beside the cave, upon the earthen platform, they laid down the root of their city: the house, the temple of Huitzilopochtli. It was a small place of worship, but they built it well.

Soon their god spoke once more through his high priest, "Settle now, and spread. Divide the land in four sections and let every Great House establish its borough. Let the gods of each group be distributed."

So the Mexica did, forming the enduring quarters of Tenochtitlan: Moyotlan, Teopan, Aztacalco, and Cuepohpan, the four districts arrayed around the ceremonial center where Huitzilopochtli's temple rose above the reed huts. It was a time of great celebration, for they were no longer simply Mexica: they were now Tenochca as well, citizens of Tenochtitlan.

For twelve years the city slowly built itself up through trade, avoiding military clashes as much as possible. But internal strife was building. In the year 1-House or 1337, the city suffered a schism. The dissidents headed to the northern end of the island, where they discovered a mound of earth that they took for a sign. They established a new city on that spot that they called Tlatelolco.

As Governor Tenoch aged and the religious responsibilities in the growing ceremonial center increased, the council decided that the executive functions of leadership should be divided. They called upon the well-respected head of House Tlacatecpan, the priestess Ilancueitl, to manage the social and religious inner workings of Tenochtitlan. Tenoch would continue to handle diplomacy, trade and defense. The title of cihuacoatl was established for Ilancueitl, whose part Colhua ancestry included the Toltec roots that the Tenochca valued as lending legitimacy to their self-determination.

In the last year of Tenoch's life, the people of Tenochtitlan learned that Tlatelolco had appealed to the new king of Azcapotzalco, Tezozomoc, requesting that he install his son Cuacuauhpitzahuac as sovereign of that Mexica city. The Tepanecan ruler had agreed. Now the Tlatelolca would enjoy the benefits of an enduring partnership with Tezozomoc's growing empire.

Not to be outdone, the Tenochca leadership sent envoys to Colhuacan. Some fifty years had passed since the Mexica had escaped Colhua lands, so King Nauhyotl was more receptive to the idea of reestablishing ties. After some deliberation, Nauhyotl suggested Acamapichtli, youngest son of Opochtli Iztahuatzin, the great Mexica warrior. The envoys found Acamapichtli in the city of Texcoco and convinced him to rule.

The coronation ceremony took place at the improved temple. There beside the altar the high priest anointed Acamapichtli with oil and water, setting the xiuhhuitzolli or emerald crown upon his brow. He now spoke for the Tenochca and was charged with protecting them and ensuring that their destiny continued to be fulfilled.

King Acamapichtli was married to the older Ilancueitl, who become the first queen. Though she never bore him a child, she managed his palace well and advised him on many successful endeavors. The king also took a wife from each of the Great Houses, including Tezcatlan Miyahuatzin, second queen, whose friendship with her sister-wife Ilancueitl was legendary. In all, Acamapichtli married eight times and sired twelve children, chief among them Huitzilihuitl II, son of Tezcatlan Miyahuatzin, who was tutored by Ilancueitl.

Trade relations between Tenochtitlan and Azcapotzalco grew stronger and stronger, but the smaller, newer city found itself increasingly controlled by the Tepanecs until finally it became a vassal state, paying stiff tribute each year to King Tezozomoc. The Tenochca were also required to fight enemies of Azcapotzalco like Chalco. Once they had proven themselves in these battles, Tezozomoc permitted the warriors of Tenochtitlan to wage war against their own enemies as well, cities like Xochimilco and Cuauhnahuac.

During one of his many diplomatic trips to Azcapotzalco, Acamapichtli saw a striking young slave in the marketplace and fell instantly in love with her beauty. He bought her and installed her in Tenochtitlan as his mistress. This Tepaneca woman, who claimed to be descended from nobility, bore the king a son, Itzcoatl, who would rise above his mother's subservient place in the world.

Though warfare and tribute took a toll on the city, Tenochtitlan continued improving itself, shipping in rock and soil to expand the island on the eastern, less briny side and establishing a system of chinampa gardens along the edges of the kingdom and on the adjacent lakeshore. Slowly, the descendants of Mexica from neighboring towns began to trickle into the city and intermarry with the Tenochca. A market was established. Soon canoes from every direction began to converge on the city, where strangers and travelers were treated with respect and allowed to sell their wares.

As the city grew more prosperous, its king and his council worked to establish a new temple atop the poor earth-and-stone construction. This small stone pyramid was dedicated not only to Huitzilopochtli, but also to Tlaloc, god of rain and fertility, whose aid the Tenochca direly needed to keep themselves alive in a place so hostile to agriculture.

The first laws of Tenochtitlan were codified during the reign of Acamapichtli. His diplomacy created many alliances and minimized military conflict. At the end of his twenty years as king, when he lay upon his deathbed, Acamapichtli had accomplished much that history would remember. His guidance had transformed nomads, exiles, and escaped captives into a viable citizenry with some influence and respect among the highlanders.

In his final days, Acamapichtli called together the calpoleh, the leaders of the Great Houses. Though the law did not specify that the kingship of Tenochtitlan was a hereditary title, only the prominent men of the city were candidates for the position. The king urged the calpoleh to elect a successor. Unanimously, they voted for his oldest son, Huitzilihuitl, a young man of some eighteen summers, battle-hardened and wise.

Confident his city was in the best hands, Acamapichtli abandoned the flesh and winged his way to paradise, where Huitzilopochtli greeted him with pomp and honor.

Tlacaelel and the Rise of the Mexica

Many kings would rule Tenochtitlan, their names emblazoned on the fabric of history forever. But one man was the true architect of the Mexica Way, his keen mind and stout heart guiding the leaders of Mexico for more than a full cycle through the dual calendar.

His name was Tlacaelel.

Birth and Childhood

The year 10-Rabbit. 1398. Morning fog was roiling thick and white from the dark expanse of brackish Lake Texcoco like the smoke that curls from the god's obsidian mirror to haze the minds of men and make them hate. Thunderheads had piled deep to obscure the rising of the vital sun. Spears of lightning jagged cracks across that amethyst gray as elemental tlaloques howled thunder.

At the heart of the mist coalesced that darkened day a swampy isle on which Tenochtitlan, the Mexica's promised home, collectively prayed. The small stone palace had become the sum of the city's hopes, the tribe's long ambition.

The date was 3-Eagle. One ceremonial year before to the hour, the first prince, Chimalpopoca, had been born to Queen Ayauhcihuatl, the lovely daughter of King Tezozomoc whom Huitzilihuitl had wed in order to cement ties with Azcapotzalco. Now the other two wives of the young ruler fought like valiant warriors to give birth.

The city's sovereign, skin crisscrossed with white scars though he had barely lived through twenty summers, stood in the throne room, ringed by his royal council, his silence contrasting with the muffled commands of midwives. Present also were his younger brothers, their wives, and his infant son Chimalpopoca, rocked by a nurse to restless sleep, a shield for his cradle. A man accustomed to battle and hard-won pact, Huitzilihuitl was now forced to idly wait and not to act. Birth was the domain of the Mother and the Protector. Men were superfluous.

Soon the midwife attending Queen Cacamacihuatl began to give war cries, praising the young mother for being victorious in battle, for having captured a baby. She held up the infant and spoke to him, "You have arrived on earth, beloved boy! Our true father, the Lord of the Near and the Nigh, the creator of human souls, has winged you to the sea-ringed world, this place of fatigue and thirst and hunger. Here there is no rest, no joy, no satisfaction. Perhaps you will survive a while, Prince. Could you be our prize? Maybe you will learn of your lineage, meet your family, join our community.

"We wonder what gifts our grandparents have given you. Perhaps the Lord of the Near and the Nigh will favor you with some ability, some small role to play. But it is equally possible you were born without merit. It could be you are destined for corruption and sin. We cannot know what was bound to you before the dawn.

"Ah, but precious necklace, rest while you may. Your struggle was long. Here you see your family gathered. You have arrived at last into their hands. Do not weep. You will endure for a time. You are a prince of the Mexica, and you will shoulder the burden of life as long as it lasts. Perhaps you have only come for a moment. It may be that our grandparents will summon you home to paradise, having given us but a glimpse of your face. Whatever the outcome, we await the word of our god."

The midwife then cut the umbilical cord and swaddled the child, handing him to the king. Later, as was tradition, a male of the family would bury the cord and afterbirth in the heart of a battlefield, ensuring the child's stature as a warrior. The family members all respectfully addressed the baby, giving elaborate advice and reminding him of his duty.

Partway through the ritual, the baby began to scream in fury. No one could silence him. His face went beet red, and he kicked viciously in his father's hands.

"I know his name," Huitzilihuitl announced as he laid the boy at his mother's breast, where he began to feed between bitter snarls. "Tlacaelel—furious man."

The same routine was repeated within a few hours when Miahuaxihuitl, princess of Cuauhnahuac, gave birth to Huitzilihuitl's third son. This baby, though he did not scream and kick during the speeches, wrinkled his brow and frowned at everyone, clenching his little fists.

"Another angry one," laughed the king. "Good. We will name him after the father of ancient Mexitli. Behold Motecuhzoma—enraged prince."

The royal diviners consulted the *Book of Days* and urged ritual bathing three mornings hence rather than four in order to avoid an inauspicious date. Artisans prepared a little shield and four arrows for each baby out of amaranth dough, as well as a little breechclout and cape. On the appointed day, the boys were taken to the palace courtyard when the sun had just begun to rise above the horizon. All the nobles of Tenochtitlan were gathered round a basin where the midwife, facing west, began to bathe Tlacaelel.

"O warrior, beloved son, you have arrived among us, sent down from the highest heavens by the Dual God. Your soul was wrought there above, and our beloved prince Quetzalcoatl gave form to your flesh in your mother's womb. Now, with the help of the goddess Chalchiuhtlicue, you take your place in the human realm."

Pouring water upon him, she continued. "Taste it, receive it. This liquid sustains all life. It purifies as well, washing away the filth from our hearts. Let the deep green of this water penetrate deep in your soul, removing the evil with which you were arrayed from the beginning of time."

Once he had been cleansed, the midwife lifted him four times to the skies, offering him to the gods: first to our grandparents, next to the Divine Mother and Protector, then to the host at Teotihuacan, and finally to the sun. Drawing forth the amaranth weapons, she asked Huitzilopochtli to provide him with the prowess necessary to shine on the battlefield and attain paradise. Then she repeated this rite with his younger half-brother.

Finally the midwife addressed each by name: "O Tlacaelel! O Motecuhzoma! Take your shield, your arrows, the spears: all the weapons that gladden the sun!"

She bent to tie on their capes and bind their breechclouts. While she was busy, their older brother Itzcoatl, quick as a flash though just nine summers old, snatched up Tlacaelel's dried umbilical cord and ran off with it in his mouth.

"O Tlacaelel, little brother, learn the ways of the battlefield! Your flesh is not your own. It will be stripped from you, and you will be honored! Your works and death will gladden the sun, giving him food and drink. Now hear me call the fallen: come, eagle warriors and jaguar knights! Come and take the umbilical cord of Prince Tlacaelel. Eat his flesh and be content!"

Once weaned and able to speak, the three brothers—Chimalpopoca, Tlacaelel and Motecuhzoma—spent considerable time at their father's side, learning the ways of noblemen in Mexica society. Huitzilihuitl was very stern with them and gave them quite a bit of responsibility, punishing them harshly with agave thorns or the smoke of burning chili peppers when they shirked their duties or did not conform to the highly formalized norms of behavior and speech of the nobility.

The boys did, of course, have time to play like all children, learning games of chance and the ever-important sport played on the ball court. They also practiced archery and the throwing of spears, matching themselves against the sons of other nobles.

Their aunt Matlalcihuatzin, Huitzilihuitl's young sister, was married to King Ixtlilxochitl of Texcoco. When the brothers were four, she had a child named Nezahualcoyotl. From time to time, Matlalcihuatzin would visit Tenochtitlan. The brothers doted on their toddling cousin.

Schooling
When thirteen sacred years of 260 days had passed since their birth, Motecuhzoma and Tlacaelel were summoned by their father. The nine-year-olds stood before him, their mothers, and the elder nobles in the throne room, listening as the king informed them of the next step in their lives as princes.

"Listen, my sons. Our spiritual sovereign, the Lord of the Near and the Nigh, has placed you here. Though you issued from my loins, though you were carried in your mother's womb, the Lord of Creation is the one who rears us all. He brings true understanding and punishment.

"So, then, understand me—when you were still swaddled babes, we dedicated you as an offering to the calmecac, the holy school of nobles. You will report there immediately to begin your studies and your sacred tasks, the sweeping and cleaning done on behalf of our beloved prince Quetzalcoatl, lord of learning. Again, you are *offerings*. You belong to the god. You are his property.

"Ah, nail of my finger, hair of my head! You boys are no longer dependent on your mothers, who fed and changed you as infants. You are strong, capable of self-defense and cunning. So go now to your new home, that house of weeping, where all nobles send their sons to be cast and drilled like precious beads. Soon you will blossom, you will sprout like quetzal feathers, and the Giver of Life will set you in his holy headdress as he sees fit.

"When the night is darkest and your sobs most intense, remember that from that holy school emerge the rulers of this city, men with authority, warriors of the great sodalities. So work diligently, without sloth. Accept the austere life with humility and stay away from vice. Let hunger be your guide. Mortify the flesh with agave spines, and let it suffer cold. Only your mind and heart matter there. Learn everything you can. Make your family, your tribe, your city proud."

At the calmecac, the boys joined Chimalpopoca, who had already entered 260 days previously. Like all noble youth, they lived at the school with the priests. Their early years were largely spent performing chores—sweeping, cleaning, carrying wood for the fires, mixing paint for ritual use, making repairs to the temples, and tending to the school's crops. Food was strictly rationed, but the boys never complained about hunger. They ran immediately to a priest's side when called, did the fasting and penance required, woke up in the small hours of the night to ritually sweep. They were the princes of Tenochtitlan, and their only flaw was barely restrained pride.

They learned the history of their nation, studied the painted codices that had been painstakingly preserved down the long centuries. The priests taught them the calendar counts, and together they pored over the *Book of Days*. They memorized all the sacred hymns, all the holy rites required to keep the gods content and the cosmic wheels turning. Math, engineering, agriculture, law, political science—the young princes were instructed in every branch of knowledge they would need to rule Tenochtitlan.

As they grew older, the boys went through a rigorous physical regimen under the leadership of young warriors and seasoned veterans, learning martial arts and pushing their bodies to their physical limits. They became adept at all the weapons used by warriors of the time as well as tactical maneuvers and command.

Each youth stood out in a different field. Chimalpopoca, normally quieter and more introspective, leaned toward administration and diplomacy. Tlacaelel, perhaps the most intelligent young man to ever attend the school, was drawn to the sciences and religious ritual, as well as military strategy. Motecuhzoma was the best warrior of the three, demonstrating incredible skill with weapons and an amazing ability to inspire others.

When they were allowed visits, Nezahualcoyotl was occasionally vacationing in the city. His admiration for his older cousins was clear. Eventually he entered the calmecac in Texcoco, however, so the four had less contact.

By the time they were sixteen, the brothers began participating in skirmishes. Eventually they were named tiachcauhuan or student leaders, responsible for showing the new arrivals the ropes. Tlacaelel even rose to the position of telpochtlahtoh or student teacher, empowered to govern and correct his fellows. With astounding speed, the brothers racked up four captives each, earning themselves the title mexihcatl tequihua, proven Mexica warrior. Their proud father presented them with their own gear, armor, and insignia.

They had, in essence, graduated.

War with the Tepaneca
The relationship between Azcapotzalco and Tenochtitlan had improved significantly during the eighteen years of Huitzilihuitl's reign. King Tezozomoc, while expanding the Tepaneca Empire north and east, had eased tribute requirements for the Mexica at his daughter's request, especially as his grandson would likely be the next ruler of Tenochtitlan. But in exchange, Tezozomoc required the assistance of his son-in-law in waging war against the Acolhua nation, in whose capital city lived Huitzilihuitl's own sister, Matlalcihuatzin, Queen of Texcoco.

Not long after the brothers had left the calmecac, sadly, Chimalpopoca's mother died. Both her native and adoptive cities mourned the passing of the queen. No sooner had their grief subsided, however, when Huitzilihuitl was slain in battle by the forces of his own brother-in-law King Ixtlilxochitl.

The calpoleh and other leaders of the city once again came together to select a new king. Given the relationship with Azcapotzalco, the choice was simple: Chimalpopoca was nominated and acclaimed by his people, anointed and set upon his throne.

Almost immediately, Chimalpopoca took up his grandfather's cause, which had the added bite of revenge. The young king eventually besieged Texcoco and drove his uncle into the sparse forest at the foot of Mount Tlaloc. There, while sixteen-year-old Nezahualcoyotl watched helplessly from the branches of a tree, Mexica warriors killed the Acolhuan king.

During the protracted war, Tlacaelel and Motecuhzoma displayed amazing skill fighting and leading men. Their older brother promoted them to higher positions of authority in the army. Tezozomoc granted Texcoco to Tenochtitlan as a tributary in recognition of Chimalpopoca's loyalty. Nezahualcoyotl, however, went into hiding in the mountains near Huexotzinco, unsure of his cousin's feelings toward him but certain that the Tepaneca wanted him dead.

After long campaigns against Chalco that ended in an uneasy truce, Tlacaelel married Princess Maquitzin of Amaquemecan, a Chalcan city-state. She would be his only wife and would bear him more than a dozen children, including a daughter, Macuilxochitzin, who would become famous for her poetry. The prince had proven himself on the battlefield and was given the symbolic staff of justice with its attendant title: topileh or constable. He helped the king to enforce laws and mete out justice in Tenochtitlan.

Aided by his uncle, General Itzcoatl, Chimalpopoca began construction of a causeway that would span the nearly four miles between his city and Tlacopan, a Tepanecan port near Azcapotzalco. At the urging of his brothers, the Mexica king also approached his grandfather and interceded with him on behalf of Nezahualcoyotl, convincing Tezozomoc to allow the Acolhuan prince to live in Tenochtitlan under Chimalpopoca's protection and watchful eye.

Finally Chimalpopoca requested his aging grandfather's permission to build an aqueduct from Chapultepec Hill and financial support to construct the project out of wood. Tezozomoc agreed, but this generosity did not sit well with his sons, many of whom ruled different cities in the Tepanecan Empire. Especially displeased was Maxtla, King of Coyoacan. To him the Mexica were mere vassals, undeserving of the gifts the emperor bestowed on them.

Tezozomoc died at last in 1426 after a reign of some four score years. His son Tayatzin succeeded him, but Maxtla incited a rebellion among the nobles of Azcapotzalco and seized the throne. Chimalpopoca sided with Tayatzin, and the two conspired together to kill Maxtla and retake Azcapotzalco. Seeking the support of the oppressed Acolhuans, the allied kings attempted to install Nezahualcoyotl as king of Texcoco. But their plans soured: Nezahualcoyotl was repulsed by Tepanecan forces, and Tayatzin was killed.

Fearing for his city and his people, Chimalpopoca sought to appease Emperor Maxtla by ritually sacrificing himself at his father's temple, but the king was captured and taken to Azcapotzalco. There he was displayed in a cage and slowly starved, until he found a means to end his own life and preserve some dignity.

News of Chimalpopoca's death reached Tenochtitlan, filling most citizens with fear. Tlacaelel, however, was gripped by a cold rage. The nobles of the city offered the kingship to Motecuhzoma, but he deferred to his higher-ranking uncle, Itzcoatl. The newly elected king, along with his council, saw no alternative. They could not take on the entire Tepanecan Empire.

"We will submit completely to Emperor Maxtla," the leaders declared. "To avoid annihilation, it is best that we take our god, Huitzilopochtli, and go to place ourselves in the hands of our uncle so that he may do with us as he wishes. Some of us yet may live. Perhaps he will pardon a few, and we can live there in Azcapotzalco as slaves."

Tlacaelel stood, appalled, and addressed the older men gathered for the deliberation. "What is this, Mexica brothers? What are you doing? You have lost all reason. Wait. Still your hearts. Let us look upon this matter with rational minds. What cowardice abounds in Tenochtitlan that you feel we must go interweave ourselves with the Azcapotzalca!" Turning to the king, he said, "Sire, what is this? How can you permit such a thing? Speak to this your people. Let us seek a means for defending ourselves and our honor. Let us not offer ourselves in such a humiliating fashion to our enemies."

Itzcoatl turned to his council. "Are you still determined to go to Azcapotzalco? It seems to me now a very ignominious act. I say we strike a blow for our nation's honor. Here you are gathered, all the Tenochca lords: uncles, brothers, nephews of mine, each highly esteemed by our people. Who among you will dare to go before the Emperor to learn what he has determined? If they are decided upon destroying us irrevocably, if they feel no compassion for the straits in which we find ourselves, then here you are, brothers. One of you must stand and go. Shrug off your fear, Mexica!"

No one volunteered, each frightened by the prospect of death. So Tlacaelel stood and declared boldly, "Good Lord my King, let not your heart be troubled. Do not lose hope. As our male kindred here seem content to simply stare at each other, refusing to respond to your entreaties, I offer myself as ambassador to Emperor Maxtla or wherever else serves your purpose. I do not fear death. We all must die. It matters little whether that destiny befalls us today or tomorrow. For what occasion should I keep myself alive? Where else will my life be put to better use than here, at this moment? I choose to die honorably in defense of my homeland! Send me, my lord. I wish to go."

King Itzcoatl rose and embraced Tlacaelel. "I marvel, dear nephew, at your spirit and your determined heart. In payment for your courage and dedication, I promise to shower you with gifts, such as this, the greatest in my power: should you die on this mission, your children will never want for anything, so that they forever remember you and this day, when you alone elected to lay down your life for the honor of our nation."

Tlacaelel, looking around at the cowed yet furious faces of his fellow princes, stood tall and strode away. He crossed the causeway into Tlacopan. From there, he approached the heavily guarded entrance to Azcapotzalco.

"What's this?" exclaimed one of the guards. "Look who's come calling! Aren't you the nephew of Itzcoatl, king of the Mexica? Name of Tlacaelel?"

"Yes, I am."

"Well, where do you think you're going? Don't you know, m'lord, that we've been expressly ordered not to let any of the Mexica enter this city? We're supposed to kill you instead!"

"I know your orders, but you surely understand that messengers are not to blame. I have been sent to speak to the Emperor on behalf of the Tenochca king and his council, so I entreat you to let me pass. I swear I will return by this same gate. If you still wish to kill me, I will put myself in your hands. Yet let me convey my message first: I assure you that there will be no reprisals."

Persuaded, they let him enter. He went before the Emperor and made the proper show of respect. Maxtla, recognizing Tlacaelel, was rather surprised.

"What way into the city did you use that kept you from being killed by my guards?"

Tlacaelel explained what had happened. The Emperor received the news with a sober, impassive countenance.

"What is it that you want, nephew?"

"I entreat Your Imperial Majesty to show mercy on Tenochtitlan. My brother's rebellion was ill-considered and has cost us dearly. Our elderly and children suffer from your embargoes. Our city still reels from the mighty blows of your army. We seek an end to hostilities now Itzcoatl has been crowned king. Can Your Imperial Majesty not work to soften the hearts of your war council? Can we not go back to serving you as we once did?"

Maxtla appeared moved by this plea. "Go with my blessing, nephew. Though I can promise nothing, I will speak to my council and to my brothers, the Tepanecan kings. Understand, however, that the decision is not in my hands. It may be that your overture is rebuffed."

"When should I return for your answer?"

"Come back tomorrow."

"And what of the guards? Can Your Imperial Majesty provide me with some sort of surety that will keep the guards from killing the messenger?"

"The intact nature of your person will be surety enough," Maxtla responded.

Tlacaelel departed with a bow. Coming upon the guards again, he saluted them. "Brothers, I have just come from speaking to your sovereign. As you can see, he has allowed me to keep my life for a time, so that I may take his message back to my king. If you would be so kind as to let me pass, I would be much obliged. I am suing for peace and have no dark designs. I will return in the morning to see this business concluded. Whether you kill me now or tomorrow, I will be just as dead. I give you my word that in the end I will put myself in your hands."

They let him go and he returned to Tenochtitlan to relate what had occurred. The king prayed and meditated for most of the night. In the morning, he summoned Tlacaelel.

"My dearest nephew, I am grateful to you for the care and diligence with which you have managed this affair, putting your life at risk in the process. Here is what you will say to Maxtla. Tell him that I insist he clearly express whether the Empire is determined to let us slip from its hand and leave us without protection or whether they desire to admit us again into their friendship. If he responds that there is no hope for us, that they plan to destroy us, take this chalky unguent with which we anoint the dead and smear his flesh with it. Then take up these plumes and feather his head as if he were dead. Give him this shield and these golden arrows, lordly insignias, and tell him on my behalf that he should beware, for we will do all in our power to destroy him."

Tlacaelel returned to Azcapotzalco. The guards let him through once more, but they murmured together their plans to attack him in the city and slay him. In the palace of Maxtla, Tlacaelel delivered Itzcoatl's ultimatum.

"Ah, nephew, what would you have me say? Sadly, though I rule the Tepanecan lands, it is the will of my people that we wage war against you. What can I do? If I move to stop them, I put my life and that of my children at risk. My brothers and councilors are furious with you, and they beg that you be destroyed."

Tlacaelel nodded. "Very well, sire. In that case, your vassal the Mexica king sends word that you should gather strength and spirit, that you should arm and prepare yourself, for from this moment he defies you and your people and declares himself your mortal enemy. Either he and his people will fall dead on the battlefield and be enslaved forever, or you and yours will. You will soon feel the heavy weight of having started a war from which you cannot escape. I have brought the chalk and feathers, the shield and arrows. Permit me to prepare you for your certain death."

Maxtla's honor forced him to allow his nephew to go through the ritual. Once it was concluded, he bid Tlacaelel to convey his thanks to Itzcoatl for observing the old forms. He had his servants sneak the Mexica general through the back of the palace.

"Nephew, do not travel through the city on your accustomed route. Understand that our guards are waiting to kill you. My servants will show you out, but first accept these gifts, with which you can protect yourself. You have been courteous and valiant, and you deserve no less."

Tlacaelel took the proffered weapons and slipped from the city by clandestine means. When he stood beyond its gates, he could not help but turn and address the sentinels.

"Ah, Tepaneca! Ah, Azcapotzalca! How very badly you carry out your charge of guarding this city! Gird yourselves well, brothers. Soon Azcapotzalco will be wiped from the face of the earth, for not one stone atop another will remain of it! Every man and woman will be bled and burned. So prepare yourselves, fools. On behalf of Itzcoatl, Mexica king, and the entire city of Tenochtitlan, *I defy you all!*"

Furious and confused, the guards rushed to kill him, but he faced them bravely. Before they understood what was happening, he had killed several of their number. A crowd gathered and Tlacaelel used the confusion to make his retreat. When he arrived in Tenochtitlan, Itzcoatl publically recognized his valor and wisdom by making him a member of the war council with the rank of tlacochcalcatl, General of the Armories. There, alongside his brother Motecuhzoma and other military leaders, Tlacaelel began to plan for the destruction of the Empire.

But the people of their city were overcome with fear: they begged the king to let them abandon the city.

"Be not afraid, my children," Itzcoatl consoled them. "We will obtain your freedom without harm befalling a single one of you."

"And what if you fail?" cried the commoners.

Tlacaelel replied on behalf of the nobility. "If we fail, we will put ourselves in your hands. Our bodies will be your sustenance. Thus will you have your revenge, devouring us on broken and dirty plates so that our flesh is defamed. However, should we be successful in this endeavor, you must swear to serve and render tribute to us, laboring and building our mansions, in serfdom to us as your true lords. You must swear to give us your daughters and sisters and nieces to do with as we will, and when we leave to war, you must carry our supplies and weapons wherever we go. Finally, you must dedicate and subject yourselves and your property to eternal vassalage."

The commoners and nobility agreed to these terms, swearing by their life's blood. The king and his generals then executed their plan: they promised to support Nezahualcoyotl as king of Texcoco and made a treaty with the dissident Tepanecan city of Tlacopan. The three Nahua kingdoms formed what was called Excan Tlahtoloyan: the Triple Alliance, remembered now as the Aztec Empire.

Nezahualcoyotl led a force of Huexotinca and Texcoca warriors across the lake in canoes, landing and marching toward Azcapotzalco from the north. Tlacopan and the Tenochca army, led by General Tlacaelel, stormed the city from the south. The forces of the Alliance converged on the enemy kingdom to the beat of war drums and began to slay its inhabitants left and right.

"Every man, woman and child!" commanded King Itzcoatl. "Leave no one alive! Take all you can and burn the rest!"

Some few nobles escaped and were pursued by General Tlacaelel into the foothills nearby. They threw down their weapons and begged quarter, promising to give the Mexica land and riches, to be their eternal tributary. Tlacaelel accepted their vow.

Meanwhile, in the city, Nezahualcoyotl dragged Emperor Maxtla from the sweat lodge where he was hiding and sacrificed him publically.

Azcapotzalco had fallen.

Itzcoatl appointed his nephew Tlacaelel cihuacoatl, minister of state, the first in almost a century. Together they engineered an even greater victory over the next months and years. The Alliance landed blow after blow against the Tepaneca. After each victory, land was given to the victorious warriors, the traditional elders, and each of the Great Houses, creating Mexica colonies throughout the highlands and expanding the noble class considerably. After the Tepaneca, the Alliance turned its sights on Xochimilco and Coyoacan and swiftly emerged triumphant.

Tlacaelel urged his uncle to gather up the books of history spread throughout the region and burn them, replacing them with an official version. "It is important that our people have a heroic past, a destiny we are striving toward with roots in the glorious civilizations of bygone eras. If we are to recreate the majesty of Tollan, we cannot allow people to even think about the lowly and ignoble parts of our history."

The king agreed. Soon a single narrative of the Mexica's rise was promoted throughout the highlands, an illustrious myth that would one day be known as *Chronicle X.*

By the time Itzcoatl succumbed to a debilitating disease, Tenochtitlan had gone from a mere vassal state to the most powerful kingdom in the basin region. The king's extravagant funeral rites, which lasted a full eighty days, demonstrated how utterly he had transformed his people in just a decade and a half.

Transforming the Mexica

Motecuhzoma succeeded his uncle on the day 3-Serpent of the year 13-Flint: May 22, 1440. The new king, dubbed Ilhuicamina or Heaven's Archer, kept Tlacaelel on as cihuacoatl. The two halted military activities for a dozen years while they solidified their administrative hold over their new territories. Working with Texcoco and Tlacopan, they engineered a web of tribute relationships and a bureaucracy to manage them. As the goods and wealth began to flow, Motecuhzoma Ilhuicamina undertook the construction of a fourth Great Temple, a large and ornately decorated pyramid that enclosed the previous iteration built under Itzcoatl.

As this massive structure went up, Tlacaelel set about persuading his people that Huitzilopochtli, the tribal god of the Mexica, was much more than they had imagined. Years among the highlanders had expanded the pantheon of the former nomads. Like most other nahuas, they adored and feared Tezcatlipoca, Xipe Totec, Quetzalcoatl, Tlaloc, and a host of other gods. But Tlacaelel insisted that Huitzilopochtli was actually the supreme divinity, responsible for keeping the sun in motion, deserving of much praise and insistent on the spilling of sufficient blood to fuel the essential fire.

In addition to elevating Huitzilopochtli to King of Heaven, Tlacaelel promulgated a host of sumptuary laws that widened the divide between the growing nobility and the commoners. The cihuacoatl prohibited the use of cotton cloth, sandals, lip plugs, or gold by the working class. Only nobles could have homes of two stories or more. Public drunkenness and other such plebeian offenses were punishable by slavery or sacrifice.

Tlacaelel also formally organized the rankings of military orders such as the Shorn Ones, the Eagle Warriors, the Jaguar Knights and the Otomies. He created compulsory military education for all males, adding the telpochcalli schools in every borough so that boys of all the Great Houses were trained for warfare.

By 1452, construction on the Great Temple had ground to a halt because Mexica territory simply did not contain stone or labor sufficient for the massive sculptures. When Motecuhzoma Ilhuicamina requested assistance from Chalco, that nation refused, sparking a bloody war. In the midst of the conflict, the highlands were stricken by a severe drought that lasted three years. Dust storms and famine ravaged the basin region. Hunger grew so severe that people began to eat their children and each other to survive.

The Tenochca finally captured hundreds of Chalcans and sacrificed them to Huitzilopochtli and Tlaloc, desperate to placate the gods they had offended by twelve years of limited bloodshed. It was not enough. King Motecuhzoma told Tlacaelel to reassemble his troops, which the cihuacoatl immediately did. He put at the army's head their younger brother Tlacahuepan, who served on the military council as ezhuahuacatl, along with two other siblings, Quetzalcuauh and Cihauhuaque.

The host departed toward Chalco by the accustomed road. Near Amecamecan, the Tenochca army was ambushed. Every Chalcan male had taken up shield and macana. They swept down on their enemy with such fury that the Mexica soon wished they had not put themselves in such straits. Seeing themselves forced to kill or be killed, they formed a ring and fought, some wishing only not to die, others hoping for victory. The fray was intense and fast, warriors falling on both sides until the battlefield was covered with the dead, fighters intermixed in a chaotic clash without strategy or order, slaying each other left and right with blazing wrath, until finally they broke apart in sheer exhaustion, dragging away what prisoners they could.

Among the dead lay the three brothers of Motecuhzoma and Tlacaelel. Other generals had their corpses brought before these two rulers, and the king began to weep and lament.

"O precious brothers of mine! Fortunate are you to have died showing your courage. Go now, festooned with lovely stones and priceless feathers, bundled and borne aloft by your deeds, having obtained the glory of our nation and the honor and defense of your brother the king."

Then, turning to Tlacaelel, who stood impassively at his side, he asked, "And what do you think, Tlacaelel, of these your brothers, lying here dead?"

The minister of state responded, "Your Imperial Majesty, I am neither frightened nor moved by their passing, as that is the purpose of war. Remember our lordly father Huitzilhuitl, who died in Colhuacan before you and I rose to power. He will never be forgotten, having acted with such valor. Why should our brothers do no less? The Mexica nation has need of such valiant dead! You and I rule in Mexico, but our betters will one day rise to replace us. Why, then, should we weep? For how long should we mourn? We have no time for sadness. There is much still to accomplish!"

The two raised an even greater army and besieged Amecamecan. Strange owls emerged from Mictlan to announce the impending doom of Chalco all through the darkness of night. With daybreak, Mexico struck, and their enemies were obliterated. Thousands were sacrificed. The rains came at last, and the Alliance slowly recovered.

Tlacaelel learned a valuable lesson. As the city continued to grow and Nezahualcoyotl lent his considerable engineering skills to create a massive dike across Lake Texcoco to dam the fresher water, the minister of state worked with priests to craft an elaborate system of monthly rituals that would require regular blood sacrifice. The Tenochca were told again and again that without the deaths of these victims, the sun might not rise and the Fifth Age might come to an end.

Motecuhzoma became concerned about a source for so many victims, especially as the date for inaugurating the Great Temple approached, a ritual that would require great spilling of blood. His brother told him not to worry.

"There is time for everything. If you wish, we can sacrifice our own children of the sun in the monthly rites. There will be no lack of men to dedicate the temple when it is ready, for I have thought upon what we must do from here on out. We can no longer wait until our god is angry and rush off to war. No, we need an easily available market where we can go with our god and purchase victims, flesh for his fire—something close at hand so that when the mood strikes Huitzilopochtli he need merely stretch forth his hand and seize. These markets will be our nearby vassal states. We will arrange regular battles with them, not to slaughter men on the field, but to capture enemy warriors to be offered to the gods here in Tenochtitlan like flowers, blossoming red upon the sacrificial stone."

So the flower wars began: blood flowed in Mexico like never before.

Greater than a King

After nearly thirty years in power, Motecuhzoma Ilhuicamina had expanded the Alliance's territory all the way to the Gulf of Mexico.

When he died, his people adored him and his enemies feared him. Tlacaelel guided the leaders of Tenochtitlan to select the son of Motecuhzoma, nineteen-year-old Axayacatl, as king. The youth ruled for thirteen years with his uncle continuing as cihuacoatl. His reign was successful in some respects: he put down the rebellion of Tlatelolco and made that sister city a permanent part of Tenochtitlan. But his campaign against the Purepecha was a failure, as were many other of his military endeavors. By the time of his death in 1481, the Alliance was rife with plots and striving factions.

Tizoc, brother of Axayacatl, inherited a fractious empire fraying at the edges. His disastrous coronation war seemed to signal ominous times. His five-year reign was marked by failures and defeat. Tlacaelel, still minister of state, and Tizoc's brother, General Ahuizotl, conspired together to have the king poisoned in order to preserve their people and stave off destruction.

With Tizoc out of the way, the 88-year-old Tlacaelel prepared to submit Ahuizotl's name to the city leadership. But he was first approached by Alliance leadership, including Nezahualpilli, son of Nezahualcoyotl. They begged Tlacaelel to assume the kingship himself.

"My sons, I certainly thank you and the king of Texcoco for coming before me. But I want you to tell me… In the nearly ninety years that I have been on this earth, during all this time since the defeat of Azcapotzalco, what have I been? What position have I held? Have I been nothing, then? Do you wonder why I never placed a crown on my head or used the royal insignias that are the wont of kings? Come, do you not understand the value of all I have judged and ordained? Do you believe I unjustly put criminals to death and pardoned the innocent? Lords were made and unmade at my command! Do you believe I have broken the laws of this kingdom, wearing jewels and clothes and sandals only permitted to kings? I have dressed in the robes and masks of gods! With these hands I have lifted the sacrificial blade and spilled blood like

Huitzilopochtli himself! And if I do these things and have done them for nearly a century, then king I am and king I have always been! What more of a king would you have me be?"

The nobles bowed their heads and accepted his recommendation of Ahuizotl, whose reign would renew the Triple Alliance and vastly expand its borders.

Yet, though Tlacaelel had refused the throne, his people crowned him with an unheard-of glory when he died a year after Ahuizotl's coronation. They wept for months at his passing, crying out a new title, one never used before or since.

They called him in cemanahuac tepehuani: Master of the Sea-Ringed World.

Conquest and Courage

Convocation

How can we weave the tale of Tenochtitlan's fall, sisters and brothers? How can we sing those anguished cries? Such an epic tragedy could fill book after book with sorrow.

Let us sketch the shape of the Conquest with smoke and ash. Let the end of the Mexica be a silhouette against the burning boroughs, the funeral pyres, the bonfires fed with painted books.

Do you tremble, friends? Do you weep here beside me?

On this battleground, littered with indigenous dead, it appears that chaos has won. The Nahuas called Tezcatlipoca—known as Hurricane to the ancients—the Enemy of Both Sides. You may see that dark god's hand at work in the destruction of Mesoamerica.

The Spanish pit nation against nation. Old rivalries heighten the destructive power of firearms, foreign disease, Toledo steel. Death spreads, conquers, reigns.

All seems lost.

But here we stand, do we not, a testament to the triumph of order and creation.

Much was torn down, many lives obliterated, many words erased. Yet something new would be built, a new hybrid people would emerge, a valiant and enduring tongue would be forged in the crucible of oppression.

Mexicans. Mexican-Americans. Chicanos. Proud inheritors of this Fifth Sun.

And if you look closely at our palimpsest souls, you can see the ghostly tracings of all we ever were, indelible if faint, ready to be read again by open hearts and minds. Ready to be emblazoned on banners like the incomparable features of Princess Donají, on seals like the noble profile of Emperor Cuauhtemoc, in paintings like Erendira upon her rearing steed.

We are their descendants, heirs to their unyielding souls.

These final stories are *ours*, mestizo missives and manuscripts and music. *We* wrote them down, recited them, shared them mind to mind. They live on in our histories, in our poetry, on our lips, in our hearts.

And we will never forget.

Malinalli and the Coming of Cortés

Thirteen years after the death of Tlacaelel, a girl was born in
Coatzacualco, a coastal vassalage located in the borderlands between the
Triple Alliance and the Mayan kingdoms of the Yucatan Peninsula. The
day was chicome malinalli, 7-Wild Rye, one of the few auspicious times
associated with that sign of twisted grain. The baby's parents, nobles
in the city of Olutla, had adopted, like most aristocrats throughout the
region, the language and traditions of their Nahua overlords, layering
these atop their Popolucan culture. As a result, in addition to the girl's
later baptismal name (which the world has forgotten entirely), she was
called by her day sign, often shortened simply to Malinalli.

The day of Malinalli's baptism was like that of any baby girl in
Mexico. A midwife offered her to heaven, then bathed her carefully,
cleaning away the vice with which all are stained when they descend.
Swaddling Malinalli, she entered the house and laid her in the cradle, a
symbol of the Divine Mother, to whom the midwife addressed a prayer.

"You who are mother to us all, Yohualticitl, Enchantress of the Night
with your cradling arms, your ample lap—the baby has arrived. She
was created there above us, in the Place of Duality, in the highest of the
heavens. Our beloved grandparents, Ometecuhtli and Omecihuatl, have
winged her down to earth, where she will face trials and suffer fatigue.
But we leave her with you, dear lady, so that in your lap, cradled in your
arms, she may find the strength to endure the tribulations prepared for
her by the Lord of the Night and his dark specters. Receive her, Mother!
Let no harm befall her!"

A few months later, her parents followed the tradition of the nobility
and took their daughter to the temple of Quetzalcoatl to dedicate her
to the future service of that god. "O master," the priests intoned, "here
is your servant. Her mother and father have brought her, dedicating
her as an offering to you. Receive the poor girl as your property. If

she survives, she will live in service to you here, cleaning this house of penance and tears, where the daughters of noblemen draw secrets from your heart, crying out to you in desolation. Show her mercy, Lord. Favor her as you will."

Malinalli grew into a toddler and was ever at her mother's side, watching the women of the household spin and weave, cook and clean, manage household and direct servants. When she was old enough, the priests scarified her hip and breast as a sign of her dedication to Quetzalcoatl. Born into a bilingual nobility, the girl learned both the local tongue, Popoluca, and the Nahuatl used by the elites and merchant class, quickly mastering multiple different registers, from the frank diction of the commoners to the highly stylized formulae of the aristocracy.

As she grew, Malinalli discovered that her town was part of a larger political unit that itself was subject to distant Tenochtitlan. Tribute and sacrificial victims flowed each year from Olutla into the hands of the new Emperor, Motecuhzoma the Younger, including occasional groups of children bound for the temple atop Mount Tlaloc. Like other youths who gradually became aware of life's injustices, Malinalli harbored resentment toward her people's overlords. But this was the way of the world, and there was little that she could do to change things. Her path was spelled out by tradition. She began to assume duties in the home when she was seven years old. She knew that in just a couple of years she would begin her period of service at the temple. After some time there, she would marry a warrior and start her own family, continuing the cycle. Malinalli accepted her role with dutiful resignation.

But then the omens began, and everything changed. First a smoking star appeared in the night sky, a red-hot comet that bled cosmic fire as if someone had gashed a wound in the very heavens. Though it vanished each dawn, the flaming sigil appeared amongst the stars at twilight, horrifying people throughout Mexico.

Not long afterward, Malinalli's father died, leaving the young girl heartbroken. After the traditional period of mourning, his widow remarried and bore her new husband a son whom the couple doted upon to a degree that made the girl jealous despite herself. Soon afterward, Malinalli's time of service to Quetzalcoatl began.

It would not last long.

One night, when she awakened in the darkness to begin her ritual sweeping, strong hands seized her and bore her away. The young girl found herself in the clutches of slavers from the Mayan state of Xicalango. They sold her to a Mayan aristocrat in the neighboring region of Tabasco, chief of a riverside village called Potonchan. Like most slaves, much of her work was difficult and physical. But as she learned both the Chontal and Yucatec dialects of the Mayan language, her value grew. Her quick mind and linguistic skill earned her the respect of her master and the nickname Tenepal: with a sharp and agile tongue.

Malinalli discovered that the Maya were not too different from her own people or the Nahuas of the Triple Alliance. They worshipped what seemed to be the same gods—Mother, Creator, Rain, Destruction, Sun, Moon—with different names. They used the same sacred and solar calendars. In fact, Malinalli was sometimes called by her day sign, Vukub Eb, just like in Nahuatl.

During her time among the Maya, whisperings and rumors began to spread throughout the region about strange happenings. Large, winged structures had been seen floating upon the water. Pale, bearded men had been sighted. In Tenochtitlan, the temple of Huitzilopochtli had burst into flames. Lightning had slammed into the shrine of Xiuhtecuhtli, Lord of Time and Fire. Lake Texcoco boiled near Tenochtitlan, devouring many houses. A bizarre bird with a smoking mirror mounted upon its head was discovered and taken before the Emperor, who saw in that glassy surface the image of an invading army, riding massive deer that glittered like silver. Two-headed men wandered the streets of Tenochtitlan and were dragged to the Black House where Motecuhzoma studied sorcery. The moment he looked upon them, rumors affirmed, the monsters vanished.

Most harrowing of all was the voice of the goddess Cihuacoatl, heard along the streets of Tenochtitlan in the dead of night, crying out in desperation: "My children, we must abandon the city! But where shall I take you? Where will you go?"

By the time Malinalli Tenepal was seventeen, Tabasco was rocked by news of an attack on the nearby coastal village of Ah Kim Pech by blond, bearded strangers from across the sea. Most of the invaders had been killed. The wounded survivors had fled upon their winged, floating castle.

People whispered that perhaps the old prophecies were true, that maybe the Wayfarer was returning at last. Could these unusual foreigners be the vanguard of the Lord of the Dawn? On Mayan lips was the name Kukulkan. Nahuas spoke of Quetzalcoatl, the beloved prince.

Twenty-four months later, the main force arrived. The year was 1-Reed, the same in which Quetzalcoatl had been born and either died or departed. A squadron of strange men landed at the mouth of the Tabasco River and began making their way upstream. Malinalli's master sent warriors against the invaders, but he lost nearly a thousand in a battle many described as magical. The bearded, silver-clad men used weapons of fire and smoke, lightning and indestructible metal, whizzing and nearly invisible projectiles that ripped away life and limb.

The chief of Potonchan consulted his priests, who declared the newcomers divine—if not quite gods, certainly possessed of celestial powers and accoutrements. Better to appease them and bend the knee than to risk the wrath of heaven. So the chief gathered rich gifts to show his respect, including twenty beautiful slaves. Among these was Malinalli Tenepal.

The young woman did not know what to expect. As the party approached the strangers' camp, the chief and his men looked warily at the massive four-legged beasts that seemed to guard the camp. They were taller than a man and clad in glittering silvery metal. Suddenly a whistling screech passed over their heads, and the trees behind them exploded, sending leaves raining down. Approaching them came a tall man with reddish-brown hair and eyes the color of thick honey. He was guiding the largest of the beasts, which reared up and made a thunderous noise before dropping to all fours and pounding the ground. The man whispered in its ear and it seemed to grow calm.

The tall man began to speak in a tongue Malinalli had never heard. An older man dressed in black robes stepped from the trees to translate into Mayan.

"The *capitán general* says that if you cooperate, no harm comes to you from these mighty weapons."

The chief then displayed his gifts, and the two leaders began to hold counsel. The tall man gave his name as Cortés, sent by a distant king in a land called Spain. The invaders seemed especially interested in the gold, asking through the interpreter, whom Malinalli deduced was a priest called Aguilar, where they could get more.

"With the Colhua-Mexica," the chief replied, pointing to the West. "Off there, in Mexico, in Tenochtitlan."

After some deliberation, Cortés accepted the gifts, giving each of his captains one of the twenty slaves. Malinalli was assigned to Alonso Hernández Puertocarrero, a dark-haired yet pale warrior not much older than she. Aguilar brought the twenty slaves together and explained that they would have to renounce their gods, whom he declared were false and evil, and embrace the one true god, Jesus Christ, and his mother Mary, Queen of Heaven.

Though it seemed foolish to Malinalli to claim that her people's gods were both false—nonexistent—and evil as well, she listened closely to Aguilar's description of Jesus Christ, born to the Virgin Mary, preaching a message of love, forgiveness, and transformation before being killed and rising to heaven. The story bore many similarities to the traditions of her people and of the Maya.

When Aguilar said that Jesus Christ's sacrifice meant no more sacrifice was needed, Malinalli took notice. Cortés apparently meant to impose this new god and his celestial mother on the people of the coast and the highlands, which would mean the elimination of sacrificial captives. The oppression of many tribes could conceivably come to an end.

She said she accepted the new faith. She bowed her head for baptism and partook of the strange new sacrament that Aguilar declared was the body and blood of their god, in much the same way as Mexica nobles were rumored to eat the flesh of victims impersonating the gods. Aguilar gave her a new name, then: Marina. A smile played across her lips. The gods were certainly at work. She had been christened with what sounded like her day sign.

Then the ceremony ended. She was escorted onto one of the floating castles to join her new master in his quarters.

The Spaniards sailed up the coast for a few days before anchoring in a broad bay. There they sighted two large canoes bearing richly dressed priests and princes. They were invited aboard. Aguilar immediately attempted to speak to them. However, none of them knew Mayan.

"Who speaks for your people?" one of the princes asked in Nahuatl. "Who is your leader?"

Neither group understood the other, and tensions were rising. Malinalli could envision the disastrous outcome—the oppressive regime of Tenochtitlan would use the confusion and conflict to consolidate power, ally even with enemies to drive the newcomers away. They were men, after all, proud and violent and rash, like those who hurt her again and again.

Yet fate had forged Malinalli into a lever. Without warning, she was overwhelmed by an epiphany, a vision of the victory she could earn over her people's enemies, the transformation she could work on the highland nations through these strangers.

So though her heart raced with hidden fear, Malinalli slipped into the gap fate had made for her. Stepping forward, she addressed the Nahua prince.

"My lord, the gentleman you seek stands over there, apart from the others." She pointed to Cortés.

Aguilar turned to her. "Marina, do you speak their language?"

"Yes, reverend priest. I learned it as a child. It is the language of the Emperor and his people."

Aguilar relayed this information to Cortés, who called Malinalli to his side. "From now on you are my tongue, do you understand?" he told her through Aguilar. "Like the priest, you must be with me at all times. Now, let us parlay with these men."

Before the wheels of time could turn, she felt the rough hands of destiny seize her willing soul and thrust it against the fulcrum.

Though the same sun still rode the hard blue skies, a new age would soon begin, arising bloody amid the clash of steel and obsidian.

The Torture of Cuauhtemoc

Aided by Malinalli, Cortés began to win to his side the great rivals of the Triple Alliance, especially the kingdom of Tlaxcalla, which lent thousands of warriors to the conqueror, pledging fealty to the Spanish crown and to the Christian god.

The Nahuas soon learned to respect the brilliant and fierce translator at the captain's side. They called her Malintzin, "Revered Marina." Cortés became Malintzineh, "Master of Malintzin." On Spanish tongues, this new epitaph slurred into Malinche. In an ironic twist of fate, Malinalli would only be remembered down the years as Malinche, the name an insult growing synonymous with treachery and treason.

As the Spanish marched ever closer to Tenochtitlan, Emperor Motecuhzoma was overcome with terror. His court shamans and priests passed down dire prophecies. Evil omens hinted at his people's doom. Striving to stave off destruction, he sent envoys with riches to bribe Cortés, bidding him come no closer, but it was to no avail. The army kept coming.

The king, desperate, sent a group of wizards, commanding them to bewitch the Spanish soldiers. Their magic failed them. As they made their despondent way back home, they were stopped by a young man who raved like a drunk.

"What are you people doing? Why does Motecuhzoma delay? What does he fear? Look at how many have been humiliated, wounded, slain because of his cowardly strategems and stupid errors! Ah, but it is too late, too late for Mexico. Soon it will lie in ruins. Look, you fools, at your city. It is fated to burn!"

Then the envoys beheld in a vision Tenochtitlan ablaze, its people dying in the streets. When the horror faded from their eyes, they realized that Tezcatlipoca himself had been among them. But not even the words of a god could goad the emperor into action. Instead, Motecuhzoma slipped more deeply into despair.

"Judgment is upon us," he cried. "All we can do is await our end."

In November of 1519, the Spanish arrived at Tenochitlan, overwhelmed by its splendor and more determined than ever to seize its riches for themselves. The crestfallen emperor welcomed Cortés with a trembling heart, allowing his armored men to march across the causeways and into the city.

The Spanish, feigning courtesy, had soon taken the emperor captive, confining him to his palace while they assumed greater and greater control of Tenochtitlan. When Cortés found himself obligated to leave the city, however, to deal with a rival conqueror, his men destroyed the tense and delicate peace. It was the festival of Toxcatl, when Huitzilopochtli was honored. Fearing revolt, the Spaniards closed all the entrances to the Patio of Dances. When the festivities began, the soldiers attacked, slaughtering thousands of Mexica.

The tide turned against the conquerors. Cortés returned just in time to witness a full-blown uprising. There was fierce fighting in the streets and along the canals, with the Mexica soon gaining the upper hand. The Spanish soldiers took up all the treasures they could carry and began to flee. As a final act of outrage, they threw Motecuhzoma to his death from a palace window. Enraged warriors routed Cortés and all of his men from the city, raining vengeance down upon them with obsidian swords and arrows.

The king's younger brother Cuitlahuac assumed the throne in the bittersweet days that followed. His reign and the Mexica victory would be short-lived. For without anyone's knowing, the foreign army had left a deadly weapon behind.

Smallpox.

Within a few months of their victory, the disease struck the Mexica. From October to November of 1520, thousands upon thousands died from the plague. Many others succumbed to hunger, for they could not get up and search for food, and their loved ones were too ill to help.

These unfortunate souls starved to death in their beds. Even those who survived were weakened to the point that they could not grow or harvest crops. An epidemic of starvation and malnutrion completed the decimation. Not even nobles were safe—Cuitlahuac himself succumbed to the plague.

In the somber aftermath, the remaining nobles selected a new emperor: Cuauhtemoc, the eighteen-year-old nephew of Motecuhzoma. When—after much of the Valley of Mexico had suffered through outbreaks of smallpox—Cortés laid siege to Tenochtitlan in the spring of 1521, the young leader managed to stave off invasion throughout most of the summer, eighty full days, despite the devastation his people had suffered.

But the city finally fell. As rainclouds piled high on the evening of August 12, 1521, Cuauhtemoc stood on the steps of the temple and addressed his people for one last time as an independent ruler.

"Our sun has hidden himself. Our sun has blotted out his face, leaving us in utter darkness. But we know he shall return once more, that he shall rise again to light our way anew. Yet while he remains there in the Underworld, let us soon reunite and embrace one another, hiding in the depths of our hearts all that we love, all that we know to be precious.

"Let us destroy our temples, our schools, our ball courts. Let our roads be abandoned and our homes seal us up until a new sun emerges. May the revered mothers and fathers never forget to guide the young. May they remind their children how good she has been to us until now—our beloved Mother Earth, this land we call Anahuac.

"Our destiny stands as both shelter and protection, along with our respect and ethics, handed down by our ancestors and planted deeply in our hearts by our honored parents. Now we must charge our children to tell their own sons and daughters—things will be good again! She shall rise again! She shall gain the strength to carry out her holy destiny, so she shall, our beloved Mother Earth, this land we call Anahuac!"

That night the rain began to fall in thick curtains. The people sealed themselves up in their homes. Cuauhtemoc led a group of canoes against the Spanish flotilla on the lake, seeking to ram a barkentine and attack it, shield and macana in hand. But the archers and riflemen sent volley after volley, and the emperor finally surrendered.

Cuauhtemoc was brought before Cortés. There was a moment of tension when the Mexica ruler reached out and seized the pommel of the captain's dagger, sheathed at his belt. Yet the emperor was kneeling, with no intention to attack.

"You have destroyed my people and my city despite every effort I could make," Cuauhtemoc declared, his heart broken. "I beg you now to take my life as well. So would you end the kingship of Mexico as you have everything else. This is the clear will of the gods."

But Cortés refused to kill the emperor. He wanted a figurehead to control the Mexica. Cuauhtemoc ordered his remaining forces to surrender. Soon Spanish soldiers were ransacking the city, avid for gold. Homes were destroyed. Corpses were piled high and set ablaze. The effigies of the gods were toppled and smashed. People fled from Tenochtitlan and its sister city of Tlatelolco, rushing to the water's edge, but there was nowhere to go.

A singer of the time composed a sad lament for this devastation:

In cruel diaspora, you conquer
Your vassals of Tlatelolco.
The burning spreads
And we learn misery
Because, through our weariness,
We became lazy, O Giver of Life.
Wailing echoes all around,
Tears spatter like rain in Tlaltelolco.
The Mexica women rush down
To the water's edge.

An exodus of souls—
But where will we go, my friends?

Thus is it true:
They abandon the city of Mexico.
Smoke rises from the ruins,
A haze shrouds everything.
This is your doing,
O Giver of Life.

Remember, you Mexica—
It is our God who brings down
His wrath, His awesome might
Upon our heads.

Heedless of the Mexica's suffering, the Spanish scoured the city. Eventually they found riches hidden away, but not nearly as much as they had imagined. Of the supposed treasure of Motecuhzoma, there was no trace. The conquerors were furious, as even the gold they had left behind was missing.

Cortés was dumbfounded that not a single native would reveal the location of the precious metals. No matter how hard his men questioned and sought, the Mexica were silent.

Cortés ordered his treasurer Julián de Alderete to force the information out of the remaining rulers through torture. Alderete called for three men: Cuauhtemoc, his counselor Tlacotzin, and the king of Tlacopan, Tetlepanquetzal. Soldiers smeared these nobles' hands and feet with oil and then held them over a fire.

The pain was excruciating, but Cuauhtemoc endured it in silence, as did his counselor. But the king of Tlacopan could barely stand the agony, so he turned to Cuauhtemoc and moaned, "My liege, I am in great pain."

Cuauhtemoc narrowed his eyes and sneered at his ally. "Do you think this is a delightful steam bath for me?"

When it became clear that the nobles would not speak, Cortés ordered an end to the toruture. Gazing upon the weakened emperor and his blackened extremities, the conqueror shook his head in disbelief.

"I do not understand you," the Spaniard muttered. "Why not simply tell me where your people's riches lie? Where is Motecuhzoma's treasure?"

Cuauhtemoc returned his gaze with dispassion. "My nation's treasure is hidden all around you, within the margins of this mighty lake. You are just too blind to see it."

For years, Cortés dredged the water, unable to understand, thinking the Mexica had hurled gold and silver into the depths as they fled the city.

But the real treasure of the Mexica was the transformation of the island, the vast canals, the rich chinampa gardens, the towering temples, the expansive marketplace, the painted books of ancient lore.

None of those things mattered to the Spanish, of course.

For three and a half years, Cuauhtemoc lived in captivity, serving as a figurehead, a puppet king. Then, on February 27, 1525, an informant named Mexicalcingo informed Cortés of a plot to kill him and other Spaniards. Cuauhtemoc and ten other nobles were hanged the next day.

The last emperor of Mexico was dead. The empire had ended.

The Anguish of Citlalli

Can you hear the cries of those indigenous mothers, lamenting
the deaths of husbands and children, sobbing bereft at the burning
of homes, howling at the pain in their own flesh, at the clutch of
conquering hands? What a heart-rending chorus, echoing still in the
shadows of Mexico.

One voice rises above the others, eerie and unforgettable. As
children we learn to flee her anguished call, to keep away from the
waters she haunts.

La Llorona, we call her, whispering the name so she cannot hear us.
The Wailing Woman.

After the fall of Tenochtitlan, the nearby city of Xochimilco—famed
for its floating gardens or chinampas—was the first to fully embrace the
transition to Catholicism and the Spanish crown. King Apochquiyauhtzin,
the last Xochimilca ruler, converted to Christianity. At his baptism in June
of 1522, he was christened Luis Cortés Cerón de Alvarado. Outfitted with
this new name, he was permitted to continue as a figurehead in his city,
overseeing its reconstruction along a more European model.

The king's family was also baptized, including his youngest daughter,
who was christened Clara Perpetua Cortés. Though she accepted the
Spanish name with impassive dignity, within herself she would always
be Citlalli—star of heaven.

By arrangement between her father and Hernán Cortés, Citlalli was
given to a low-ranking officer, Diego Fernández. Arranged marriage
was the norm among the nobility in Xochimilco, so the princess
accepted her father's will wordlessly, even as she quailed at the unending
changes to her people's culture.

Don Diego was kind to her in that strange barbaric way the Spanish
had. He lavished her with gifts and attention from time to time while

largely ignoring her otherwise, leaving the management of their modest household to her alone. Aside from the occasional visit from Don Gregorio Villalobos, a fellow officer of Diego's who leered at Citlalli with a wolfish grin, she had few complaints and suffered no overt mistreatment.

In time, Citlalli bore Diego two sons—Martín and Sebastián, whom she named in secret Ehcatzin and Pocuixin. The boys were a delight, impish and brave. The little family lived in relative peace and joy, despite the social upheaval all around them. Diego took some interest in the history and traditions of his wife's family, and their relationship deepened into a sort of easy friendship. Even the strange mysteries of her husband's god became clearer, dovetailing with the lifelong beliefs of the princess in unexpected ways.

Citlalli—Clara Perpetua—began to embrace her new life. Her Spanish improved. She learned to read, reviewing the scriptures of the Catholic priests. Blending cultures in the house that she ruled, Clara was just making peace with life when Diego came to her with devastating news.

"Clara, I must return to Spain," he explained. "My father has taken ill, and there is important family business I must attend to. In the interim, I entrust to you the care of my land and my sons. I have asked Don Gregorio to look in on you when I am away. Should you need anything, he will take care of it."

"But Diego, you have brothers in Spain. Can they not manage your family affairs? And if not, will you not take us with you?"

"Take you...surely you jest, Clara. I can only imagine my mother's reaction were I to bring an Indian woman into her home."

Citlalli bristled at this slight, her pride stung. "I am a *princess*, Diego. She should feel honored at my presence."

The Spaniard shook his head and gave a feeble laugh. "You understand nothing. Listen, I cannot take you with me. You and the boys will be fine—I shall only be gone six months at the most."

Diego left, and Citlalli made do without him. All went well until Gregorio began to visit. Without her husband around to impose a sense of respect, the cruel Spaniard began to take advantage of Citlalli's hospitality, first by demanding food and drink while he berated her in ugly racial terms.

The mistreatment soon edged into harassment and physical abuse.

"If you say anything, try to go to your brothers or your father with complaints," he murmured one day, pushing her against a wall and attempting to kiss her, "I'll see to it you and your half-breed brats are thrown into the streets or worse. Doubt me not, wench."

Citlalli did not doubt him. She knew what men were capable of, especially these Spaniards. So she endured as long as she could, awaiting Diego's return. Even if her husband refused to believe her, his presence would impose some respect on his villainous countryman.

Then a letter came.

It began with pleasantries and well-wishing as if to soften the blow, but Citlalli skipped down to the meat of the matter.

"To secure financial stability for our family, I have had to agree to a marriage. Isabel Zúñiga is her name, from a wealthy and aristocratic lineage. When I return to Xochimilco, she will be with me. It will be challenging for you, I know, but I shall have to make adjustments to our household. As my concubine, you cannot possibly live under the same roof as my wife, Clara. I shall arrange for you and the boys to stay in a nice home nearby, unless you prefer to move back to your father's estate."

The letter went on in this vein, but Citlalli dropped it into the fire. Her heart was raging. *Concubine?* As far as Xochimilca traditions went, she and Diego were married, and by one of his people's effeminate priests. How dare this simple barbarian treat her like a whore? What kind of savages were these Spaniards that they understood so little of the civilized intricacies of conquest? When the Mexica had conquered Xochimilco, they had not ripped down its buildings, shattered its gods, renamed its nobles. They had not treated its royal family like beasts.

Looking around at her Spanish-style home, Citlalli clenched her fists, wanting to obliterate every trace of Diego Fernández.

The door swung open without a knock. It was Gregorio Villalobos, drunk and leering.

"I'm hungry, little Indian princess," he slurred. "Want some food. Then I want you."

Seizing the statue of the Virgin from its niche in the wall, Citlalli gritted her teeth and struck the captain in the temple. He dropped to the floor and lay unmoving.

The next few minutes were a blur. Dragging the body from the entrance, Citlalli woke her two sons and walked them through the starlit night toward the flower-edged canals for which her city was renowned.

"Where are we going, mother?" Martín—Ehcatzin—asked in a groggy little voice.

"To pick flowers," she answered with distracted calm. "We shall sell them in the market."

Inwardly, though, her furious thoughts swirled around different women. Chief among them was Cihuacoatl, goddess of motherhood and fertility. Though she had created life, working with Quetzalcoatl to form human beings at the beginning of this age, she had also abandoned her son at a crossroads. Legend had it that she returned to that place again and again, crying out in anguish for her lost child. Reflecting this pattern were the Cihuateteoh, women who had died in childbirth and whose mighty spirits returned every four years to scour crossroads, looking for the children they had never had the chance to meet.

Cihuacoatl was also said to provide protection for any zohuaehecatl—a woman transformed by tragedy and hate into a weeping ghost of revenge. In her youth, Citlalli had been taught that this fierce divinity lived with her wailing protegees within the lake and its canals. When the Spanish had begun to cross the great expanse of sea, the goddess had emerged from the water to wander the streets of Tenochtitlan, Xochimilco, Chalco, announcing her people's coming doom.

Citlalli remembered awakening in the dead of night as a child to the sound of sobbing and cries. She had gone to the window and heard a voice calling out in eldritch tones, "Oh, my children, your destruction has arrived, for we must soon depart! My children, where shall I take you?"

Mother and sons were now standing by one of the canals, edged with floating gardens and flowers that gleamed bone white under the baleful eye of the moon. The boys, too, looked pale, their Xochimilca blood effaced by lunar light.

Citlalli thought of Marina, the concubine of Hernán Cortés himself. After all she had done, the devastation she had wrought alongside that conqueror, Cortés had recently taken their son from her and moved with him back to Spain.

Pride, fury, fear, despair—these all came together in Citlalli's heart in a deadly conflagration. Stepping into the water, she called to her sons. "It is easier to pick the flowers down here, boys. Come to your mother. I shall take care of you." When they waded toward her, she pulled them into one last loving embrace before plunging them with her beneath the moon-silvered surface of the canal.

It was the price of her transformation, the heavy cost of her revenge. Among the roots of the chinampas, Citlalli died with her children.

Then she was reborn, a spectral embodiment of vengeance, a sobbing creature of the night hungry to strip the joy of motherhood from others, just as it had been stripped from her.

A zohuaehecatl, her people whispered when children began to disappear.

La Llorona, the Spaniards called her, trembling at her unbridled, weeping wrath.

As a cathedral was erected and Xochimilco transformed, she remained. Nightfall would be announced each evening by the tolling of church bells. If there was a moon high in the sky, children sought refuge in their beds, trembling in fear of those moans, echoing out from the twisted mouth of a woman in great moral and physical pain.

Adults at first simply crossed themselves at the fearful sound of that mournful cry that surely came from some strange native beast. But the moans were so long and repeated that a few brave souls dared the darkness, wanting to see with their own eyes what the source of the sobbing could be. First from doorways, windows or balconies and later upon the very streets, these bold or mad adventurers managed to make out a whispy figure of fog and moonlight making its way through the night.

It was a woman, dressed in white blouse and skirt, face obscured by her wild shock of hair. With slow and silent steps, she walked through the entire city, searching, weeping. From time to time she would lift her crazed eyes and turn her ghastly head from side to side, calling out, "Children! Children! Where are my children?" as she fell to her knees in horror.

Those witnessing this scene would be terrified, standing mute and immobile like marble statues, shuddering at the depths of such despair.

Then, at the very witching hour, the Llorona would make her lonely way back to the lake, followed perhaps by some intrepid spectator, who would watch her slip into those black waters, disappearing beneath the surface without a trace.

From time to time, that sobbing revenant would bear a living child in her arms.

Erendira

Desperate, broken, brave, rebellious—the women of Mexico found many ways to resist. But no image embodies this resistance like figure of proud Erendira, mounted on a white stallion that rears to kick at the enemy.

The Spanish Conquest soon spread from the Nahuas of the central highlands. Cortés, ever-greedy, sought to bring all the nations of Mesoamerica under Spanish rule. One region he set his eyes on was Michoacan, home of the Purepecha people.

They would prove difficult to conquer.

Generations had passed along the teeming shores of Lake Patzcuaro. The Purepecha Empire had become legendary. The air was clear and clean, the landscapes of indescribable beauty, and those fortunate enough to be born in that region felt themselves blessed by the gods. They lived in harmony with their surroundings, developed a unique culture, expanding their nation, acknowledging the gods for the rich natural bounty.

The economic and social splendor of the Purepecha Empire, under the rule of its venerable king, Ziguangua, made itself manifest in the peaceful existence of its inhabitants, guided by a responsible government. Among the councilors of the aging king, Timas was the most respected, known for his sage opinions and advice that fortified the decisions made by the noble elders for the benefit of the empire.

Timas had a daughter named Erendira—"the smiling one." At sixteen, she radiated a fearsome beauty heightened by her particular grin, a haughty and mocking smirk that set her apart from other young women. As she turned this terrible smile on her swooning admirers, her black eyes scintillated with cruel playfulness, catching the glinting light of the Tarascan sun.

Among the many warriors yearning for that dark-complexioned nymph was Nanuma, commander of the Purepecha army, whose thoughts often turned to the wind and water of the lake or the silhouettes of the mountains, accompanied always by the incomparable face of Erendira. Nanuma's love for her was more than just desire—he admired over all her great intelligence and wit.

But Erendira lacked such easy emotions—instead, the one great passion she felt was for the plains and mountains of her nation, for the vast lakes and woods, its winds and sky.

Still, Nanuma made every attempt.

"Erendira, how can you be so cruel to the man who loves you most?"

"Well you know, Nanuma," the young women replied, her features slack, "that I love no man. I think I may be incapable of ever loving anyone."

"A thousand times you have said that you refuse to become a priestess of the lunar goddess, Xaratanga. So a day will come that you must accept a husband."

"Never. I refuse to have a master. The idea disgusts me."

"Master? I shall be nothing more than your slave if you will only accept me as your companion for life. My love for you has no limits. I worship you."

Erendira gave him that arrogant sneer. "For a warrior like you, there is something more worthy of worship than a woman."

"I do not understand you, Erendira."

"No, I did not imagine you would."

How could she belong to anyone more than she belonged to the wind and the trees? Why swear eternal love to someone when she had already sworn her life to her motherland? How could she forget about the vastness of nature just to center her existence on one man?

The health of King Ziguangua failed at last. His son Timzincha succeeded him. Beyond this change, much in the government continued as always—Timas gave wise counsel to the new ruler and Nanuma led the young Purepecha Warriors.

Yet on the horizon, despite this peaceful existence, worrisome rumors began to spread about invading barbarians, sent by bloodthirsty and vengeful gods. They used tongues of fire to burst apart the very homes of the ancestors.

One day news came, born by messengers from Tenochtitlan—soldiers from beyond human ken had broken the greatest empire on the sea-ringed earth, spilling the blood of a majestic civilization into the immensity of Lake Texcoco.

Sad songs drifted over the waters of Patzcuaro. Warriors girded their souls in silence for battle, inspired by pride in their unconquered nation. These young Purepecha were willing to fight till the end to defend that soil, the country that belonged to them, where men were free and eagles flew.

But of what use was an army ready to die for the motherland if its king trembled before the enemy? Tzimtzicha was a weak and cowardly monarch. His indecision brought chaos to Michoacan. Would he repeat Motecuhzoma's error and surrender before the invaders? Would he follow Cuauhtemoc's example and fight?

Erendira's heart ached at the thought that the clear, fresh water that she cupped in her hands might run red with the blood of her people, that the joyous wind that whistled through the trees might become the laments and screams of women and children, burning in the strange fires of distant, alien gods.

The news filled the hearts of warriors with grief. The moon rose fearful and its reflection in the lake found the steady gaze of Erendira, full of desire to recreate in the clouds and sky the freedom of the land of her birth.

The invaders drew nearer and their unwanted presence clung to the petals of flowers, loomed in the gloomy shadows of forests, muddied the crystal clear streams.

Behind the smile of the haughty princess lurked a grimace of hate, taunting the words she addressed to the venerable Timas.

"My father, root of my blood, do not let weakness and fear stop the warrior spirit of our eagles from flying. Our men cannot abandon their desire to defend these lands so our children may live in the eternal garden of happiness that our gods promised. May the hand that will stop the enemy not be weak and never desire to press in friendship those hands that have been washed with the blood of our brothers."

Timas looked at his daughter, feeling pride rise in his chest. When he finally spoke, he sought words that would calm the fears that everyone now felt.

"We must be patient, dear child. Let us await news from the messengers we have sent to the edges of the empire. We will pray the invaders curb their hunger for destruction. Now we must protect our young ones and beg the gods to allow flower songs of peace and hope to endure."

Erendira, echoing her father's words, spoke to the women and children, teaching them how to best protect themselves from the possible aggression and danger they all might be facing, how to best help each other at the most critical moments of the struggle.

Word came—the conquistadores had crossed the border and were heading toward Taximaroa, where the Purepecha had defeated the Aztecs long ago. At the head of the Spanish army came Cristóbal de Olid, one of the greatest soldiers of Cortés, astride a strange beast like some unnaturally massive deer.

The king, nervous, agreed to let his army face the invaders. Before the warriors set forth, Erendira found Nanuma alone and spoke to him with tears in her eyes.

"Listen, Commander. Long have you courted me, hoping to win my love. Though I cannot give you what now belongs to the empire, I promise you my body and mind if you can protect the immaculate clarity of the imperial lakes, if you can keep the enemy from destroying our homes and slaying our people. My thoughts and my flesh will be yours forever, here in Michoacan. Together we shall gaze upon the many-hued flowers in our gardens, in the countryside, along the banks of rivers and lakes. As the seed of liberty grows, we shall watch our children grow into men and women, and we shall proudly say that no one could break us, no one could enslave these lands. Do you hear me, Nanuma? Go and fight for what is ours!"

Her words echoed in his heart as he galloped at the head of his army, rushing toward Taximaroa there at the edge of the empire. They arrived before the Spanish host, which was supported by native warriors of other nearby kingdoms, and Nanuma learned the truth of the rumors. The invaders wielded unbreakable weapons that spat fire and death, sat upon gigantic beasts with glittering armor that trampled warriors beneath their weighty hooves at the barbarians' slightest touch.

The battle was a whirlwind of destruction. The Purepecha stood no chance.

Sentinels on the horizon bore word of the defeat back to the capital city of Tzintzuntzan. King Tzimtzincha sought counsel from his advisors. Ignoring those like Timas who urged better strategy and another battle, the king fled to take refuge in the mountain stronghold of Uruapan. There he received an embassy from the encroaching army. Hernán Cortés had learned of the riches in Michoacan. He persuaded the monarch through intermediaries to surrender and swear fealty to Carlos V, the king of Spain.

In Tzintzuntzan and throughout Michoacan, depair and doubt haunted every face. Young men burned with patriotic pride. Old men had resigned themselves to defeat, knowing that a king like Tzimtzicha, without ambition, would lead their nation to as humiliating a defeat as the Aztecs had suffered.

Erendira led women and children to refuges in the hills and island, far from dangers. She encouraged young men to trust in the divine strength that would give them victory over the invaders.

Nanuma watched his beloved's actions from afar, not daring to come close or look her in the eye. His fighting spirit had been mutilated by the crushing defeat and by his own self-doubt. Should he return to face these alien conquerors or hand himself over to those inscrutable gods of theirs, becoming a hated slave?

The forces of Cristóbal de Olid marched closer and closer to the capital, scouts reported. The host moved without haste, confident in their victory.

When the Spanish were a day away from Tzintzuntzan, an envoy came to the city gates with heavy cargo. Presents for King Tzimtzicha, they explained, who had given his friendship and obedience to Cortés. Along with the chests of riches, the messengers brought an enormous sighthound, property of one Francisco Montaño, to reward the Purepecha sovereign for his loyalty to Carlos V.

"Captain de Olid will enter the city tomorrow," the messengers concluded before taking their leave, "to visit the crown jewel of Michoacan and report its beauty to its new lord in Spain."

The city was horrified at the cowardice of the king. Its leaders came together to debate a course of action. Nanuma, impassive, listened from afar as counselors and generals argued whether to commit treason and ignore the king's wishes, taking up arms against the Spanish as best they could.

As they expressed with passion their feeble hopes, Nanuma felt the desire to surrender grow stronger and stronger within him. Erendira's voice had begun to fade.

It was Timas who sided with the priests at last—they would call upon Xaratanga, the vengeful and inexorable goddess of the moon, in the Great Temple. She would guide them true.

At the hour the Purepecha call inchantiro, when the sun has dropped below the horizon and the moon rises like a silver disc until all bask in her glory, conches and copper cymbals struck up a plaintive melody. The people of Tzintzuntzan gathered 'round in wordless communion as the councilors and priests took their appointed seats.

Then a scream like none they had ever heard burst the silence of the night, filling the hearts of all present with terror, the discordant cries echoing with erratic rhythm. Into the temple came four warriors, leading between them the horrible beast given to their king in payment for his treachery. Many of the citizens panicked as they contemplated its mad, spiraling eyes and long, narrow muzzle, from which that horrific voice came squealing.

It was Montaño's sighthound, raging and growling, snapping and barking in fury as it struggled to get free.

The warriors lifted the beast to the sacrificial stone, its belly and snout facing the sky. The hound's crazed eyes fell on the bright moon that hung just above the horizon. It ceased its frantic barking then. Sad howls came from the depths of its chest.

Blanching, the priest took up his obsidian knife and plunged it into the beast's breast, extracting its steaming heart.

The echoes of the hound were slow to fade.

Nanuma shuddered at the scene, but then an even more terrible voice whispered at his ear.

"Today this monster, tomorrow the Spanish must die as well, in just this way!"

The commander turned to face Erendira, whose face was cracked by that uncanny sneer.

"You do not know what you ask," he began.

"Yes, I do. You are the one who will defeat that army, Nanuma. Did I not swear this to you? When you return, victorious, I shall be your reward."

"And if I fail?"

"Then I shall go cry upon your tomb. I shall plant upon your funeral mound the most beautiful flowers of our fields."

The idea made Nanuma shudder.

"Do not worry, my love." His voice grated between clenched teeth. "I shall fight to the death if I must."

Erendira looked at him curiously as if trying to see into his soul.

"We cannot surrender, Commander. We are greater, stronger. Have the gods not always protected us? Did we not defeat the Aztecs with clever stratagems both times they attempted to conquer this nation? Is it not true, perhaps, that Curicaueri, God of Fire, made man from clay? And when we broke apart in the water, did he not attempt again with ash? And so that we would be harder still, did he not remake mankind of metal? *Are your soldiers not made of metal, Nanuma?* Or will they turn into simpering women on the battlefield once they face these barbarians? Have no mercy, then, Commander Nanuma, when you are out on the battlefield. I know you are the most valiant of our warriors. You and only you can guide our army to triumph over the invaders and protect our empire."

Words failing him before her unyielding national faith, Nanuma bowed his head and left to ready the troops.

When the Spanish approached the gates the following morning, the Purepecha fell on them like birds of prey. The war cry of Michoacan echoed across the lakes and throughout the small isles. Spears and arrows darkened the skies, obsidian blades hacked and stabbed, large stones were lobbed against the barbarian horde.

But these efforts were in vain. The superior arms and horses of the Spanish outmatched the Purepecha army. The sun itself was tinged red with young blood. The smell of death and gunpowder filled the air along with dust and smoke. The neighing of horses drowned out the native battle cries.

Nanuma sounded the call for retreat. Decimated, the army drew back inside the city.

Erendira stood furious, glaring at the commander. His heart breaking, Nanuma strode to her side, seized her shoulders with his bloody hands.

"We are outmatched, damn you!" he cried. "Tell me, then—what would you have me do?"

"Die!" she spat. "Like a warrior! You disgust me, Nanuma. But soon enough the Spanish will teach you the way of men who refuse to die for their motherland."

Watching her haughty back recede, the commander's spirit finally broke. He decided to immediately send word to his king and Captain de Olid. He and his army would lay down their weapons and submit to Cortés.

As soon as Timas learned of the military's impending surrender, he went to Erendira. "We must flee the city, taking as many able-bodied men with us as possible if we are to mount a resistance."

Livid and trembling at the commander's betrayal, she agreed at once. As night fell, they led a group out into the hills. There, far from the cowardice of the man she had admired, away from the people that revered her, Erendira wept hot tears of rage and bereavement. Her nation now hung in the balance. Its champion had abdicated. She would have to find another way.

That morning, the captain entered Tzintzuntzan as promised, greeted by Nanuma, who bent his knee before the foreign warlord. The conquerors celebrated their triumph there in the heart of the Purepecha Empire, destroying the symbols that tied its peoples to their beliefs, to the mistaken vision of themselves as invincible in a world that stretched only as far as their gods allowed them to see.

The city became a specter of desolation, devouring the past with every step of the invaders, covering the remaining inhabitants with expressions of pain.

A great cross, symbol of the alien religion, was lifted in the temple after the gods had been shattered.

Nanuma nodded, unable to feel regret or despair. It was fitting.

What chance did he have against these barbarians if their one god could so handily defeat an entire pantheon?

Smoke curled in the distance above the capital. Erendira's tears of powerlessness left a bitter taste on her lips. As she and the rest of the former residents sought refuge in the city of Patzcuaro, she stoked the fires of her anguish.

With her father, Erendira began to organize volunteers from the refugees and the local population at the edge of the lake. A resistance was formed that took over an entire borough of the city, positions fortified in preparation for the worst.

Thus began a series of skirmishes against the Spanish, probing attacks to determine their weaknesses. Nanuma knew who was behind the rebellion. When King Tzimtzincha returned—to kneel before de Olid in public and be baptized with the Spanish name Francisco—the commander expressed his will to quell the uprising himself. His numb heart wanted nothing more than to find Erendira, to make her kneel before him, not so that she would look up with the admiring and loving gaze that he had long coveted, but so that he could break her once and for all, wipe that haughty trace of a smile from her pretty face.

As Purepecha turned against Purepecha, Erendira cringed and screamed to see what had been a mighty empire slowly disappearing as when the rain is whipped about at the mercy of the wind and drowns out the song of the mockingbird.

Then something miraculous occurred.

During a raid, a group of rebels managed to overcome their fears and trap one of the Spaniards' great beasts, those steeds that merged with rider to become a single harbinger of devastation and terror. Without its barbarian master, the creature came with them calmly, offering no struggle.

The warriors presented the white stallion to Erendira as a sign of hope. The people of that great land could—somehow, in some way—repay the Spanish usurpation in kind.

Erendira was fascinated by the horse. She spent several days in the woods with the steed, learning to bond with it in ways that surpassed its owner, drawing on her deep respect for nature.

By the end of the week, she galloped from the forest on its back to the amazement of the resistance. Their respect for the young woman deepened into awe. Her black hair streamed out behind her as the horse dashed around their camp, a study in contrasts and harmony. Barely seventeen summers old, Erendira had wrested the secrets of the enemy from them by dint of her own courage and will.

She began to accompany the warriors on raids and skirmishes. The sight of that teen astride her white horse helped turn the tide against their enemies again and again, filling her faithful soldiers with valor and her traitorous countrymen with fear.

Old Timas, seeing his daughter so regal and vicious upon that beast, realized that these monsters could be the key to retaking the capital. His idea was to steal as many more of the horses as possible so that Erendira could train others to ride them.

Steeds became the objects of raids. Within weeks the rebels had a dozen or so of the creatures in their power. Timas selected the most robust and agile young men to serve as mounted warriors. Erendira taught them all she knew, helping them to bond with their horses. After several successful skirmishes in which the horsemen proved their mettle, Timas decided it was time to invade Tzintzuntzan and wrest it from enemy hands.

With the mounted warriors at the vanguard, ten thousand Purepecha flooded their capital, ready to fight until the death for the motherland, armed with slings and arrows, spears and macanas. Timas had begged Erendira to remain behind with the civilians, but she, undaunted, brought up the rear.

The fighting was fierce, lasting well into the night. Many died on either side. But Cristóbal de Olid had Tlaxcallan and Mexica allies with him, as well as Nanuma and all his men. Timas was pushed back into the Great Temple, where the insurrection made its last stand.

They fought well, but in the end they lost.

In the aftermath, de Olid walked in the darkness, checking corpses, searching for his fellow countrymen. Dawn lit up the sky—the extent of the ruin was made clear.

The ground was carpeted with the dead, mostly Purepecha, together with Mexica and Tlaxcallans and Spaniards. The waning of one of America's greatest cultures had truly begun, the last stand of Michoacan's mighty sons.

The cries of survivors came from the temple. To Captain de Olid's surprise, a group of warriors rushed into its interior, attacking with cruelty the surviving rebels within. This was the remnant of Nanuma's army, whom he had ordered in fierce tones to have mercy on no one. His hate had one objective: to find Erendira and then humiliate or harm her. He shouted her name in a maddened voice that blended with the screams of terror and pain. No answer came. His wild, searching eyes scoured the victims to no avail. Erendira was not among them.

One by one, Nanuma and his men slaughtered their surviving brothers, ignoring outstretched hands and pleas for compassion.

Among the wounded was old Timas, his blood watering the soil that he so loved. Stepping with indifferent cruelty on the corpses of his kin, Nanuma rushed toward the father of the woman he despised, his obsidian sword raised to strike.

Then, bursting through the doors on her white stallion came Erendira, hurtling toward the traitor with a scream of righteous fury on her lips. The hooves of that horse were her weapons, and she used them with deadly precision to obliterate the shameful coward to whom she had once promised her heart.

Dismounting, Erendira went to her father's side as he trembled in his final moments.

"Be ever true to yourself, dear child," he breathed. "Michoacan awaits you with open arms. Let no man be your master."

Closing his eyes with a steady hand, Erendira leapt onto her stallion and spurred it out the temple door, past the startled Spaniards, through the city gates, and into the distant hills.

Horse and rider disappeared within the forest.

Erendira was never seen again.

Donaji

Two hundred kilometers south of Tenochtitlan, the Zapotec Empire
had crumbled. The mighty city of Monte Alban had been erected upon a
mountain whose peak had been sheared away by skillful Zapotec hands.
Yet it lay abandoned and empty for centuries until the Cloud People
took it for themselves. The Mixteca and Mexica harried the remaining
kingdoms in those central valleys of Oaxaca. Many valiant warriors lost
their lives defending the noble Zapotec people—the Be'ena'a, in their
native tongue.

Zaachila was the last capital of the Zapoteca, a mighty city governed
by battle-hardened kings. Cosijoeza was its fourth sovereign, ruling
when the Emperor Ahuizotl of the Aztec Triple Alliance sought
to expand Nahua territory. When Cosijoeza discovered pochteca
merchant-spies in his territory, he had them executed. Ahuizotl took
this as an act of war.

The first Zapotec city to fall to the Aztecs was Huaxyacac, then
Mitla. Ahuizotl's military campaign then spread across the Isthmus of
Tehuantepec, which prompted Cosijoeza to forge a historical peace
accord with his Mixtec rivals. Their combined force of 50,000 warriors
pushed the Aztecs back. After a protracted war of many months,
Emperor Ahuizotl understood that diplomacy would be the only
solution to the conflict.

The Aztec overlord offered Cosijoeza the hand of his daughter,
Coyolicatzin. Their marriage cemented an alliance with the Aztecs,
ensuring the stability of Zapotec lands. Coyolicatzin bore the
Zapotec king several children, including the next king of Zaachila,
Cosijopii, and the lovely Princess Donaji—"great soul" in the
Zapotec tongue.

Not long after Donaji's birth, her mother and father visited Tiboot,
a priest and astrologer who used ancient lore to peer at possible futures.

Consulting kernels of maize and a painted codex, Tiboot revealed with great solemnity what he had seen.

"This beautiful baby will grow healthy and strong, with dignity and graceful bearing becoming a princess of our people. The Zapotec nation will feel great love and respect for her, and she will love them in kind. But in the future, she may be required to lay down her life for her people."

Though Tiboot stressed that this was only one possible outcome for the royal child, the queen was devastated.

Years passed. Donaji did indeed grow into a beloved and beautiful princess. The citizens of Zaachila showed her deference and respect, inspired by her generosity and genuine affection for her people.

The first part of the prophecy had proven true. The king and queen fretted in secret that the rest might come to pass as well.

The alliance between the Aztec and Zapotec nations did not sit well with the Mixteca. The delicate peace between those age-old foes frayed till it broke. Prince Cosijopi was sent to rule the region of the Isthmus of Tehuantepec, guarding it against incursions from the enemy.

For a time the might of the Aztecs helped keep Dzahuindanda, king of the Mixteca, at bay. But then strangers arrived from across the jade-green sea, and Tenochtitlan found itself grappling with a new and powerful enemy. It was not long before Spanish troops under the command of Francisco de Orozco arrived in Zapotec lands and attempted to seize Huaxyacac.

Violence exploded throughout the region as the Mixteca took advantage of the political chaos. Princess Donaji, though not a warrior like her brothers, did her part in these battles, tending to the injuries of fallen soldiers, even Mixteca who had been taken prisoner.

Among these enemy combatants was Nucano, son of Dzahuindanda. The handsome prince had been gravely wounded, and Donaji nursed him back to health. As war raged around them, the two young aristocrats came to know each other well. Respect and even affection blossomed in their hearts.

"We are not so different, you and I," Donaji told Nucano as she applied herbs to his wounds. "My parents also come from nations with a history of mutual hate, but they have come to love each other. Perhaps together we can overcome these conflicts, sue our royal fathers for peace. With the Spanish wielding steel upon their massive steeds, it hardly makes sense for Zapoteca and Mixteca to slaughter one another."

"You are as brilliant as you are beautiful," Nucano replied. "Soon I shall be strong enough to travel. If you can find a way to help me escape, I shall take this plan to my sire and convince him of its merits."

Their scheme was sealed with an unexpected kiss. A few days later, Nucano slipped past sentries that the princess had distracted. There was no turning back.

However, Princess Donaji did not know of her father's secret meetings with the Spanish, who had finally taken Huaxyacac and now sought to ally themselves with the Zapoteca. Though his wife was Mexica, of royal Aztec blood, Cosijoeza understood what must be done. Breaking his ties with Tenochtitlan, he pledged fealty to Cortés and his distant king, Carlos V.

Francisco de Orozco, the commander in charge of Huaxyacac, used his position and the threat of further conquest to force both the Zapotec and Mixtec kings to cease hostilities. These lands now belonged to the king of Spain, he decreed, their only sovereign, whom they would respect and obey from that day forward. There was no more reason to wage war.

Nucano, who had at last arrived in Monte Alban, urged his father to comply. He spoke to the king of Donaji, of the unity that could exist between their two peoples.

"Even if you wish to resist the Spanish," the prince explained, "you will need Cosijoeza and his sons at your side. Only together can we answer this threat."

The Mixteca king spat in disgust. "Twenty years ago Cosijoeza betrayed our alliance by joining with the Aztecs. I have no guarantee that he will not attempt to deceive me again, bringing destruction down upon our heads."

"I tell you, father, his daughter will intercede."

A retort died on Dzahuindanda's lips as he saw another way to ensure Cosijoeza's loyalty and truthfulness. Traveling to meet with Orozco, he announced his willingness to bend his knee to Carlos V and put an end to the war.

With one condition.

"We Mixteca," he pronounced, "having been victims more than once of King Cosijoeza's political trickery, require a guarantee from the Zapoteca that they will not attack our fortifications at Monte Alban or any other of our towns. A hostage whose life will be forfeit if the accord is broken: Princess Donaji."

Queen Coyolicatzin refused to hear her husband's arguments.

"I was given to you, was I not, to seal a compact? And have you not broken that alliance to side with the bearded destroyers of my people? I do not trust you to protect our daughter. Tiboot's words lie heavy on my heart."

But word came that Tenochtitlan had fallen. The Zapotec king felt he had no other choice. He agreed to Dzahuindanda's terms.

Donaji stood stunned as her father broke the news to her.

"Princess, our conqueror has imposed peace, but the Mixteca want you as a guarantee. Dear Donaji, you must go reside in Monte Alban, in the palace of your ancestors. Never forget your homeland as you live among the Cloud People. We shall not forget you."

She pleaded with him, but the king was unmoved.

"You love your people, do you not? This is what is required of you to ensure their safety."

The princess surrendered at last, travelling with her brothers and Spanish soldiers to Monte Alban, where she was remitted into custody of the Mixteca. They received her with the honors due a woman of her rank, bending their knee before her.

Their obeisance felt like mockery.

Confined to sumptuous quarters that were nonetheless a prison, Donaji was soon visited by Prince Nucano, shame reddening his features.

"For this I helped you escape?" she demanded. "So that you could convince your father to take me hostage? As I remember it, our plan did not include my imprisonment."

"Forgive me, Donaji. I had nothing to do with this arrangement. I tried to reason with him, but the chasm between our peoples is deeper and broader than we had imagined."

"Indeed it is," the princess spat. "Now leave me to my cell. I cannot bear to look at you."

Weeks passed, and Donaji, the great-souled princess, suffered her captivity with stoic resolve. Her lips never smiled. With haughty mein, she paced the high balcony of her prison. When the birds of the surrounding woods sang their songs, and she saw the mockingbird nests rocked by the evening wind, Donaji felt sadness flood her heart.

The birds that flew past were harbingers of misfortune. She meditated. In her mind's eye, the princess reviewed her noble, happy past. And she gave a radiant smile, murmuring, at the image of her mother Coyolicaltzin, brought by the gods to Ninza Rindani to capture her father's heart.

In that vision, the stern visage of her grandfather Ahuizotl stepped from the shadows and urged her to action.

"Flee, noble Donaji. Abandon this captivity. You are beautiful, yes, with a voice as melodious as a wood thrush. But in your veins flows the blood of warriors, girl! You must save your nation from enslavement. Be implacable. Shrug off your bonds. Return to Roalo and delight in the cooing of the pigeons that kiss in the brush. Return to your sun-gilded lagoon, where bone-white herons flirt with the moon."

The figures faded from her mind, but the hunger for freedom remained.

The humiliation of Donaji's condition worsened when the Spanish priest Juan Díaz arrived in Monte Alban to baptize the nobles into the Catholic faith. When her turn came, the princess was christened Doña Juana Cortés.

The chill spreading through her heart was sharpened by the December winds that Donaji braved as she paced again and again that high balcony. Prince Nucano, desperate to afford her some solace, convinced his father to bring a Zapotec handmaiden to attend to Donaji's needs.

The woman was from Guiengola. She spoke proudly to her princess of the great battle fought in her town, during which Cosijoeza had brought the Aztec emperor to his knees and wrested a daughter from him.

"Though what has been done to you is abominable," the older woman whispered, "my pride in our people is unshaken. Your father may have laid down his arms, but your brother Cosijopii is camped a few leagues away, hoping for a miracle, an opening that will let him win your freedom."

At these words, Donaji's heart swelled with determination.

A fortnight later, after a riotous celebration of the winter equinox, the Mixteca host sprawled drunken and unconscious. Donaji, viewing them from her balcony, went inside and woke her handmaiden.

"My stay here is a humiliation to my house and my tribe. Go! Slip past those besotted guards. Get word to my brother. The enemy is sleeping. Come kill them all."

Cosijopii did not hesitate. He led his warriors with great stealth into Monte Alban, where they proceeded to slaughter the Mixtec army without hesitation. Cries of warning reached the palace before the invaders, however. The captain of the guard burst into Donaji's chambers, rage twisting his features.

"You're a hostage, girl, a peace offering. Now that your king has broken his word, your life is forfeit. Tonight you die."

The guards dragged Donaji away, heading for the Atoyac River in accordance with the plan their king had made known many months before.

The princess gave a disdainful smile as they forced her to her knees among the reeds at the river's edge. In the distance, the Zapotec cries of victory filled the broad streets of Monte Alban. Their echoes, winding down the mountainside, became a dirge for brave Donaji.

Lifting his obsidian-edged macana, the captain of the guard cut off her head. The water of the Atoyac went scarlet beneath the sorrowful moon.

The drums of war still sounded. Warriors shrilled their battle songs. But as Cosijopii and his men searched the city, they found no sign of Donaji.

The Mixteca refused to speak. No one would reveal her whereabouts.

Until Prince Nucano emerged from his hiding place and knelt before Cosijopii, tears staining his cheeks.

"Search for her no longer, my lord. My father had a protocol in place. At your arrival, her guards carried out his will. Your great-souled sister is dead."

The guards had escaped after meting out their king's justice. The Zapotec army searched for days before they finally discovered Donaji's resting place, there on the banks of the Atoyac. Blossoming on the mound of earth was a purple lily of incomparable beauty.

With respect and veneration, her countrymen dug up her remains. They recoiled in surprise when they found her head on its side and facing East. Despite the time that had passed since her death, her flesh was perfectly preserved, untouched by rot. From her forehead and temple emerged the roots of that majestic lily.

A miracle, the priests declared. A sign of the gods.

For now the Spanish ruled their mountains and valleys. But one day the Zapotec people would rise up once more to claim those ancestral lands.

Three hundred years later, the government of Oaxaca had to select an emblem for the city's coat of arms. They turned to the people, asking their advice.

The people choose the face of their beloved princess, great-souled Donaji.

Guide to Pronunciation

Indigenous Mexican languages like Nahuatl and Mayan were transcribed after the Conquest using Roman letters and Spanish spelling conventions. As a result, pronunciation rules for these languages are broadly similar and are combined below.

Vowels
a as in "father"
e as in "bet"
i as in "police"
o as in "no"
u as in "flute"

Diphthongs (vowel combinations)
ai like the "y" in "my"
au like "ow" in "cow"
ei like the "ay" in "hay"
eu a blend of "e" of "bet" and "u" of flute
ia like the "ya" of "yard"
ie like the "ye" of "yellow"
io like the "yo" of "yodel"
iu like "you"
ua like the "wa" in "want"
ue like the "whe" in "where"
ui like "we"

Consonants
b as in "baby"
c like "k" before "a," "o" and "u"; like "s" before "e" and "i"
d as in "dog" at the beginning of a word; like the "th" in "that" elsewhere
f as in "four"
g like the "g" in "go" before "a," "o" and "u"; like "h" before "e" and "i"
h silent before vowels; a glottal stop like the middle sound of "kitten" after vowels
j like "h," but harsher
l as in "like"

m as in "moon"
n as in "no"
ñ roughly like the "ni" in "onion"
p as in "pet"
r like the "dd" in the American pronunciation of "ladder"
s as in "see"
t as in "ten"
v like "b" in "baby"
x like "sh" in "she" (indigenous languages) or like "h" (Spanish only)
y as in "yes"
z like "s" in "see"

Digraphs (two letters always written together)
ch   as in "check"
cu/uc   "kw" as in "queen" (primarily Nahuatl)
hu/uh   like "w" in "we"
ll   like "y" in "yes" (Spanish only)
qu   like "k" in "key"
rr   a "rolled r" (Spanish only)
tl   roughly like the "ttle" in "bottle"
tz   like the "ts" in "cats"

Note also that most words are stressed on the next-to-the-last syllable:

Hapunda—ha/PUN/da
Citlalli—ci/TLAL/li
Tezcatlipoca—tez/ca/tli/PO/ca
Quetzalcoatl—que/tzal/CO/atl

Glossary

This glossary contains most, but not all, of the people and places referenced in this book. It is intended as a guide to those names that show up repeatedly, allowing readers to reference and refresh their memories. An approximate pronunciation is also included to facilitate reading.

A

Acamapichtli (ah-cah-mah-PEECHT-lee): a king of Colhuacan, son of Coxcoxtli

Achitometl (ah-chee-toh-MEH-tul): a ruler of Colhuacan who chased the Mexica into Lake Texcoco

Achiutla (ah-CHOOT-lah): mythical city of the Mixteca.

Acolnahuacatl (ah-kol-nah-WAH-kah-tul): a Tepanec king.

Alux (ah-LOOSH): a mystic elfish being, protector of nature and wielder of magic.

Azcapotzalco (ahz-kah-poht-SAL-koh): a Tepanec city-state with ties to the Mexica.

Aztlan (AHST-lahn): ancient homeland of the Nahua (Aztec) tribes.

C

Camaxtli (kah-MAHSHT-lee): leader of the Centzon Mimixcoah. Also known as Mixcoatl or Xipe Totec. Chief god of the Toltecs.

Ce Acatl Quetzalcoatl (SEH AH-kah-tul quets-al-KWA-tul): ruler of Tollan. Incarnation of the Feathered Serpent.

Centzon Mimixcoah (CENT-son mee-meesh-KOH-ah): the "Four Hundred Cloud Serpents," demigods who roamed the earth in the early years of the Fifth Age.

Centzontotochtin (cent-son-toh-TOHCH-teen): minor gods of drunkenness.

Chalchiuhatl (chal-chee-OO-ah-tul): the blood of the gods, "precious liquid."

Chalchiuhtlicue (chal-chee-oot-LEE-kweh): goddess of rivers and lakes.

Chapultepec Hill (chah-pul-teh-PEK): located on the southwest bank of Lake Texcoco.Served as a base of operations for the Mexica.

Chichimecah (chee-chee-MEH-kah): the nomadic peoples of Northern Mexico.

Chicomecoatl (chee-koh-meh-KOH-ah-tul): goddess of agriculture. Wife of Tezcatlipoca.

Chicomoztoc (chee-koh-MOHS-tohk): a series of seven caves used by the Centzon Mimixcoah and the Nahua (Aztec) tribes.

Chimalman (chee-MAL-man): mother of Quetzalpetlatl and Ce Acatl Quetzalcoatl.

Chinampa (chee-NAM-pah): a floating garden.

Cihuatlampa (see-waht-LAHM-pa): Western paradise for women who die during childbirth.

Cipactli (see-PAHKT-lee): the primordial reptile that becomes both the earth and the earth goddess.

Cipactonal (see-pahkt-TOH-nahl): the first man, created at the beginning of the First Age.

Citlalatonac (seet-lah-lah-TOH-nahk): god of the stars.

Citlalicue (seet-lah-LEE-kweh): goddess of the stars.

Coatlicue (koh-aht-LEE-kweh): a fierce but loving deity whose nature encompasses the duality of motherhood. Wife of Camaxtli. Mother of Coyolxauhqui, Huitzilopochtli, and the Four Hundred Gods of the South.

Colhuas (KOL-wah): a Nahua tribe that takes the Mexica captive (also Colhuahqueh).

Colhuacan (kol-WAH-kan): the kingdom of the Colhuas (also Colhuahcan).

Copil (KOH-peel): wizard king of Malinalco. Son of Malinalxochitl. From his heart grows a prophesized cactus.

Coxcoxtli (kohsh-KOHSHT-lee): king of Colhuacan who enslaved the Mexica.

Coyolxauhqui (koh-aht-LEE-kweh): a goddess who leads her four hundred brothers in a revolt against their mother, Coatlicue. Dismembered by Huitzilopochtli. Her head is transformed into the moon.

Cuauhcoatl (kwau-KOH-ah-tul): a high priest of the Mexica.

Cuauhtlequetzqui (kwaut-leh-KEHTS-kee): (1) Governor of the Mexica (2) His son, a godbearer who hurls Copil's heart at the command of Huitzilopochtli.

E

Ehecatl (eh-HEH-kah-tul): god of the wind. An aspect of Quetzalcoatl.

H

Hapunda (hah-POON-dah): Purepecha princess of Yunuen.

Heart of Sky: brother to *Feathered Serpent*. God of chaos.

Huitziltzin (weet-SEELT-seen): high priest of the Mexica. Avatar of Huitzilopochtli.

Huitzilopochtli (weet-see-loh-POHCHT-lee): god of the war and patron of the Mexica.

Hunahpu (hoo-NAH-poo): one of the Hero Twins.

Hurricane: a name for *Heart of Sky* in his most destructive form.

I

Ihuimecatl (ee-wee-MEH-kah-tul): an evil priest of Tollan allied with Tezcatlipoca.

Ihuitimal (ee-wee-TEE-mal): king of Tollan before Ce Acatl Quetzalcoatl.

Ilancueitl (ee-lahn-KWEH-ee-tul): a priestess who became the Mexica's first cihuacoatl or counselor to the king.

Itza (EET-sah): the "Water Witches," a Maya nation.

Itzpapalotl (eets-pah-PAH-loh-tul): patroness of women who died giving birth and children who died in infancy. One of the tzitzimimeh.

Itztacxilotzin (eets-tahk-shee-LOHT-seen): a Toltec queen.

Ixchel (eesh-CHEL): goddess of fertility, childbirth, and war.

Ixmukane (eesh-moo-KAH-neh): a maize goddess, mother of One and Seven Hunahpu.

Iztaccihuatl (eez-tahk-SEE-wah-tul): a Tepanec princess who is transformed into a dormant volcano upon her death.

K

Ku (KOO): divine energy.

Kukulkan (koo-kool-KAHN): a Mayan name for *Feathered Serpent*.

L

Lady Blood: daughter of Blood Gatherer (one of the Lords of Xibalba) and mother of the Hero Twins, Hunahpu and Xbalanque.

Lady 1 Deer and *Lord 1 Deer*: creator gods of the Mixteca.

Lady Egret: mother of One Monkey and One Artisan.

M

Malinalco (mah-lee-NAL-koh): kingdom founded by Malinalxochitl.

Malinalxochitl (mah-lee-nal-SHOH-chee-tul): sister of Huitziltzin, a great shaman who led a schism within the Mexica.

Mayab (MAH-yab): land of the Maya people on the Yucatan Peninsula.

Mayahuel (mah-YAH-wel): goddess of the maguey plant. The only tzitzimitl to renounce destruction and join with Quetzalcoatl.

Mecihtli (meh-SEET-lee): Earth Goddess and source of fertility.

Mexica (meh-SHEE-kah): the last Nahuat tribe to emerge from Aztlan. Founders of Mexico Tenochtitlan.

Mexitin (meh-SHEE-teen): original name of the Mexica.

Mexitli Chalchiuhtlatonac (meh-SHEET-lee chal-chee-wut-lah-TOH-nahk): first recorded leader of the Mexica.

Michoacan (meech-wah-KAHN): a seaside kingdom established by Purepecha people and a rogue group of Mexica.

Mictecacihuatl (meek-teh-kah-SEE-wah-tul): goddess of death, queen of the Underworld.

Mictlantecuhtli (meekt-lahn-teh-KWIT-lee): god of death, king of the Underworld.

Mimich (MEE-meech): one of the Centzon Mimixcoah. Helps capture and kill Itzapapalotl.

Mixcoatl (meesh-KOH-ah-tul): another name for Camaxtli.

Mixteca (meesh-TEH-kah): the Cloud People, Nahuatl name for the Ñuu Dzaui of Oaxaca.

N

Nahualli (nah-WAHL-lee): double or animal spirit form.

Nanahuatzin (nah-nah-WAHT-seen): decrepit and old god, covered in pustules. Son of Quetzalcoatl. Becomes the sun at the beginning of the Fifth Age.

Nene: the first woman created in the Fourth Age.

O

Ometeotl (oh-meh-TEH-oh-tul): the dual god from which the universe was formed.

Omeyocan (oh-meh-YOH-kahn): place of duality, abode of *Ometeotl*.

One Hunahpu (hoo-NAH-poo): a minor god of the milpas, brother of Seven Hunahpu, father of One Monkey and One Artisan as well as the Hero Twins.

One Monkey and One Artisan: gods of the arts.

Oxomoco (oh-shoh-MOH-koh): the first woman created at the beginning of the First Age.

P

Patecatl (pah-TEHK-ah-tul): god of medicine and discoverer of peyote.

Patzcuaro, Lake (PAHTS-kwah-roh): a large, island-dotted lake in Michoacan.

Piltzintecuhtli (peelt-sin-teh-KWIT-lee): son of Oxomoco and Cipactonal.

Popocatepetl (poh-poh-kah-TEH-peh-tul): a volcano in the highlands of Central Mexico.

Popocatzin (poh-poh-KAHT-seen): a Mexica warrior descended from exiled nobles living in Azcapotzalco. Transformed into Popocatepetl.

Q

Quetzalcoatl (quets-al-KWA-tul): Nahuatl name for *Feathered Serpent*, god of creation and order.

Quetzalpetlatl (quets-al-PET-lah-tul): older half-sister of *Ce Acatl Quetzalcoatl*.

Quilaztli (kee-LAHST-lee): an earth goddess associated with the *Mother*.

Q'uq'umatz (koo-koo-MAHTS): a Mayan name for *Feathered Serpent*.

Seven Hunahpu (hoo-NAH-poo): a minor god of the milpas, brother of One Hunahpu.

T

Tabaosimoa (tah-bow-see-MOH-ah): the most respected women and men on earth at the beginning of the Fifth Age.

Tamoanchan (tah-moh-AHN-chahn): Nahuatl name for the home of the gods.

Tata: the first man created in the Fourth Age.

Tecciztecatl (tek-sis-TEH-kah-tul): handsome young god of shell and stone. Son of *Tlaloc* and *Chalchiuhtlicue*. Becomes the moon at the beginning of the Fifth Age.

Tenoch (TEN-ohch): led the Mexica out of Colhuacan to establish the city of Tenochtitlan.

Tenochtitlan (teh-nohch-TEET-lan): city founded by the Mexica on an isle in Lake Texcoco.

Teotihuacan (teh-oh-tee-WAH-kahn): city of the gods and its copy on earth.

Teotl (TEH-oh-tul): divine energy.

Tepalcatzin (teh-pal-KAHT-seen): Toltec king who married Xochitl.

Tepanecas (teh-pah-NEH-kah): a tribe of Nahuas.

Tepeyollotl (teh-peh-YOHL-loh-tul): "Mountainheart," the *nahualli* or double of *Tezcatlipoca*. A massive jaguar.

Texcoco, Lake (tesh-KOH-koh): southermost of the lakes in the highlands of Central Mexico.

Tezcatlipoca (tes-kaht-lee-POH-kah): Nahuatl name for the god of chaos. Brother of *Feathered Serpent*. Also referred to as *Heart of Sky* and *Hurricane*. Later incarnated as a priest of Tollan.

Tezozomoc (teh-soh-SOH-mohk)—a Tepanec king with blood ties to many Mexica rulers.

Tlaloc (TLAH-lohk): Nahuatl name for the rain god.

Tlacahuepan (tlah-kah-WEH-pahn): an evil priest of Tollan allied with Tezcatlipoca.

Tlalocan (tlah-LOH-kahn): Tlaloc's paradise, where the spirits of the drowned, diseased, and deformed go upon death.

Tlaloques (tlah-LOH-kehs): Elemental spirits that serve the rain god.

Tlaltecuhtli (tlahl-TEKW-tlee): "sovereign of the earth," an epithet of Mecihtli.

Tlatelolco (tlah-teh-LOL-koh): a sister city of Tenochtitlan established after a schism in the Mexica tribe.

Tollan (TOL-lahn): the legendary capital of the Toltec empire

Toltecs (tol-TEHKS): the Toltecah, a mighty people who controlled Central Mexico before the Aztecs.

Toltecayotl (tol-tehk-KAY-yoh-tul): Nahuatl term for master craftsmanship.

Tonacacuahuitl (toh-nah-kah-KWAH-wee-tul): the Mother Tree, source of human souls, which stands at the heart of *Omeyocan*.

Tonalli: spiritual essence contained in sunlight. The source of a nahualli.

Tonantzin (toh-NAHNT-seen): "Our Revered Mother." Nahuatl name for the mother goddess.

Tonatiuhchan (toh-nah-TEE-oo-chahn): Eastern paradise of the sun where the souls of brave warriors go after death.

Tzitzimimeh (tseet-see-MEE-meh): an order of goddesses who seek to devour the sun.

X

Xaltocan (shal-TOH-kan): northernmost of the lakes that once dominated the highlands of Central Mexico.

Xbalanque (sh-bah-LAHN-keh): one of the Hero Twins.

Xibalba (shee-ball-BAH): the Mayan name for the Underworld.

Xinantecatl (shee-nan-TEH-kah-tul): a proud and fierce Tepanec warrior from an illustrious family. Rival of Popocatzin.

Xipe Totec (SHEE-peh TOH-tek): god of spring and renewal.

Xiuhtecuhtli (shoo-teh-KWIT-lee): god of time and fire.

Xiuhcoatl (shoo-KOH-ah-tul): *nahualli* of the God of Fire. Used as a weapon by Huitzilopochtli.

Xiuhtlahcuilolxochitzin (shoot-lah-kwee-loh-shoh-CHEET-seen): a Toltec queen.

Xiuhtlaltzin (shoot-LALT-seen): a Toltec queen.

Xmucane (sh-moo-KAH-neh): a Mayan name for the Grandmother. One of the two oldest gods, source of all others. Corresponds to the Nahuatl Omecihuatl.

Xochiquetzal (shoh-chee-KEHT-sal): goddess of flowers and fertility.

Xochimilco, Lake (shoh-chee-MEEL-koh): smaller lake to the southeast of Texcoco.

Xochitl (SHOH-chee-tul): Toltec queen who discovered pulque,

Xolotl (SHOH-loh-tul): the *nahualli* of Quetzacoatl. A massive hound that accompanies the sun through the Underworld.

Y

Yaushu (YOW-shoo): the opossum who ruled the world in the early years of the
Fifth Age.

Yacoñooy (yah-koh-NYOH-oy): legendary hero of the Mixteca.

Yunuen (yoo-noo-WEN): island on Lake Patzcuaro.

Notes on Sources

Origins: Synthesis of passages from the *Popol Vuh*, the *Florentine Codex* (books 2, 4, 6 and 9), *La historia de los mexicanos por sus pinturas* (chapter 1), Pedro Ponce's *Breve relación de los dioses y ritos de la gentilidad*, *Historia Tolteca-Chichimeca*, and *Histoire du Mechique* (part VI).

The Heavens and the Underworld: Drawn from *Histoire du Mechique* (part VI), *La historia de los mexicanos por sus pinturas* (part III), and the *Florentine Codex* (the appendix to book 3).

The First Three Ages of the World: Synthesis of passages from the *Popol Vuh*, book 5 of the *Florentine Codex*, and the *Codex Chimalpopoca* (*Annals of Cuauhtitlan* 2:24 to 2:38 and *Leyenda de los soles* 75:6 to 75:33), with additional information from Pedro Ponce's *Breve relación de los dioses y ritos de la gentilidad*, *La historia de los mexicanos por sus pinturas* (chapters 3 and 4), and *Histoire du Mechique* (part VI).

The Hero Twins: Translated and adapted from the *Popol Vuh.*

The Fourth Sun and the Flood: Synthesis of passages from the *Popol Vuh*, chapter 5 of *La historia de los mexicanos por sus pinturas*, the *Codex Chimalpopoca* (*Annals of Cuauhtitlan* 2:39 to 2:41 and *Leyenda de los soles* 75:34 to 76:7),

The Creation of Human Beings: Synthesis of passages from the *Popol Vuh*, chapter 6 of *La historia de los mexicanos por sus pinturas*, the *Codex Chimalpopoca* (*Leyenda de los soles* 76:18 to 77:24),

The Fifth Sun and the Harbingers of Darkness: Synthesis of passages from the *Popol Vuh*, chapter 7 of *La historia de los mexicanos por sus pinturas*, the *Codex Chimalpopoca* (*Annals of Cuauhtitlan* 2:42 to 2:51 and *Leyenda de los soles* 76:18 to 77:24), *Histoire du Mechique* (part VI) and *Cantares de Dzitbalché.*

Lord Opossum Brings Fire to Man: Drawn from the folklore of the Cora, Mazatec, Otomi and Huichol peoples.

Itzpapalotl and the Cloud Serpents: Adapted from the *Codex Chimalpopoca* (*Annals of Cuauhtitlan* 1:10 to 1:15 and *Leyenda de los soles* 78:30 to 80:17), chapter 8 of *La historia de los mexicanos por sus pinturas,* and "The Song of the Mother of the Gods" from *Primeros Memoriales.* Additional information on the identity of the *Xiuhtetecuhtin* or Fire Lords has been drawn from book two of the *Florentine Codex.*

The Birth of Huitzilopochtli: Translated and adapted from book three of the *Florentine Codex.*

Archer of the Sun: Retold from the popular legend, drawing from *Codex Vindobonensis Mexicanus I, Arte en Lengua Mixteca* by de los Reyes, and Burgoa's *Geográfica Descripción.*

Tollan and the Toltec Queens: Some material adapted from the *Codex Chimalpopoca* (*Annals of Cuauhtitlan* 1:1 to 1:5, 3:16 to 3:24, 4:17, 9:12 to 9:28), Torquemada's *Monarquía Indiana* and the *Historia Chichimeca* by Fernando de Alva Cortés Ixtlilxóchitl.

The Brothers Incarnated: Adapted from the *Codex Chimalpopoca* (*Annals of Cuauhtitlan* 3:56 to 7:41 and *Leyenda de los soles* 80:29 to 81:46) and the *Florentine Codex* (book 3). Additional information drawn from Diego de Landa's *Relacion de las cosas de Yucatán* and Antonio de Herrera y Tordesillas' *Historia general de los hechos de los castellanos en las islas y tierra firme del mar océano que llaman Indias Occidentales.*

The Dwarf King of Uxmal: Retold from oral traditions among the Maya of Yucatan, adapting elements of the version narrated to American explorer John Lloyd Stephens in 1840.

The Rise of Hunak Keel: Drawn from Landa's *Relación de las cosas de Yucatán,* the *Book of Chilam Balam of Chumayel,* the *Book of Chilam Balam of Mani,* and the *Book of Chilam Balam of Tizimin.*

Sak Nikte and the Fall of Chichen Itza: Adapted from *La tierra del faisán y del venado* (1928), by Antonio Mediz Bolio, with additional material from the *Book of Chilam Balam of Chumayel,* the *Book of Chilam Balam of Mani,* and the *Book of Chilam Balam of Tizimin.*

The Tale of Xtabay: Retold from traditional oral tales of Yucatán and Quintana Roo.

The Mexica Exodus: A synthesis of passages from *Crónica Mexicayotl* (parts I and II), *Historia de los mexicanos por sus pinturas* (chapters 9-18), and *Histoire du Mechique* (chapters 3 and 4), with additional information drawn from the *Codex Chimalpopoca* (*Annals of Cuauhtitlan* 3:56 to 7:41 and *Leyenda de los soles* 80:29 to 81:46) and the *Codex Chimalpahin*.

Hapunda and the Lake: Retold from traditional tales of Michoacán state, drawing upon *Relación de Michoacán*.

The Volcanoes: Retold from the popular legend, with the inspiration of images from the poems "El idilio de los volanes" by José Santos Chocano and "La leyenda de los volcanes" by Rafael López.

Tenochtitlan: A synthesis of passages from *Crónica Mexicayotl, Historia de los mexicanos por sus pinturas,* and *Histoire du Mechique*, with additional information drawn from the *Codex Chimalpopoca*, the *Florentine Codex* and the *Codex Chimalpahin*.

Tlacaelel and the Rise of the Mexica: A synthesis of passages from the *Florentine Codex, Crónica Mexicayotl, Historia de los mexicanos por sus pinturas,* and *Histoire du Mechique*, with additional information drawn from the *Codex Chimalpopoca* and the *Codex Chimalpahin*.

Malinalli and the Coming of Cortés: Drawn from the *Florentine Codex* and Bernal Díaz del Castillo's *Historia verdadera de la conquista de la Nueva España*.

The Torture of Cuauhtemoc: Drawn from the *Florentine Codex* (book 12), Fernando de Alva Ixtlilxochitl's *Relación*, the *Anales de Tlatelolco, Cantares Mexicanos*, and *La historia de la conquista de México* by Francisco López de Gómora, along with oral tradition about Cuauhtemoc's final words to his people.

The Anguish of Citlali: Retold from the wide-spread legend, with additional information drawn from the *Florentine Codex*.

Erendira: Adapted from *Michoacán: Paisajes, tradiciones y leyendas*, by Eduardo Ruiz Álvarez, along with other tradition oral variants in Oaxaca.

Donaji: A synthesis of traditional tales in Oaxaca and excerpts from *El rey Cosijoeza y su familia* by Martínez Gracida.

Bibliography

Benítez, Fernando. *Los indios de México*. Tomo III. Mexico City: Ediciones Era, 1970.

Bierhorst, John. *Ballads of the Lords of New Spain: The Codex Romances de los Señores de la Nueva España*. Austin, TX: University of Texas Press, 2009.

Bierhorst, John. *Cantares Mexicanos: Songs of the Aztecs*. Stanford, CA: Stanford University Press, 1985.

Bierhorst, John. *Codex Chimalpopoca: The Text in Nahuatl with a Glossary and Grammatical Notes*. Tucson: The University of Arizona Press, 1992.

Bierhorst, John. *History and Mythology of the Aztecs: The Codex Chimalpopoca*. Tucson: The University of Arizona Press, 1992.

Blombert, Lennart. *Tequila, mezcal y pulque: lo auténtico mexicano*. Mexico City: Editorial Diana, 2000.

Bowles, David. *Flower, Song, Dance: Aztec and Mayan Poetry*. Beaumont: Lamar University Press, 2013.

Burgoa, Fray Francisco de. [1674] *Geográfica Descripción*, Volumes I and II. Mexico City: Editorial Porrúa, 1989

Carrasco, David. *Religions of Mesoamerica: Cosmovision and Ceremonial Centers*. Prospect Heights, IL: Waveland Press, 1990.

De la Garza Camino, Mercedes. *Literatura Maya*. Caracas: Fundación Biblioteca Ayacucho, 1980.

Díaz del Castillo, Bernal. [1585] *Historia verdadera de la conquista de la Nueva España*. Mexico City: Editorial Porrúa, 1976.

Garibay Kintana, Ángel M. *Teogonía e historia de los mexicanos: tres opúsculos del siglo xvi*. Mexico City: Editorial Porrúa, 1965.

Jansen, Maarten and Gabina Aurora Pérez Jiménez. *Paisajes sagrados: códices y arqueología de Ñuu Dzaui*, en *Itinerarios* Vol. 8. Warsaw: Instituto de Estudios Ibéricos e Iberoamericanos, 2008.

Lockhart, James. Trans. and ed. *We People Here: Nahuatl Accounts of the Conquest of Mexico*. University of California Press, 1991.

López Austin. *Los mitos del tlacuache: caminos de la mitología mesoamericana. Alianza Estudio: Antropología*. Mexico City: UNAM, 1996.

León-Portilla, Miguel. *Broken Spears: The Aztec Account of the Conquest of Mexico*. Boston: Beacon Press, 1962.

León-Portilla, Miguel. *Fifteen Poets of the Aztec World*. Norman: University of Oklahoma Press, 1992.

León-Portilla, Miguel and Earl Shorris. *In the Language of Kings: An Anthology of Mesoamerican Literature, Pre-Columbian to the Present*. New York: W.W. Norton & Company, 2002.

Markman, Roberta H. and Peter T. Markman. *The Flayed God: The Mesoamerican Mythological Tradition*. San Francisco: Harper Collins, 1992.

Miller, Mary and Karl Taube. *An Illustrated Dictionary of the Gods and Symbols of Ancient Mexico and the Maya*. London: Thames & Hudson, 1993.

Peniche Barrera, Roldán. El libro de los fantasmas mayas. Mexico City: Maldonado Editores, Biblioteca Básica del Mayab, 1992.

Reyes, Antonio de los. [1593] *Arte en Lengua Mixteca*. Nashville: Vanderbilt University Publications in Anthropology, 1976.

Ruiz Álvarez, Eduardo. *Michoacán: Paisajes, tradiciones y leyendas*. Mexico City: Oficina Tipográfica de la Secretaría de Fomento, 1891.

Sahagún, Bernadino de. *Florentine Codex: General History of the Things of New Spain*, Books I-XII, 2nd edition. Trans. and Ed. Charles E. Dibble and Arthur J. O. Anderson. 12 volumes (1950-1969). Santa Fe: University of Utah, 2012.

Stephens, John Lloyd. *Incidents of Travel in Yucatán*, Volumes I and II. New York: Harper & Brothers, 1858.

Sullivan, Thelma. *Scattering of Jades: Stories, Poems, and Prayers of the Aztecs*. Ed. Timothy J. Knab. Tucson: University of Arizona Press, 1994.